Jack & Susan in 1953

Jack & Susan in 1953

Michael McDowell

FELONY & MAYHEM PRESS • NEW YORK

All the characters and events portrayed in this work are fictitious.

JACK & SUSAN IN 1953

A Felony & Mayhem mystery

PRINTING HISTORY
First edition (Ballantine): 1985
Felony & Mayhem edition: 2012

ISBN: 978-1-937384-40-1

Manufactured in the United States of America

Printed on 100% recycled paper

Library of Congress Cataloging-in-Publication Data

McDowell, Michael, 1950-
Jack & Susan in 1953 / Michael McDowell. -- Felony & Mayhem
edition.
    pages cm
ISBN 978-1-937384-40-1
1. Nineteen fifties--Fiction. 2. Americans--Cuba--Fiction. 3. Mystery
fiction. I. Title.
PS3563.C35936J35 2012
813'.54--dc23
                        2012045489

For My Father

Other "Wild Card" titles from

FELONY&MAYHEM

MICHAEL McDOWELL
Jack & Susan in 1913
Jack & Susan in 1933

BONNIE JONES REYNOLDS
The Truth About Unicorns

SARAH RAYNE
A Dark Dividing
Ghost Song

Jack & Susan in 1953

The Hep Cast of 1953:

JACK, who handles Libby's finances and discovers he's got his hands on much more—

SUSAN, who is as wise and witty as her last name implies—

LIBBY, who wants Jack at any cost and has all the money it would take to get him—

RODOLFO, whose mysterious Cuban past throws everyone into a life-and-death struggle—

And, of course, Woolf, who can't help wiggling into trouble and who sniffs out with Jack and Susan a mystery deeper than simple murder...

CHAPTER ONE

THERE WAS NO doubt the restaurant had an atmosphere. It was dim, quiet, full of odd angles, and it seemed to wind off in peculiar directions so that there was plenty of wall space on which to hang old-fashioned, sepia-tinted views of Paris. Many small tables, accommodating two or three, were placed against the walls, while the small number of larger tables in the middle suggested that the management didn't relish groups. Charles' French Restaurant, in fact, discouraged large parties of diners. In Greenwich Village large parties of diners frequently made a racket and got very drunk.

Most of Charles' clientele were uptown. Uptown felt comfortable at Charles'. The waiters were quiet and discreet; they looked not into your face but into the knot of your tie. The menu was substantial, in French, and high-priced in comparison with the rest of Greenwich Village.

Libby Mather looked around with ostentatious misgiving as Jack helped her off with her jacket. Jack Beaumont was an old friend of Libby Mather's. He also served as her investment counselor, and in time, he feared, he might be even more to the young heiress. Libby hadn't wanted to come so far downtown. She'd heard all the stories about the Village, and not one of them interested her. Libby had often expressed her certainty that between Wall Street and Thirty-fourth there was a wide social ditch inhabited entirely by maids and alcoholics.

In 1953, Greenwich Village was—at least to Libby and her uptown friends—a bohemian wasteland of ex-Harvard students perpetually clad in tweed jackets and dungarees; drunken artists of doubtful talent supported by young women of equally doubtful virtue; men and women with confused and perverse attitudes toward so simple a concept as physical attraction; and droves of unhappy young men disaffected by World War II.

There wasn't anything down there, in Greenwich Village, Libby's friends said, except bars seedier than those around Times Square. You never knew who you'd find yourself standing next to in a Village bar. It was true that rents were cheap, even in buildings that weren't condemned. Rents were cheap in Newark, too, but that was no reason to live in Newark.

Absently adjusting her bright blue monkey-fur helmet, Libby peered suspiciously into the dark corners of the restaurant. "Oh, goodness," she exclaimed in not a particularly happy tone of voice, "I was wrong!"

"Yes," Jack concurred hopefully. "I knew you'd like this place."

"Not that," Libby whispered. "There's actually somebody I know here."

The maître d' approached and gazed into the knot of Jack's tie. It was a Countess Mara tie, hand-painted. In the shop it had looked adventurous and special; now Jack was certain it looked as if his ten-year-old cousin had made it at summer camp.

"Beaumont," said Jack, adjusting the knot of Countess Mara and wishing he could twist it around and conceal the painted side. "For two."

"Yes sir," the man replied in a quiet voice. "This way, please, madam."

"I want to sit there," said Libby, nodding in a direction different from the one in which they were being led. She spoke in a loud slow voice, as if everyone in the restaurant were deaf and stupid.

"Madam?" said the maître d' turning, and looking with deep disapproval at Libby's left shoulder.

"Over there, that empty table. We want to sit over there." She indicated a table next to the person she knew.

"If it's convenient," said Jack, reaching forward with a dollar bill secreted in the palm of his hand.

"Yes sir," said the maître d', palming the bill neatly so that Libby did not notice the transaction. "Of course. The table *is* free—though rather exposed."

"Don't you see who it is?" Libby demanded of Jack, as they changed direction behind the maître d'.

"No," said Jack, without curiosity. Jack knew all Libby's friends, and they fell into two categories. Those who were boring, and those who made the boring ones seem interesting by comparison. The problem, Jack thought with a sigh, was that in the past few years, those people had become *his* friends too. There had been a time, he seemed to remember, when he knew exciting people, people who...

"It's Susan Bright," said Libby, interrupting his thought. "I can't believe it. Susan Bright. What in the world is she doing down here, do you suppose?"

Jack took a moment to answer. "Maybe she's having dinner," he said offhandedly but his voice was at once uneasy and annoyed. It *was* Susan. In the flesh. For a few moments Jack looked at her. He'd forgotten nothing.

Though cut differently, her hair was still thick and black, and had that familiar luster of blue in dim light. Her lashes were long, thick, and curled. Her skin was creamy and unflawed, and Jack knew she hadn't been out in the sun recently, for he recalled how easily Susan burned. Most of all he remembered the dark blue eyes set in a face that otherwise seemed all black and white—as if God, at the very last, had decided to paint a little color on Susan's face before he let her go.

The maître d' reached the empty table and pulled out a chair. As Libby was seating herself, with some commotion, Jack glanced over at the man with whom Susan was dining. One look sufficed; Jack immediately disliked him. He was a direct descendant of the Arrow Shirt man, though perhaps a trifle darker-skinned. He seemed to be a mass of all those attributes that Jack lacked—and wanted desperately. He was well-proportioned; whereas Jack, at six-three, was gangly. Above features that were regular and pleasing, the man's hair was of a definite color—black as Susan's; whereas Jack's was brown, sandy, or even blond, depending on the light or what he was wearing. Moreover, the man seemed to have found exactly the right amount of Vitalis to use—every hair was in place, yet didn't appear oily. If Jack used any hair oil at all, he looked as if he'd stuck his head into a vat of frying grease; if he used none he looked as if he'd stuck his finger into an electrical socket. The man had a perfect, natural demeanor and he was the perfect dresser. His suit was exactly the right shade and cut; the shirt was right—with that new rounded collar; the tie was right—not hand painted by Countess Mara, but a discreet blue-and-yellow silk. It appeared to Jack that Susan, seeing Libby and Jack coming, had pulled the perfect specimen out of a bandbox and planted him in the seat across from her.

Now Jack was aware that he was wearing the same clothes that he'd put on at seven o'clock that morning. With a drop of gravy—acquired at lunch—on the front of his jacket, and his trousers knees wrinkled at the back, Jack felt positively filthy.

All this whirled through Jack's mind in only a couple of seconds. In the meantime, Libby reached out and placed her hand on the other young woman's arm. "Susan Bright, I can't believe it! I don't think I would have been surprised to sit next to you in a restaurant in Paris or Vienna, but I cannot believe you are having dinner in Greenwich Village. I cannot believe it, I said to Jack—"

Susan looked up sharply. As her eyes locked with Jack's, the left side of her mouth tightened in a momentary grimace. A moment later it evened out, though with apparent effort.

"Hello, Libby. This *is* a surprise."

Jack had not forgotten. The most distinctive thing about Susan was her voice. It was low-pitched, a little slow, and always seemed tinged with sarcasm. As a result, almost everything she said seemed to be smart and deliberate, even when it wasn't actually cutting. "May I introduce you?" Susan said. The man opposite her had risen halfway from his chair, clutching his napkin against his lap. Libby gave the man a cold smile. "Libby Mather, this is Rodolfo García-Cifuentes."

At the sound of the Spanish name, Libby's eyes narrowed slightly, and her smile, if possible, became even colder. "How do you do?" she said, as if she'd just been introduced to someone's chauffeur.

Rodolfo García-Cifuentes had started to extend his hand to Libby, but she smoothly turned her eyes away before the motion could get well under way, and Rodolfo aborted it. Only a slight tinge of red on his dark skin showed any embarrassment.

"May I—" began Libby.

"I know Mr. Beaumont," cut in Susan.

Jack turned to García-Cifuentes and put out his hand. "Jack Beaumont," he said, hoping that the man's palms sweated, or that he was missing a finger or two.

"How do you do," replied the other, and they shook hands. All Rodolfo's fingers were there, and the palm was bone dry. Jack consoled himself with the remote hope that Mr. García-Cifuentes would turn out to be an utterly ruthless murderer.

"I just can't believe this coincidence," continued Libby, leaning toward the next table. "I mean we all know each other, or most of us do. And here we all are, in *this* place."

"This place?" echoed Rodolfo.

"Libby thinks that Greenwich Village is on the edge of the civilized world," explained Jack.

"No I don't," said Libby. "I think it's *over* the edge. I mean, I just can't believe that I actually know somebody who comes to eat down here. Oh Jack, this is fun after all! Like camping out in the woods and eating pork and beans out of a can. Don't you think that's what it's like?" she said to Susan.

"Very much," replied Susan dryly. "In fact, pork and beans out of a can would be a wonderful accompaniment to the *escalopes de veau* I've ordered."

Libby opened her menu, took a quick look at it, then sighed and said, with a smile that coyly announced her helplessness, "Oh Jack, you order for me. And please get something that I can eat. Honestly, Susan, once Jack took me to *Chinatown*. It was dreadful. Birds' nests and sea slugs, that's all they had. Jack, you know what I like."

"Porterhouse steak, mashed potatoes, and Jell-O," said Jack, opening up his menu.

Jack did order for Libby the items he could find on the menu that were closest to steak and mashed potatoes. It wasn't close enough, however, and Libby merely picked at her food. Jack ordered exactly what he wanted and thought he relished—*boudin blanc*, a kind of white sausage.

(The waiter had assured him that it had been made in the kitchen that morning.) But when it arrived he found he didn't like it after all. Besides that, the *haricots verts* seemed mushy, the bread was stale, and the butter had an off taste. And every time he turned even a few degrees to the right, he glanced into the face of Susan Bright. That wasn't often, but sometimes he couldn't help it.

As Jack grew more uncomfortable, Libby grew brighter. Libby, in general, tended to seize upon Jack's unhappiness, and if possible, to increase it. She couldn't fail to notice the obvious strain between Jack and Susan. Rather than jealously imagining some past liaison that would account for the ill-feeling, Libby took advantage of the situation and relentlessly maintained a three-way conversation. This plan had the bonus, for Libby, of rudely excluding Susan's friend Rodolfo. Despite Rodolfo's perfect manners and bearing, Libby objected to him because he was a foreigner. It would have been bad enough if the man had been French—but a *Spaniard*. Every time Libby looked at Susan it was with a smile that was composed of one third pity, one third condescension, one third derision. Libby did all she could to increase Jack's discomfort and spoil what little pleasure he was able to take in his food. She did this in perfect good humor; it was the way that Libby treated anyone she liked.

"I had forgotten," breathed Libby through a wreath of smoke from her Camel cigarette, "I had totally and absolutely forgotten, Susan, that you and Jack already knew each other. But was it here? It wasn't here, was it?"

"In this restaurant, you mean?" asked Susan with obviously spurious innocence.

"New York, I mean," said Libby. "*Here* in New York, not this restaurant."

"It was in Boston," said Jack. "About six years ago. Right after I finished Harvard."

Libby made a great show of dredging weed-covered facts up from the silty floor of her memory. "And Susan, you went to Boston after you left Smith. Right at the end of the war. You went to Boston because you...you..."

"Got a job in Boston," said Susan. "I went to work."

Libby drew back, took a meditative puff on her Camel, and asked, "A job? You went to work? I don't remember that at all. I thought you went to be in a regatta or something." She turned to Jack. "Does a regatta have anything to do with Quonset huts, whatever they are?" Libby asked Jack. "I have this distinct memory of Susan going to Boston to do something with regattas and Quonset huts."

Susan, biting her lip, simply shook her head. "I was doing some translating for military intelligence. I didn't live in a Quonset hut. And I didn't—as far as I can remember—take part in any regattas. You must have me mixed up with someone else, Libby."

"I don't think so," said Libby, as if she were the authoritative historian of Susan's past, and her most recent article on the subject was being disputed. "But Boston *is* where you knew Jack."

"We had friends in common," said Jack in a tone of finality.

Rodolfo García-Cifuentes had sat silently through this exchange. He slowly drank his coffee, smoked a Lucky, and listened with his hand on his chin. When Libby made a trek to the ladies room, he spoke quietly to Susan in Spanish. Susan replied fluently in his language.

Jack could not help but listen. He cursed himself for never having studied a foreign language. He had seen Linguaphone language lessons advertised in *Esquire*, but had never given more than a passing thought to enrolling. He ached to know what Susan and Rodolfo were saying. Susan was talking out of the side of her mouth; her sarcastic mode, so the subject was probably Libby. Now she was speaking with her tongue drawn slightly back from her teeth. That was her holding-in-anger mode, so she was probably telling Rodolfo who Jack was.

"He means nothing to me," she concluded in English. Jack at least knew for whom *that* statement was meant.

For a second, Jack lifted his eyes to the face of Susan Bright, and found his gaze returned. He felt blood rush up through the veins of his neck, and he knew his face was suffusing with a blush. There were many things in life over which Jack Beaumont had assumed control: his finances, his career, his relationship to most women and almost all men. But he had never learned how to control his blushes. He remembered how violently he'd blushed when he had spilled iced tea on his shirt at his first dinner dance, when he was fourteen. He blushed as violently now, at twenty-seven, as he looked into the eyes of Susan Bright.

Susan smiled. Susan never blushed at anything. But she knew that Jack did, and she smiled at his lack of control.

Jack put down his cup and rose as Libby sidled back into her chair.

She now smiled at Susan and asked relentlessly, "Did you two meet at a regatta?"

"No," replied Susan evenly, "Rodolfo knows my uncle. I believe they met in the casino at Havana."

"Oh!" exclaimed Libby, with a total alteration of expression in her face and in her voice. "I love casinos. I was never so happy in all my life as the time I spent in Monte Carlo. Somebody has since told me that Monte Carlo is on the water, but let me tell you this, I had no idea. I never saw the outside of the casino. Not once. Roulette," Libby whispered. "I love roulette. Do they really have a casino in Havana?"

"Gambling has recently been made legal in Cuba," Rodolfo explained.

"Rodolfo is *from* Cuba," said Susan.

"Really?" said Libby excitedly. "Gambling really is legal in there? Do they have roulette wheels?"

Rodolfo laughed. "Yes," he said. "Really and truly. But you know, Miss Mather, you do not have to go as far as Havana—or even Nevada—in order to find a roulette wheel."

"Are you talking about Montreal? Call me Libby. May I call you Rodolfo?"

Jack stared at Libby. It had been a long time since he'd seen her so excited about anything. Libby Mather lived in a part of town and moved in a crowd of people that considered enthusiasm ill-bred, even unwholesome. It ruined the complexion and wrinkled your *ensemble*. But just now, Libby positively bubbled.

"Not Montreal," said Rodolfo. "I am speaking of Fifty-fifth Street."

Libby sat back in her chair as if thunderstruck. "A gambling house on Fifty-fifth Street?" she echoed. "East or west?"

"East," said Rodolfo.

"My God," whispered Libby, and actually seemed to tremble with the thought of it. "I know where that is."

"You should," said Jack, "since you live on East Sixtieth. It's a five-minute walk." Jack noticed an expression of curious surprise cross Susan's face. Then she saw Jack looking at her, and she suppressed it just as quickly. *Aha*, thought Jack, *there is something in this...*

"Is it legal?" asked Libby in a low voice.

Rodolfo smiled slightly, and shook his head once. "No, no. Gambling is not legal in New York. This place is very private. Like a club."

"Oh, my goodness," whispered Libby, gasping for breath that surprise had taken away. "I can't believe this. Do you need a password to get in? Is it like a speakeasy? Does it get raided?"

"No passwords," said Rodolfo. "But one does need a friend. And no raids." He smiled a knowing, secretive smile that seemed to melt Libby.

"Could you..." she began, and seemed to lack the strength to finish the question, so fearful was she of a negative reply.

"Yes, of course, I could," he said, with a gallant half-bow in his chair.

"Tonight?" Libby asked, her eyes ablaze.

"By all means, if..." replied Rodolfo, looking across the table at Susan Bright.

"Why not?" said Susan.

Jack was by no means convinced that this was a good idea, but he did not object. "Yes, why not?"

"Oh, good-good-good-good-good," burbled Libby. "This is going to be an evening to remember."

CHAPTER TWO

AFTER THAT, LIBBY'S undisguised anxiety to leave was amusing to Susan. She had been in other restaurants with Libby Mather, and she remembered that Libby always ordered two desserts and nibbled off of everybody else's plate as well. But now she was foregoing dessert altogether, announcing that the Baby Ruths in her bag were perfectly sufficient. "Get the check," Libby said to Jack in a low insistent voice.

Once the bill was obtained and paid, the two men got up and fetched coats.

Libby leaned over toward Susan, and whispered—though whispering was hardly necessary—"He's so handsome. Does he use something on his skin?"

"I beg your pardon?" Susan returned, not understanding.

"To lighten it," explained Libby. "I wouldn't have known he was Spanish until I heard his name. I've heard that the first thing Spaniards do when they get off the boat is invest in a case of lightening creams."

"Rodolfo is Cuban," said Susan. "Havana? The gambling casinos? Remember? And so far as I know, he doesn't use lightening creams—if there are such things."

"Well," said Libby thoughtfully, "maybe he's a half-breed."

Libby was pleasant to Rodolfo, though that had more to do with the fact that he knew the whereabouts of a gambling den, than it did with any real sense of politeness. They found a cab a few doors up from Charles', and all crawled in the back. The two men were on the outside, with Susan and Libby squeezed together between them. Libby wouldn't hear of anybody sitting in the front. She maintained a belief, which she stated quite loudly, that all cabdrivers were infested with fleas picked up on trips to other boroughs.

Retaliating, the cabdriver deliberately took the long way and drove into Times Square. It was half-past ten, and the sidewalks were thronged with people. Beneath the enormous brightly lighted marquees of the Broadway theaters, well-dressed crowds were milling about and talking and making supper decisions and keeping eagle eyes out for empty taxis. Polite lines had formed in front of Longchamps and Lindy's, and teenagers in open-topped cars shrieked with laughter and waved at the pedestrians. At Broadway and Forty-fourth Street the cab became embroiled in a massive jam of cars and pedestrians. This gave Libby the chance to launch once more into a stream of chitchat.

Libby's arm pressed against Susan's ribs. Libby's arm was firm and fleshy, just like the rest of her. She wasn't fat—she wasn't even plump—but Libby had flesh where men thought a young woman should have flesh. Libby had curves that gave her a silhouette enticing from the back as well as from the sides. Susan, on the other hand, was slender. No curves. Enemies—and Susan herself—sometimes pronounced her figure *bony*, but in better moments Susan knew that wasn't the case. She just didn't have flesh to spare. She hoped she'd be around when—and if—thinness and flatness came into style once more. When was the last time? Susan wondered. Oh yes, the twenties. Her mother's generation. Well, maybe if Susan herself gave birth to a daughter tending to thinness, the eighties would be kind to the girl.

Susan was also annoyed by the fact that the young woman chattering in her ear always managed to dress in the teeth of fashion. It was a talent Libby had, of always looking as if she'd just walked out the door of a smart avant-garde shop. It was a discouraging habit, as far as Susan was concerned. Sometimes Susan tried to dress in the teeth of fashion as well. She would spend more than she ought on clothes that were exactly right; would take them home, and put them on and look at herself in the mirror, and *know* that at that moment she stood at the pinnacle of style. Then she'd go downstairs, and by the time she got to the street, the avant-garde style would be old hat, and every secretary in town would be wearing Susan's outfit. At a restaurant or nightclub Susan would see where she'd made her mistake. The new color today was red, not violet. The covering for the head was a tiny feathered helmet, not the wide-brimmed toreador hat with ball fringe that she had purchased with an impulsiveness she had regretted almost immediately. With a little inward sigh of despair, she would admit to herself that she'd probably never be on the cutting edge of modern fashion.

Before Susan could elaborate mentally on further differences between herself and Libby Mather, the taxi began to move. In another five minutes they pulled up in front of an ordinary-looking brownstone on East Fifty-fifth Street between Park and Madison. They climbed out, and Jack paid the driver.

Drawing her arm through Susan's, Libby leaned over and said, with evidently unfeigned relief, "Oh Susan, I feel so much more *comfortable* uptown, don't you?"

Only two minutes earlier Susan had told Libby that she was living in an apartment on the east side of Washington Square.

Whatever reason Jack had for seeing Libby, Susan wished him joy in the company of her old friend.

Mr. Vance's establishment—it had no other name—was located on the upper floors of the brownstone. On the ground floor was a small restaurant wholly inadequate to accommodate the considerable number of well-dressed persons who tried to get through its front doors. But in the lobby of the restaurant was a door leading to a narrow curving staircase that wound up to the second floor. At the top of these narrow steps was a wide door padded in red leather. It wouldn't open for Libby. She peered into the diamond-shaped mirror on the door and said, "I bet there's somebody behind here. I bet this is a three-D mirror."

"Two-way mirror," Jack corrected.

"May I?" said Rodolfo. Jack pulled Libby out of the way. Rodolfo stood directly before the door and tapped with his knuckles on the mirror. Almost immediately the door opened. The doorman was dressed in an ill-fitting dinner jacket that plainly outlined a shoulder holster beneath his left arm. Perhaps, Jack considered, that visibility was intentional.

Libby swept in and immediately declared herself enchanted. The carpet beneath her feet was deep and red; crimson damask draperies closed thickly over tall windows. Even the two ladder men who oversaw the room's gambling operations were seated on high platforms lacquered Chinese red. The floor–through establishment boasted two craps tables, three blackjack tables, and a roulette wheel in the far corner. The clientele was well heeled, if not precisely fashionable. While the men checked their coats, Susan sized up the room; she saw lots of expensive clothes and what appeared to be diamonds. The ladies looked as if they had paid for their adornment—one way or another. All the gentlemen seemed to be wearing new blue suits of a style comparable to Rodolfo's.

Libby didn't even glance at the other gambling tables as she made a beeline for the roulette wheel, Jack tagging behind.

As they made their way across the room, Libby abstractedly reached into her pocketbook and brought out a small wallet. "This is all I have," she said with a hasty sigh, as if she were too busy to spare a longer one. "Jack, be a darling, please, and go get me some chips."

Jack looked around, and Libby—who didn't appear to have noticed anything in the room except the roulette wheel—pointed toward the opposite corner with exasperation. "Over there, you silly," she said impatiently. "Over *there.*"

Over there consisted of a tiny, dark triangular booth half hidden behind a screen in one corner of the room. In it sat a man in a tuxedo whose eyes were so heavy-lidded he appeared not to have slept for days.

Jack put the money on the counter, and said, "Chips please."

"Yeah?"

"Yes, what?" asked Jack. Jack had just decided that he didn't like this place, and when Jack Beaumont didn't like a thing, his voice became short and surly. It was sometimes a disadvantage not to be able to disguise his feelings, and Jack had scars to prove it.

"Yeah what kind of chips. Fi'-dollar chips, ten-dollar chips, hunnert-dollar chips, or what—what kind of chips I'm asking is what I'm asking."

"Five-dollar chips," said Jack. He objected to the obvious illegality of the operation and distrusted the aspect of the men who were hired to run it. But most of all, he was forced to admit, he didn't like the fact that it was Susan Bright's companion who had brought them there.

As it happened, Libby Mather was further indebted to Mr. García-Cifuentes for an introduction to the roulette croupier, and was standing quite close to Rodolfo at the edge of the table, anxiously awaiting the arrival of her chips. "You are so slow, it makes me furious," Libby complained as Jack approached. "I could have made five hundred dollars in the last ninety seconds. How much are these worth? How much money did I give you?"

"These are five-dollar chips, and you gave me two hundred dollars," said Jack. "Why on earth do you carry around so much money, Libby?"

"In case I'm asked to elope," returned Libby archly, "I want to make sure I have decent shoes for the wedding." She lurched forward and placed ten of her chips, which were red, on black.

Though he had not gone to the cage in the corner, Rodolfo had chips as well, and Jack wondered for a moment where he might have gotten them. Was he such an habitué of this Mr. Vance's establishment that he carried them about in his pocket at all times? Rodolfo was working with ten-dollar chips and was betting on even, as well as directly on the number twenty-seven.

Jack stood behind Libby and was watching as the croupier spun the wheel in one direction and snapped the small white ball into its trough, sending it around in the opposite direction. "It's very bad luck to have someone standing over your shoulder at a roulette wheel," Libby said severely.

"I just thought I'd watch and see how it works," Jack returned mildly.

"I'll buy you a book," said Libby. "I don't have time to teach you. Now go away. Rodolfo," she went on in a whisper, "ask the croupier how the table's been going tonight. Has it been running black or red?"

Jack backed off, and headed for the bar that ran down one long side of the room. Susan was seated on a stool at one end, looking a little self-conscious, as women sitting at bars alone often did in 1953.

"Rum Collins," Jack told the barman. With the memory of how he and Susan had parted four years before, it was with some apprehension that Jack turned to her and remarked, with as much inconsequence as he could muster, "We've both been abandoned, it appears."

"I haven't been abandoned," said Susan. "I just have no interest in gambling. Of course, I had no idea that Libby was so..."

"Yes?" Jack prompted. For the first time Jack could smell the perfume Susan was wearing. It startled him. Lilacs.

"...enthusiastic," said Susan. "About roulette."

"I didn't know either," returned Jack. "Has Rodolfo brought you to this place before?" He looked about with an air of unsettled mistrust. *What was that perfume called?*

"I've never been here," said Susan. There was an evasiveness about her answer that piqued Jack's interest.

"At the restaurant," he said, "you did look surprised when Rodolfo mentioned it." *Duchess of York. White lilacs. He'd bought Susan Duchess of York perfume their last Christmas together. She was still wearing it—but for another man. Very annoying.*

Susan paused only a moment before answering. "Rodolfo hasn't been in New York long. I'm always surprised how well he can find his way around. It takes most people years."

"You've been showing him about?" asked Jack with a pleasant smile.

"Rodolfo is a friend of the family," replied Susan shortly. Then, with a smile as pleasant as Jack's had been, she remarked, "You know I was a little surprised to see you at the restaurant with Libby."

"Really?" said Jack. "What was so surprising about it?"

"Well," said Susan, "I had heard that you'd married a New Orleans demimondaine and that she attacked you at the reception with a cake knife when she found out that you'd made her maid of honor pregnant."

"Sorry," Jack replied after a moment, swallowing his anger to see what it would turn into. It turned into quiet sarcasm. "It wasn't quite like that. I'd gotten the bride's *mother* pregnant." Jack lifted his head and rubbed his neck with two fingers.

At this meeting, their first in four years, Susan could have been coldly polite and distant, to indicate how little she cared for him now. Instead, she chose an undisguised attack, showing that her animosity was still very much alive. That was interesting, Jack decided, but he couldn't make any more out of it than that. Susan shook her head. "Isn't it strange how the truth gets distorted?" Susan briefly pondered whether she should jump down off the barstool and stalk away. Jack's mistrust of Rodolfo was apparent. His questioning of her was rude, and he ought to be punished. But if she did jump down, and in the process manage to land with her spike heel on Jack's foot, where in the room would she go? She stayed where she was.

"Yes," said Jack. "It is strange what passes for truth these days. For instance, I'd heard that you'd married a senator's son and moved to Washington, but that he'd abandoned you for a Brooklyn laundress. I felt so bad I nearly wrote to you. I wouldn't have believed it to be true, but so many people came to me with the story..."

"No," said Susan, looking into her glass, nearly empty. "I haven't accepted any proposals of marriage lately." She waved to Rodolfo across the room.

"And I haven't made any." Jack smiled in the direction of distant Libby. "Not this week anyway."

Susan Bright signaled the bartender for another drink. "And I wouldn't either, if I were you. At least not till you've learned to take a little better care of yourself. Has that suit been pressed in the last year? Or *cleaned*?" she added, peering at the spot on the front. "I see your hair has continued to recede. Have you considered the advantages of a toupee?"

Susan knew she was touching a sensitive point. Jack had straight brown hair that he combed straight back. Now that his hair was thinning in front, his forehead—always high, broad, and unlined—seemed even higher and broader. But that brow lent him a certain nobility of expression and a suggestion of intellect—at least when he was in repose. His face was sculpted, with a sharply defined jaw and high cheekbones, giving him an enormous expanse of shaven cheek. Susan had always thought him handsome, but she knew that Jack had always felt his features were too angular. Though, so far as Susan was concerned, the features of a man's face could never be *too* distinctly defined. "Or perhaps," she went on, "you're just worrying too much about what it would be like to be married to a margarine heiress..."

Jack suddenly stood up straight. He cast a cold eye on Susan. "The intervening years haven't dulled your tongue. Don't start in on Libby, and I won't say anything against Señor García-Cifuentes."

"I can't imagine what you *could* say against Rodolfo. Sometimes I think he's the only *real* man I've ever met." She looked at Jack meaningfully.

"I have nothing to say against Rodolfo personally," said Jack, paying no attention to the insult, "but I have been wondering about his friends. Do they all have such heavy jowls? And such dark beards? And smell of bay rum? And carry guns?" Jack nodded around the room, at the doorman, the croupiers, and the tuxedoed ladder men perched on their platforms like overfed penguin lifeguards.

"These aren't Rodolfo's *friends*," said Susan. "Rodolfo just knows them. Rodolfo likes to gamble—all Cubans do, I'm told. He told me his entire Harvard education was paid for by his mother on a winning lottery ticket—you know, the Havana lottery."

"I don't remember him from Harvard," said Jack. "And since we seem to be about the same age, we would have been there about the same time. Are you certain—"

"Neither Rodolfo nor I can be responsible for your memory, Jack, any more than we can be responsible for your extraordinarily peculiar taste in female companions. Libby has one of the most—"

Susan left off abruptly, and for a woman who never blushed, she came very near it at that moment. Jack turned to see what had interrupted her, and found Rodolfo standing directly behind him. Jack wondered for a moment how long the Cuban had been there, but if he'd heard any of the conversation, he gave no indication. He said, "Mr. Beaumont, I think you'd better see to Miss Mather. She's..."

Jack immediately moved away from the bar to a position that gave him a clear view of the roulette wheel. But even before he could see Libby, he heard her voice, strident as only Libby's could be: "That's the fourth time in a row! That doesn't—"

Jack moved toward Libby and, glancing back over his shoulder, saw Rodolfo and Susan conferring. In seconds, Jack reached the roulette table. As before, perhaps a dozen persons were gathered around. The ball was spinning, but not a single bet had been placed on the board.

Libby spoke loudly. "I'm not betting. And I'd advise everybody else here not to bet."

"Make yer bets," said the croupier. "Make yer bets, please, ladies an' gen'men."

"Don't," Libby advised the company airily. "That's four times in a row that the zeros have come up. *Four times.*"

Jack reached her side. "Libby," he said quietly, "what's the matter? I could hear you all the way across the room."

"Then you know what the matter is," she said. "The matter is that I've only got two damn chips left because this wheel has landed on zero or double zero four times in a row, and it's fine for me because that was mad money for my possible elopement and nobody's made any proposals of marriage *yet* tonight, but these other people are losing lots more money than I am—"

"Lady," said a harsh masculine voice. "Lady, why don'tcha shut up? Why don'tcha take yer goddamn two chips and stick 'em where the sunlight won't fade 'em? Wouldja do that for everybody?"

Libby was about to retort, but just at that moment, out of the corner of her eye, she saw the tiny white ball bounce down onto the wheel. Grimly she turned and watched. "It's going to do it again. I know it is. You wait, Jack. Here it comes..."

The fuss Libby had created had attracted gamblers from the other tables, and they gathered around now, watching with bated breath as the ball came to rest...

At double zero.

"I told you!" cried Libby triumphantly, as the red-faced croupier raked in all the chips. No one had bet on double zero, so the house cleared the table. "Five times now! I'm sure that's never happened before—anywhere. It would *never* happen in Monte Carlo, because in Monte Carlo," she explained for those around the table who just might not be apprised of the fact, "gambling is legal. It's government-controlled. The tables in Monte Carlo are *honest*."

"Libby—" Jack began, with a strong note of caution in his voice. He glanced around and saw that Rodolfo and Susan were now standing a few feet away. Rodolfo's expression was apprehensive. Jack glanced up at the nearest ladder man. He was a fat, greasy-looking man with slick hair. He was now awkwardly climbing down from his lacquered perch, saying, "Lady, listen, you got some—"

"Do it again, I dare you!" cried Libby at the croupier. "You watch," she said to the assembled crowd, "everybody watch what I'm doing. I have two chips left, and I'm putting one on zero and the other on double zero, and see if I don't win. I'd advise everybody in this room to put their chips on zero or double zero."

"Place your bets," said the croupier weakly, grasping the small pointed spire in the middle of the wheel and spinning it. He hesitated a moment before snapping the ball into motion in its trough, but did so when the ladder man cried out, "Go on, goddamnit!" As the ball spun around and around, several persons who had been hesitating placed their bets alongside Libby's meager chips.

Libby had squeezed in right next to the croupier, and grasping the edge of the roulette table, was feeling around underneath it with her foot. The croupier tried to nudge her out of the way, but Libby held her ground. "See," she said to the crowd, "they have these buttons on the floor and when they step on them the ball falls in zero or double zero. That's what they do, that's what they did in here tonight, five times. It's like loaded dice, and—"

Her face was wreathed in a sudden, triumphant smile. "*I found it.*"

"Lady—" cried the croupier, nervously.

"Watch, everybody, wa—"

At that moment the hulking ladder man finally broke through the crowd to Libby. "All right," he said to her, at the same time casting a menacing eye toward Jack. "All right, that's it. That's enough. No more. We go home—we all go home and we don't never come back. You got me, lady? Mister, you got a leash for this one? You got a muzzle?"

"Unfortunately not," said Jack, barely beneath his breath.

"Of course. Now that I've placed a bet on the zeros and pressed their little button, they're going to try to get me out before I win—before my little bet closes down the whole damned table."

"Move," said the ladder man.

The white ball rolled around and around.

Susan suddenly looked at Jack, with a surprised look on her face. Surprised and frightened. She raised a single finger and pointed; only Jack saw the movement. He saw in an instant what had startled Susan. The ladder man was holding a small revolver at Libby's back, pressing it against the black material of her dress.

The ball slowed.

"Just go," said Jack quietly to Libby. "Let's just get out of here. Let's—"

The white ball clattered down onto the wheel and came to a stop.

On zero.

Unfortunately for everyone, Libby saw it. Despite Jack's pleading, Libby—who had never denied herself anything in her entire life—screeched, "Cheat! Cheat!"

There was a sudden moment of silence all around the table, and then underneath Libby's shrill protestations, the croupier gasped out, "Zero. Pays thirty-six to one."

"Cheat! Cheat!" Libby continued to chant, and there was a surging movement of the crowd toward the wheel. Jack and Libby and the ladder man were caught between the table and the pressing mob. The gun was pressed sideways against Libby's back, and when she felt that, she whirled around and began to beat her fists against the ladder man. Her tiny hands beat ineffectually against the lapels of his dinner jacket.

Jack, hoping to take advantage of this moment of distraction, made a grab for the gun. But the ladder man was too quick for him and pulled the weapon away. Libby could see that her fists weren't getting anywhere, so she opened them, and dragged her sharp painted nails down the bare cheeks of the man. Still crying out, "Cheat! Cheat!" she drew narrow gullies of blood like war paint below both eyes. The ladder man was thrown off balance by this surprising, painful attack. Confused and humiliated, the big man pointed the revolver at Libby Mather again, pressed the barrel into her stomach, and pulled the trigger.

CHAPTER THREE

THERE WAS, HOWEVER, no gunshot; only the heavy click of the weapon's hammer.

Without thinking, Jack Beaumont flung himself at the ladder man. Not just his hands or his arms or his shoulders—but his whole body. He flew at the perspiring, bleeding penguin whose gun was still against Libby Mather's belly. There was an instant in which Jack had an entirely new sensation: of flying horizontally through the air. But before he had the chance to reflect on the very great strangeness of this he made physical contact with the ladder man.

The ladder man was propelled sideways onto the roulette table. Chips scattered, and the ladder man's cheek was pierced by the spirelike point of the roulette wheel. He screamed in agony, and in another moment blood began to gush out of the small puncture wound and splash into the circular cavity of the roulette wheel—rather like a Burgundy wine poured into a punch bowl.

Jack was unharmed; the ladder man himself had acted as a cushion. Jack rolled off onto the table, and then stood shakily.

Pandemonium had broken out around him, with croupiers, the doorman, ladder men, and bouncers hurtling toward the scene, and with guests at that illegal establishment rushing away in the opposite direction as quickly as possible. With people screaming uncontrollably, Jack could see Libby nowhere.

He looked around frantically—locking eyes with Susan Bright for a brief moment before she was hurried away by Rodolfo—and then he found Libby again. Calm and unruffled, she had crawled beneath the roulette table in order to retrieve the gun the ladder man had dropped when Jack hit him. Jack reached beneath the table, and dragged her out. As he pushed her away toward the door of Mr. Vance's establishment, Libby deftly slipped the pistol into her purse.

Jack had already decided to abandon his coat. It was much more important to get out of there. He was glad that Mr. Vance's establishment had been so well-attended this evening; Jack and Libby were easily hidden in the panicky crush at the door. With their heads down, in the middle of the mob, it would have been nearly impossible for Rodolfo's friends to get at them.

"Aren't we going to say good-bye to Susan and her friend?" Libby demanded, grimacing—even under the circumstances—against the lapse of etiquette.

"You can send a little note in the morning," said Jack, pushing her out the door, "telling her how much we enjoyed the evening's entertainment."

In a couple of minutes, they were down on the street. There was a large group there, trying frantically to flag taxis, and everyone recognized Jack and Libby as the couple who had precipitated the brawl and cut the evening short. Jack and Libby were the recipients of a panorama of hostile stares. Jack blushed violently. Libby appeared not to notice, but loudly voiced the opinion that since they were so many, perhaps they ought to form a line for taxis.

Libby's suggestion was not acted upon, and she said petulantly to Jack, "There's no point in waiting around here. By the time all these people have got taxis you could be arrested for assault and battery."

Jack blinked. "I saved your life."

"No you didn't," returned Libby, and held up her opened purse for his inspection.

Jack peered inside it. There lay the gun with the chamber open. It was empty.

"It wasn't loaded," said Libby.

"Let's get out of here," said Jack, taking her by the elbow and hurrying her along toward Park Avenue.

"We're going to *walk* home?" Libby wailed.

"It's exactly five blocks to your place," said Jack.

"It's really quite a nuisance," said Libby.

"Five short blocks?" asked Jack.

"No. I mean, now that you've attacked one of the men who runs the place, we won't ever be able to go back there."

"If the wheel was crooked," asked Jack, "why would you want to?"

"Oh, you're right!" laughed Libby, then cried out in pain as one of her spikes slipped and she twisted her ankle. "Slow down, Jack. Nobody's after us."

Jack slackened his pace, but glanced nervously over his shoulder and kept close to the façades of the buildings along Park Avenue.

Libby Mather owned a penthouse duplex on the east side of Park Avenue, between Sixtieth and Sixty-first streets. She had inherited it from her father, and she redecorated it every eighteen months, always around a particular theme. Most recently the theme had been Arabia, so the floors were covered with Oriental carpets, the walls and ceiling were hung with patterned fabric, the lighting was dismal and yellow, and there was nothing to sit on except big spangle-covered red pillows. It was so decidedly uncomfortable that Libby spent as little time there as possible.

"Would you get rid of this please," Libby said to the elevator man as they were getting out. With a little grimace of distaste, she pulled the unloaded gun out of her purse—handling it gingerly by the barrel—and dropped it into the elevator man's outstretched hand.

"Yes, Miss Mather," said the elevator man politely, and the doors slid smoothly shut behind them.

The elevator opened directly into the apartment, and Jack, who badly wanted a drink, groped his way forward into the entrance hall. "The problem with this place," said Jack, "is that even with the lights on, you still need a flashlight to get around. I need a drink."

"Well, you know where the booze is," Libby said.

With so much hanging drapery and fabric it was hard to know with any precision where to find walls and doors, but Jack made his way into the kitchen—one of the few rooms that hadn't been altered beyond recognition by the decorators. The lighting was very white and bright. He rummaged through the liquor bottles in one of the cabinets until he found the rye he was looking for.

Libby came up behind him and snaked her arms around his chest as he was pouring a big slug of the whiskey into a highball glass, neat.

"You're so sweet," she said.

"Because I tried to save your life?"

"Yes—and because you probably killed that ugly man. Just for me."

"You're welcome," said Jack. "But I wish I had known that gun wasn't loaded." He swallowed off a fair amount of the liquor at one gulp, then turned around within the confines of Libby's embrace, and she pressed her cheek against his chest. "I'm not used to a lot of action," Jack said. "At least not since I took up investment counseling."

"Hold me close, Jack, please—I was so scared..."

Jack looked down at Libby with surprise. He felt her breasts pressing hard against him. It was a nice feeling. Libby had the type of breasts that men vulgarly—and privately—referred to as "bullet tits."

"You weren't frightened," he said, pushing her off a little—before he became embarrassed. "Not one bit. I was the one who was scared. Didn't you feel that gun?"

"Of course," said Libby. "But I knew it wasn't loaded."

"How did you know?"

"I figured that a gambling house wouldn't shoot their clientele. Bad for business."

"So when he pulled that trigger he was just trying to frighten you?"

"Of course. I was so scared, Jack," she added with brazen inconsistency. "Please hold me tight. We can..."

She was pulling in close again, and Jack tried to take another long swallow of his rye. Libby however came in too fast, hitting the bottom of the glass with her head. The edge of the glass knocked sharply against Jack's teeth, causing his whole head to vibrate, and sloshing the liquor down the front of Libby's dress.

"Oh darn!" exclaimed Libby and, without a single moment of hesitation, she drew down the dress at both shoulders, exposing her brassiere in the harsh kitchen light.

"Libby!" Jack exclaimed.

"This *was* a good dress," Libby complained, as she wriggled out of it entirely. "A very good dress." She tossed it into the sink. Jack stared at her in her underwear. Maybe the incident at Mr. Vance's establishment had unsettled her brain. Libby appeared to take no notice of the fact that she was standing temptingly half-clothed in front of him. Something was going on, he felt certain, but what it was exactly he had no inkling. "I had no idea you were so clumsy, Jack. Do these little accidents always happen around you?" She peered at him closely. "There's a gravy stain on your jacket."

Jack mixed a pitcher of highballs and carried it into the living room. He piled up a couple of the spangled red pillows and made himself as comfortable as was possible under the circumstances. Libby had disappeared into her bedroom, and now emerged wearing a blue Chinese robe. Jack could tell that beneath the robe she was no longer wearing those underclothes which had seemed to him—in the harsh light of the kitchen—to be as formidable as the armor plating on an armadillo.

"I'm calling the decorators tomorrow, and I'm having the whole place redone. Marie Antoinette, I think. She may have had her head cut off, but at least while she was alive she got to sit on chairs."

"I remember when this apartment had chairs," said Jack, looking around. "And it once had views, too."

"Oh, they're still there," said Libby, seating herself voluptuously on a pile of pillows only inches away from Jack. Libby's perfume was a good deal stronger than the light in the room. Not just lilacs, but a whole damned arboretum of sweet-smelling blooms. "The views are behind this fabric somewhere. All this will come down—I hope. You can have views with Marie Antoinette, I think. Not everything has to be covered up with thick curtains, does it?"

"Libby, you have all the money in the world. You can do anything you want to."

"That's right," said Libby, gratified with the thought. "Absolutely anything. What went on between you and Susan tonight?" she asked suddenly.

"Nothing much, except that she insulted me relentlessly," said Jack.

"Did she insult me, too?"

"I didn't let her."

"You're so gallant. Not only did you save my life—sort of—but you prevented another woman from saying terrible things about me behind my back. When did you two come to a parting of the ways?"

"Years ago, Libby. She and I..."

"What?"

He shook his head. "We came to a parting of the ways. That's all."

"Then there wasn't any real...unpleasantness?"

"Oh, there was plenty of that," said Jack. "And you'd think she'd be over it by now."

"Oh no, darling, Susan holds a grudge forever. For *eons*. Remember, I went to school with her. We were confidantes. She's never forgiven me for something perfectly horrible I did to her when we were at Smith. So I know she'll never forgive you. And what did you find out?"

"Find out? About what?"

"About Rodolfo. That dark-skinned person—except he wasn't as dark-skinned as a Cuban should be."

"Nothing," said Jack. "Nothing at all."

"You didn't ask?"

Jack hesitated. He suspected this was a trick question, but everything about this evening was so peculiar that he hadn't any idea how he *ought* to answer. "It wasn't any of my business, Libby. Susan Bright has every right to keep company with whomever she pleases. Even if the company she keeps has friends who run gambling casinos and carry weapons."

"Unloaded weapons," said Libby.

"But weapons nonetheless," Jack insisted.

Libby, in a surprising movement, leaned over Jack's reclining body, snatched up the pitcher of highballs, and placed it on the floor on her opposite side. "No more," she said. "I want to talk."

"We are talking," said Jack, reaching for the pitcher. "I

may have killed a man tonight, and I'd like to deaden my conscience a little."

"That man got a little hole in his cheek—that's all. So don't worry about him. I want to talk seriously."

The evening was growing odder by the moment. He suddenly realized that Libby somehow had turned on music somewhere. Probably on her new Zenith Cobra-Matic radio-phonograph that Jack had helped her pick out the previous week. It was very pleasant music. Romantic music, in fact. Maybe all this strange business was leading up to something. He steeled himself for something large and surprising.

"What is it, Libby?"

She paused a moment, sighed deeply, and said solemnly, "Jack—"

"Yes?"

"—I hate your apartment."

He stared at her.

"I hate your apartment," she repeated. "I hate where it is. I hate what it is. And I hate what's in it."

"You've only been there once," said Jack, not understanding the attack.

"An experience I will never forget," said Libby. "I cannot believe it. Those three...tiny...little...rooms. That *location*. Nobody lives between Second and Third avenues, Jack."

"Actually, a great many people do," Jack argued. "I just happen to be the only one you know."

"You have to move," said Libby.

"Why?" said Jack.

"Because when people ask, I will *not* tell them that my fiancé lives between Second and Third." She threw up her hands. "I just won't do it!"

"Your...fiancé..." Jack repeated slowly.

He asked for the pitcher of highballs. Libby reluctantly allowed the indulgence, and he poured himself another.

"When did I become your fiancé?" Jack asked. Her

statement was so unexpected that he felt he ought to explore the curious situation as logically and as slowly as possible. "I thought I was your investment counselor."

"This afternoon you were just my investment counselor. Tonight you're both."

Jack nodded slowly, but didn't comment. Had he proposed to Libby, and forgotten the fact in the melee at the gambling club? That didn't seem likely.

"You just said that with my money I could have anything I wanted," Libby pointed out.

"I did say that," Jack acknowledged, and as he finished off that highball he began to wish that he hadn't had any.

"And as it appeared," Libby went on, "that you had no intention of asking me, I decided—"

"—that you would ask me," said Jack, completing the thought.

Libby drew back in horror. "I would *never* ask a man to propose to me," she protested. "But that's no reason that I can't accept." She smiled a ravishing smile, and altered the position of her voluptuous body on the pillows so that it was even more alluring than before. The lighting in this room, Jack decided, had been designed precisely for the purpose of complementing the gold of Libby's hair.

"You must get at least twenty offers of marriage a week," said Jack. "From all sorts of men. Why have you decided to accept the one offer that wasn't made?"

"I think it's very rude of you to quiz me on such a delicate subject," said Libby. "It's not every day that I accept a proposal."

Jack cleared his throat, and held out his glass. It was strange that the more he drank, the soberer he felt.

The funny thing was, Jack *had* thought about proposing to Libby. Often. His friends had suggested it to him as a wise course. The men above him in the firm had made jokes to him about it. He had received long-distance telephone calls from his father on the subject. Beyond the fact that he was truly fond of Libby, despite her obvious shallowness of character and often idiotic behavior, Jack could think of four reasons to marry Libby Mather: Libby was rich, Libby had a fabulous figure, Libby was very rich, and Libby was evidently in love with him. Besides those four, there was the additional argument that Libby was very *very* rich.

It was Jack who had handled Libby's finances for the past three and a half years, so he had an even better idea than Libby just how much money she had. To Libby, Jack's yearly income was like the pennies that gathered at the bottom of her purse.

She held out her hand to him. He took it politely.

"See?" she said.

"See what?" he said.

"You even bought me a ring."

Four or five karats' worth, he judged. Square-cut. Tiffany setting.

Jack smiled at the ring, and he smiled at Libby; then he asked, "Why me?"

She pulled her hand back, and pondered the question, as if she thought it surprising, but interesting.

"You're probably the only man I know—the only man in our circle—who hasn't courted me for my money. I'm like a cow to them. To be led to slaughter for the meat I'll bring. That's what I feel like. You've never done that."

Jack blinked. "Libby, all I *do* is think about your money."

"Yes, but that's your job. That's different. And—as far as I can tell—you've done a very good job."

"Thank you," said Jack modestly.

"So now it's time for you to take *real* control of my money, by marrying me. Then we can get rid of that awful place where you live. It doesn't matter to me if you propose because of my money, or because you like my figure— that's why so many people hate me, you know, because first they see my figure, and *then* they hear how much money I've got. Anyway, I don't care why you ask me to marry you. Because"—and Jack had never found Libby Mather to be so candid, so straightforward, or so attractive—"I'm in love with you. I always have been. That's why I dislike Susan so much—because I think you used to be in love with her. So I would be saying yes to your proposal because I love you. And you would be proposing because...well, I don't really care why you propose to me, as long as you do it, of course."

For a few moments Jack said nothing.

Then he spoke briefly and to the point.

CHAPTER FOUR

SUSAN SAW THE gun in the hand of the ladder man, and her first instinct was to rush forward in an attempt to warn Libby of the danger. She took a half-step forward, and her mouth was open to shout, but then Rodolfo had a hand on her arm and was pulling her in the opposite direction.

Before she had time to protest his interference, the fight had broken out, and the crowd had begun to rush for the exit. At any rate, Libby was obviously still alive.

"It is their fight, not ours," explained Rodolfo, as he led her away from the uproar toward a far corner of the room where there was a small folding screen that Susan had not noticed before. They slipped behind the screen and Susan saw that it concealed a small door. Rodolfo opened the door and pushed her through into a small room on the other side.

"You will be safe here," he said. "I will make sure your friends are all right."

Before Susan could say a word he had shut the door. To her astonishment, when she turned the knob she found it was locked.

She blinked, trying to dissolve her surprise, and looked around the room.

It was an office of some sort, expensively done up with a huge mahogany desk, leather furniture, paneled walls, and an Oriental carpet, but she somehow got the impression that it was rarely used. It didn't have a window, and the only other door led to a tiny bathroom, also without a window. Either the commotion in the gambling room had suddenly stopped or the room was soundproof, for Susan heard nothing.

She didn't know what to do or to think. How had Rodolfo known about this room? And why was he so anxious for her to be out of the main room?

She seated herself in one of the chairs facing the great desk, and was uncomfortably reminded of the half dozen times she had been interviewed by prospective employers. She felt as if she were being kept waiting for the entrance of the great man himself.

Then she noticed that there was no telephone.

Nothing about this place made any sense; then she decided that it was better to snoop than to conjecture.

She stood up and stepped around to the other side of the desk and began opening drawers. In the top right-hand one were three number 2 pencils, unsharpened. In the second drawer was an unopened ream of bond paper. The third held only a cast-iron paperweight in the shape of the Statue of Liberty. In the center drawer was a box of Gem paper clips and an envelope filled with large rubber bands. The left-hand drawers were locked.

In one corner of the room were two wooden filing cabinets, but these were also locked. Susan tried unsuccessfully to tilt one of them and from its weight she felt certain that the cabinet was filled with papers.

She went into the bathroom and peered into the medicine chest, which was recessed into the wall: a box of

Doeskin tissues, a tube of Ipana toothpaste, three brand-new toothbrushes, a tin of Band-Aids, and a canister of Stopette spray deodorant.

There was nothing else at all in either room; no sign that anyone used the office as an office. Nothing to read; nothing with a letterhead; nothing bearing a trace of use, abuse, origin, or purpose. It was like a movie set office—it looked right from a certain angle, but didn't stand up to close inspection.

The more she thought about the room, the greater its mystery.

She returned to her interviewee's chair in front of the desk and sat down again. Then she thought about Rodolfo, to see if that would help make a little sense of the business.

What Susan had told Jack was true—Rodolfo was a friend of the family, though the connection was tenuous at best. Rodolfo had called with a recommendation from her uncle, James Bright. But, Susan had met her uncle James only twice, and then not since she was fourteen, which was the last time—as far as she knew—that he had visited the United States. So it was on the basis of his acquaintance with that slightly known relative that Rodolfo had one day called her up, and asked her to take pity on a poor, ignorant foreigner cast into the wilds of New York City. That had been six weeks ago, and out of boredom at first, and now out of habit, Susan was seeing Rodolfo twice a week or more. He was always charming, always polite, and—it occurred to her now—always a little mysterious. He never talked about his job; in fact, she wasn't absolutely certain he had one. He said he did "work for the consulate," and he claimed, occasionally acted as cicerone for wealthy or important Cubans visiting the city. He lived in a small sublet on Ninety-fourth Street between Fifth and Madison. Once she had visited it for a drink, and found the place strangely cold, with tubular steel furniture on rattan carpets. She hadn't liked it.

All men lied, Susan supposed, but she had never caught Rodolfo in a falsehood. He said little, but every word had the crystal ring of truth. That gave her confidence in him. He was very handsome—*extraordinarily* handsome in fact, almost too good-looking for a man. Large dark eyes with lashes as long as hers. A mouth that had a genuine smile, and a genuine frown, and teeth that were incandescently white. His body was firm and lithe and when she took his arm, or was thrown against him in the back seat of a taxicab, she could feel how strong he was. He had two physical flaws. The first was a scar at the top of his right shoulder she'd glimpsed once when he wore an open-collared shirt. The second was that his beard was heavy and black and grew so quickly that he had to shave at least twice a day.

Most of what Susan liked about Rodolfo, however, was his manner. She had never met a man so supremely confident. And not an iota of that confidence was bravado. He was collected and secure. He thought about what he wanted to say before he spoke, and when he spoke his words conveyed his meaning precisely. His opinions were forthright and tended toward the simplistic, but Susan liked this.

"I like this object and I want it for myself," was the sort of thing Rodolfo tended to say. Or, "I do not want to go to this place, so I will not go."

But he had never made love to her, had never attempted to seduce her; he was as formal, polite, and collected on their tenth meeting as he had been on their first. Now she wondered why she had never found that peculiar. (She had, in fact, found it a relief after so many other, dissimilar experiences with other young men.) Susan had come to no conclusion about Rodolfo by the time he returned, about fifteen minutes later.

"Your friends are perfectly safe," he said, with a smile, closing the door behind him.

Susan's brows wrinkled. She'd thought little about Jack and Libby for the past quarter-hour, so intent had she been on her exploration of the office and her ruminations about Rodolfo.

"That's good," she said, after a moment. And then, coming right to the point: "Why did you put me in here, Rodolfo, and lock the door?"

"I wanted to make certain you would be all right."

"How did you know this room was here?"

"This is Mr. Vance's office," he explained without hesitation. "I have been here before. During the day. Shall we go?"

Susan nodded uncertainly.

He opened the door and stepped back out into the gambling room of Mr. Vance's establishment. As Susan followed, she tried to imagine what she'd find. A woman rhythmically sweeping the floor with a broom? The overfed penguins counting the receipts of the aborted evening? Maybe the room would be empty.

She was wrong. The gambling room was exactly as it had been—filled with well-dressed people enjoying themselves at the blackjack and craps tables. The injured ladder man was no more to be seen, and Jack and Libby were gone, too. The only evidence of the violent altercation was a dark cloth that had been draped over the bloody roulette table.

"Did everyone come back?" she asked, but a moment's observation answered the question. "No, this is a different crowd. None of these people were here before. Where did they all come from?"

Rodolfo shrugged. "I know nothing of the gambling business."

She glanced at the croupiers, the ladder men, the bouncers. All were as she had remembered them—except that a different man sat atop the elevated chair over the roulette wheel.

What had happened while she was locked in Mr. Vance's office?

"Would you like to stay and play for a little while?" Rodolfo asked.

"No, no," Susan replied. "I'm quite ready to go..."

Rodolfo took Susan back down to Washington Square in a taxi. It was a little past midnight.

"Is she very rich?" asked Rodolfo as they rode down Park Avenue.

"Who?" returned Susan, mystified once more.

"Miss Mather. Your friend."

"She's a margarine heiress," returned Susan. "Lots of money. She's one of those people who have even more than you imagine they have."

Rodolfo laughed.

Susan shrugged, and grimaced with the same mild envy she'd felt for Libby Mather's money ever since they'd been in school together. "I could live off the interest on her interest. So could the Netherlands. I've got my trust fund, of course, but my money looks to Libby like the loose change that falls between the cushions of a sofa."

They were silent for a few moments. Susan's thoughts kept returning to what had happened at Mr. Vance's establishment. How long had it been since she'd seen any sort of violence? Not since she'd last seen Jack, she deduced. How strange it was that Jack—an investment counselor— should be a magnet for guns and ambulances. Perhaps, however, this was just an isolated incident. Perhaps...

"You used to be in love with Jack," said Rodolfo matter-of-factly.

Susan turned her head and stared at the Cuban. "Why do you say that?" she asked, trying to keep the sharpness out of her voice.

"There are some things one need not be told in so many words."

"Yes I was. But I'm certainly not now. How did you know? I don't—"

"I saw it in his eyes," said Rodolfo. "Not yours." Susan relaxed. "Do you think he will marry her?" Rodolfo asked.

"Jack?" said Susan. "Marry Libby?"

"Yes."

"I hadn't given it the slightest thought." She looked out the window—the taxi was going down Fourth Avenue now, passing Fourteenth Street. "I hadn't considered it at all. Though he might. Libby's certainly always been after him. Or at least since we were all teenagers together. Jack's prep school held dances with our prep school."

"Would he marry her for her money?"

Susan considered this for a moment, then said, "No, I don't think so. Not directly anyway. Though Jack is peculiar about money. His family used to have a great deal, but after his father died, his mother squandered it all. Every penny. I think that's why he became an investment counselor. So that he could keep other people from squandering their fortunes."

"Then he might marry Miss Mather to keep her from spending all her money unwisely." Susan wasn't certain why that remark made her uncomfortable, but it did. "May I see you tomorrow night?" Rodolfo asked. "I'd like to make amends for tonight."

"Amends? It wasn't your fault what happened. Libby—"

"If you will not allow me to apologize..."

"Yes, of course," said Susan, realizing that this had been merely an excuse for the invitation.

But as she was getting out of the taxi at the door of her apartment building, she wondered why she'd accepted...

That night, in the tiny back bedroom of her small apartment on Washington Square, Susan Bright dreamed that she married Rodolfo García-Cifuentes in Mr. Vance's peculiar, windowless office, with the officiating minister a large, overfed penguin.

Susan Bright had a job at the Metropolitan Museum of Art giving lecture tours of the Gothic, Renaissance, and

Classical collections—two a day in each, with fifteen-minute breaks to rest her feet and massage her throat. It's what a degree in art history got you these days: fifty-two dollars and fifty cents a week, before taxes. It was a good thing she had her small trust fund to lean back on, otherwise she'd have been one of the million other unfortunate twenty-seven-year-old girls in Manhattan with looks, brains, and ambition, who were fighting to get ahead in a system that held about half a dozen positions worthy of their talents.

When Susan wanted extra money she translated Soviet agricultural pamphlets for U.S. military intelligence, though why on earth the army cared by what means the Russians achieved such miserable harvests year after year was quite beyond Susan's power of reasoning. Russian agricultural policy not only dictated the actions of seventy-five million farmers, it provided Susan Bright a very nearly up-to-date wardrobe.

Yet there was something missing from Susan's life. It was hard to fool yourself into thinking your life had true shape and purpose when day after day, six days a week, you glibly expatiated on the glories of Western art to groups of tourists who hadn't the slightest idea what you were talking about. When your odd-hours were spent in the contemplation of soybean, alfalfa, and wheat quotas for the Ukrainian steppes. When your address read Washington Square, but your only view was of a windowless expanse of brick not ten feet away.

"What I need," Susan often said to herself, "is someone to complain to."

Someone-to-complain-to, of course, had certain unspoken qualifications. Male. Handsome. Accomplished. As intelligent as Susan herself.

And Susan had no intention of objecting if someone-to-complain-to also turned out to be quite rich.

Once she had thought it might be Jack Beaumont who filled that particular bill, even though Jack's family fortune had been squandered away by his mother. But things with Jack hadn't worked out, which was the politest way of remembering a relationship that had been a series of cloudy misunderstandings, thunderous arguments, and lightning-bolt accusations only occasionally interrupted by brief spells of sunlit happiness. More and more she had been thinking of Rodolfo García-Cifuentes as one who might fill out the desiderata of the perfect someone-to-complain-to. Susan had taken to lingering in the Spanish rooms of the European painting galleries of the museum, studying the Velàsquez portraits. Handsome men in general, though they tended to be poisoners as often as they were royal councilors.

She was still thinking about Rodolfo when she left the museum on the day after the incident in Mr. Vance's establishment, and that's why it was such a surprise to find not Rodolfo, but Jack, waiting for her on the steps outside.

CHAPTER FIVE

"THIS IS ALL TOO sudden," said Jack to Libby Mather, in response to her demand that he ask her to marry him. Then he wondered where he'd heard that line before.

"Would you like another highball?" asked Libby, pouring one without waiting for his answer, and in the process moving much closer to him. Her garden of perfume seemed to envelop him, but the scent now brought to his mind the thorns that grew around Sleeping Beauty's castle.

"What's the name of that perfume you're wearing?" he asked.

"Quelques Fleurs. Do you like it?"

He nodded yes, which was at least more polite than the emphatic no that first had popped into his mouth.

Libby put her head into his lap. The Cobra-Matic Arm of the new Zenith—the manufacturer had indeed made it look like a snake—did its business and yet another long-playing record began to play on the turntable, and it was even more romantic than the last music had been. The sash of Libby's blue Chinese robe loosened, and with the nail of her middle finger Libby drew a line down the middle of her breast parting the robe—just in case Jack had not noticed her cleavage.

It was a superfluous gesture. Libby looked romantically up into Jack's eyes.

"Yes, yes," she whispered.

"Yes what?" he asked, feeling stupid.

"Yes, Jack, darling, I will marry you. Absolutely. Any time, any place—as long as it's not in the morning, and as long as it's in an Episcopal church on the Upper East Side."

She waited. She breathed in romantically, and her cleavage grew deeper.

Jack finished off the highball Libby had poured for him two minutes before; it was the last of the pitcher. The emptiness of that vessel seemed to act as a signal that it was time Jack did something. He said, "Libby, I can't give you an answer tonight."

"I don't want an answer," said Libby. "I want to hear the question."

"Libby," Jack said, "I can't ask you a question tonight."

"Not *a* question. *The* question."

"Not tonight."

"When, then?"

"Next week," said Jack, and then immediately wondered why he had. He didn't even know what it meant.

"What day next week?"

Jack didn't think at all as he answered: "A week from today."

"Thursday," breathed Libby sultrily. "Next Thursday I'll—"

Jack checked his watch. "Actually, a week from today is Friday. It's past midnight."

Libby breathed deeply and gazed soulfully up into Jack's eyes. At the same time her fingers were busily untying the knot of her sash. Jack struggled to his feet.

"Not a word, Libby. You can't say anything to anybody."

"I won't," she said. "I promise. Next Friday night I'll have a little party—a little engagement party." Her eyes brightened. She was crying. For joy. She grabbed Jack's hand and peered at his watch. "Is it too late to start calling people?"

"I have to go, Libby."

She made no objections; she was already thinking about other things. It was as if she'd made out a list headed Things I Have to Do to Get Married, at the top of which was (1) Find a Husband. Now that she'd accomplished that, she was ready to go to work on (2) Plan the Engagement Party.

Jack staggered out of Libby's apartment; he leaned against the wall of the elevator on his way down to the street; his voice was thick as he mumbled good-night to the elevator man and the doorman of Libby's building. What had he done? Well, he hadn't proposed to Libby; he'd only agreed to propose to her. Now he had a week to figure out some way either to convince himself that the proposal was a good idea, or somehow to convince Libby that it was a bad one.

Jack wasn't certain if a week was going to be long enough in which to recover from the hangover that he had laid down tonight.

Jack was waiting for her on the steps of the Metropolitan Museum of Art. Not Libby, but Susan.

The day was one of the first warm days of spring. Behind the museum the white crabapples were in bloom, and the red crabapples were close to flower. Jack had dressed too warmly, and now sat on the steps with his coat decorously over his arm, pretending to be a tourist; investment counselors did not sit on concrete steps with their jackets draped over their arms, fanning their overheated faces with the brims of their hats. But Jack had a hangover—though it was not as bad as he thought it was going to be—and the night before he had agreed to propose marriage to a woman whom he did not love, so he didn't care just then *what* the prescribed conduct was for up-and-coming Wall Streeters.

He saw Susan emerge through the front doors. It only then occurred to him that if she had exited through the employees' door he would have missed her. He stood and hurried to her, and had opened his mouth to speak, but something stopped him. The lilac perfume again. The simple sheath of a black dress, the red shoes. The black hair, shining in the light of the warm sun. It became very clear to Jack at that moment—despite his hangover, and despite his promise of the night before—that he would never totally love Libby Mather. Susan spoke.

"The museum is closing," she said, "in half an hour."

"I was waiting for you."

"I'm meeting Rodolfo in a few minutes," she said, checking her watch. She went down a few steps, out of the crush, and seated herself quietly. The steps in front of the Metropolitan Museum are wide and shallow, perfect for a woman of Susan's small size. They accommodated Jack less easily. His legs seemed to stretch all the way down to the sidewalk.

"I wanted to talk to you about..."

"About?"

Jack cleared his throat. He looked away. He straightened the crease in his trousers.

"About?" Susan prompted again.

"Rodolfo," Jack got out at last.

Susan just nodded. As if she'd seen this coming two miles away.

"I think I'll move farther down," said Susan. She got up, and walked down nearly to the sidewalk. After a few moments of surprise, Jack followed her. "You are as persistent as you are rude," she said quietly. Now when Jack stretched his legs out, they did reach the sidewalk.

"I'm not trying to be rude," said Jack, straightening the crease again, and fanning his face with his hat. "It's just..."

Susan wouldn't look at him. An unaccompanied off-white mongrel dog with a singularly dopey expression on his face wandered by on the sidewalk, and Susan called out softly, "Come here, Jack, come here, boy."

The dog, which was of medium size but had paws that would have looked more natural at the extremities of a mastiff, immediately trotted over to Susan and lapped a generous amount of saliva into the palm of her hand.

"How did you know that dog's name is Jack?"

She lifted the animal's long ears and let them drop. If dogs grin, that dog grinned. It licked Susan's shoe. Then her ankle.

"If his name isn't Jack," said Susan, "it should be. He's awkward, overly eager, and none too smart. Aren't you, Jack?"

"He seems a very noble dog, with an engaging disposition," said Jack. "Maybe I should buy him a hot dog. If I buy him a hot dog, will you call him something else?"

Susan wouldn't answer. Jack rose and went over to the man selling hot dogs from a cart at the curb not far away. He purchased two—with ketchup and relish—and brought them back over.

"I don't think dogs like ketchup and relish," said Susan.

In two bites the dog gobbled down the hot dog Jack gave him. He barked his pleasure, and the bark sounded like "Woolf!"

"That's what I'll call him," said Susan, and imitated the happy bark. "Woolf!"

Woolf sat down on his haunches, and looked at the other hot dog Jack was holding.

"I want this one," said Jack, but Woolf cocked his head, and looked so forlorn that Jack relented and gave him half—after he'd scraped all the relish on to his side.

"I thought you came here to make snide remarks about Rodolfo," said Susan.

"Questions," said Jack, who had been trying to put it off. "Not snide remarks. Who is he?"

"What right do you have to ask me that question?"

"An old friend's right," Jack said.

"Is that what we are?" asked Susan. "After four years, sworn enemies dwindle into 'old friends.'"

"We were never sworn enemies. You just couldn't bear the sight of me. Rodolfo doesn't exist."

"What?"

"He doesn't exist. He didn't go to Harvard. The Cuban consulate has never heard of him. The Cuban embassy in Washington has no record of his being here in America. He has no account at the Banco de Habana. He doesn't belong to that club down on Sixtieth Street where all the rich South Americans go. He's not—"

"Did you hire a detective?" asked Susan coldly.

"I did all this myself," said Jack quietly. After a moment he added, "Libby and I were worried."

Woolf stood with his front paws on the wax paper Jack had brought the hot dogs over in, and was licking off every dab of relish and ketchup that remained on it.

"You might have saved yourself some trouble," said Susan. "I know exactly who Rodolfo is."

"Who is he?" asked Jack in some surprise.

"You still don't have the right to ask me that question."

"Granted. But I'd feel better if you told me."

"Do you remember my uncle?" she asked, glancing at her watch.

"I remember you had one."

"I have two, actually. The one on my mother's side lives in San Francisco. Do you remember where the other one—the one on my father's side—lived?"

Jack tried to recall. Suddenly, the light of remembrance came into his eyes. "Cuba?"

Susan smiled coldly. "That's right. Do you remember what he did there?"

"He..." This Jack couldn't remember.

"...owned a plantation," said Susan. "Tobacco and sugarcane. Evidently Rodolfo's family is from the same area. Everybody around there raises tobacco and sugarcane."

"Then why is there no record of him here?"

"Perhaps the people you called felt you had no right to make those inquiries," Susan suggested. "Perhaps they thought you were incredibly rude and presumptuous. Perhaps they felt that you were being a snoop. A busybody. A troublemaker. Someone who tries to interfere in other people's business for no good reason. Someone who..." She broke off with a shrug, seeming to indicate that she might have gone on in that vein for some time to come.

"Is that what you think?" Jack asked.

"Oh no, of course not! I think you had every right in the world to pry into my affairs! Every right to play the role of a cheap detective. Every right to intrude yourself where you're not wanted, not welcomed, and not needed."

"That's not what I meant to do," Jack protested mildly.

"Rodolfo's late," Susan said, looking at her watch again. "It's his principal fault. Maybe if you'd have done a little more investigating, you'd have found that out."

"I'll go," said Jack, and got to his feet. "It's just that..." He couldn't think how to finish.

Susan gazed up at him with a steady eye.

"It didn't work out between you and me," she said. "So I don't understand why you..."

Woolf had finally given up on the wax paper and abandoned Jack and Susan in favor of the hot dog stand, where he waited in patient expectation of the vendor or another kind customer to give him another wiener, preferably with the works.

The vendor once or twice tried to kick Woolf away, but Woolf cannily stationed himself out of the reach of the vendor's extended leg.

"No!" said the vendor. "You don't get none! Go 'way, pooch. Scram!"

Woolf, as if he understood every word, set his sights on another vendor on the opposite side of Fifth Avenue, and with a tongue-lolling insouciance, padded eagerly out into the street.

Susan saw the traffic light change from red to green, and she saw that Woolf, in the middle of Fifth Avenue, was directly in the path of a taxicab and two trucks, behind which were a blue DeSoto convertible and a municipal bus. They were now speeding forward with the energy of mismatched racehorses released at a starting gate.

She raised her hand and pointed, but she never screamed. It was yet another of those things that distinguished her in Jack's mind from all other women.

But Jack had already seen Woolf's danger, had leaped to his feet and was now in the middle of Fifth Avenue, with the traffic bearing down on him.

Woolf had turned with a sloppy grin to greet him, and Jack scooped the dog up in his arms.

Horns were blowing frantically, and a truck slammed past on either side of Jack, plunging him and Woolf into a long canyon of metal and enormous rubber tires. And when those high walls disappeared, Jack found himself staring at the rapidly approaching grille of an enormous blue convertible.

And behind the wheel of the DeSoto, Jack saw a face he recognized.

Rodolfo García-Cifuentes' face.

CHAPTER SIX

Dogs ARE SUPPOSED to possess a sense of danger. They are reputed to be able to identify hypocritical strangers in all their hidden perfidy; to smell out rabid squirrels in the underbrush of the park; to warn of the prowler at the gate.

With Rodolfo García-Cifuentes' blue DeSoto convertible rushing at them down Fifth Avenue, Woolf eagerly lapped at Jack's face.

Unable to fling himself either to the right or the left for safety, and it being nonsensical to try to outrun the speeding DeSoto, Jack heaved the dog away from him—toward Rodolfo in his car—as if the impact of dog and automobile would save him.

Then he jumped himself.

Woolf landed in the front passenger seat of the DeSoto, and Jack crashed with a hard thump onto the hood of the vehicle, rolled over the metal hot from the engine beneath and grabbed hold of the edge of the windshield. His hat flew off and was instantly crushed by a Piels beer truck.

"Stop, please," Jack begged Rodolfo.

Rodolfo pulled over to the curb as soon as traffic permitted.

Woolf, with an appropriate appreciation of his miraculous escape, generously licked the back of Rodolfo's hand. Rodolfo gently pushed the dog's muzzle away from him, and cautioned him, in Spanish, not to drool on the seat.

A small crowd gathered around the automobile, curiously examining Jack, but carefully refraining from touching him. Jack still clung to the windshield.

"Our friend is very lucky," said Rodolfo to Susan, who had pushed aside the crowd to get to the car.

Susan began to pry Jack's fingers one by one from the rim of the windshield.

"Woolf," she said, "you are a very silly dog."

Jack was peering at Susan. His scraped cheek was pressed against the glass. Then he tried to raise his head, but the collar of his shirt had caught and held him fast on the windshield wiper mechanism.

"Jack," said Susan, "do please get up before the police come and we have to explain everything and make out a written report. Rodolfo, you do have a license that's good here in America, don't you?"

Rodolfo blinked, and said quietly, "Yes of course, but I'd rather not show it. Police..."

"Yes, I know," said Susan. "More trouble than they're worth. My mother always advised me against getting arrested. Jack, *please* get down from there."

She reached under his arms, got a good hold on his torso, and pulled.

His shirt, still caught, ripped a bit, but did not come loose. By the time Susan had pulled him off the hood of the car onto the sidewalk he had pulled off the wiper mechanism entirely.

The crowd, curious and silent, had gathered in a tight circle, still watching the proceedings.

"Here comes a policeman," warned an old lady in a feathered hat, tugging politely at Susan's sleeve.

Woolf stood with his forepaws on the back of the seat, and began barking at the approaching policeman.

"All right, stand up," said Susan to Jack, with exasperation. She dragged out the windshield wiper that dangled from his shirt collar. "And pretend nothing happened. You got dizzy. You can say it must have been the hot dog."

Jack, dazed and bruised, leaned against the side of the DeSoto. Remaining in the front seat, Rodolfo smiled a tight smile at Woolf, and tried without success to keep the dog from barking.

The policeman had also been eating a hot dog and was now wiping mustard from his mouth with the back of his hand. He gently parted the crowd and approached the convertible.

"We stopped for a hot dog," said Susan without preamble, "and our friend got dizzy. He'll be all right."

The policeman looked at Susan, looked at Jack's torn shirt and the windshield wiper, looked at Rodolfo in the driver's seat, and then threw his glance slowly over the small assembled crowd.

"It was the mustard," someone ventured. "The mustard on the hot dog must have gone bad."

"He got dizzy when he tried to fix the windshield wiper," someone else said. Then after a pause, to Rodolfo, "You'll have to take it to a garage now."

The policeman said to Susan, "Is your friend drunk?"

Jack shook his head no, with exactly the care a drunk takes when he's trying to show someone that he's not had too much to drink.

Woolf had jumped into the back seat of the car, and was barking incessantly directly at the policeman's back.

"Does that dog have a collar?" the cop demanded, turning around suddenly, and staring at the mongrel.

"We were on our way to get one," said Susan. "But Jack hadn't had any lunch so we stopped for a hot dog, and I think the mustard must have gone bad. Like the man said."

The policeman sighed a deep sigh, and said, "Get out of here. Drive away please, and let that guy throw up on someone else's beat, would you?"

"Yes sir," said Susan quickly, "thank you." She smiled at the policeman, and threw an appreciative glance at the small crowd. The people smiled back at Susan, and then began to drift away. "Get in the car," she said in a low voice to Jack, pushing him toward the door. Rodolfo pushed the seat forward, and Susan shoved Jack into the back with Woolf.

In another moment, just as the policeman was staring thoughtfully at Rodolfo's license plate, the vehicle eased its way back into the traffic. Rodolfo turned off the avenue at the next corner.

As soon as the policeman was lost to sight, Woolf quit barking, turned around, and again began licking Jack's face.

The following morning, directly after tour number 3 (Spanish Renaissance), Susan stuck a nickel into the pay telephone in the employees' lounge of the museum and dialed Jack's number. She had looked it up that morning before coming to work; someone invariably stole the directories in the employees' lounge, no matter how often they were replaced.

Jack answered, groggily.

"It's Susan Bright," she said hesitantly. "I called to find out if you'd recovered."

There was a small pause before he answered. "I'm all right. I think."

"I woke you up."

"That's all right."

"Did you go to the doctor? I wish you had let Rodolfo and me take you to the doctor."

"I'm fine. I didn't need to see a doctor. I was just a little shaken up."

"You wouldn't even let us take you upstairs," said Susan. "I would have felt better—"

"I had seen enough of Rodolfo García-Cifuentes."

Susan decided to remain silent. In the ensuing pause, she heard violent barking on the other end of the telephone.

"Shut up, Woolf!" Jack said, away from the receiver.

"I forgot about him. Are you going to keep him?"

"I guess so. Until he throws himself out the window. This dog has no sense of height. I think he was raised in Kansas or somewhere. And then wandered off the prairie onto Fifth Avenue."

"Are you feeding him hot dogs?"

"Cheese, actually. I cut it into hot dog shapes. Are you going to continue to see Rodolfo?"

"Jack—"

"He tried to kill me, you know."

"You jumped out in front of his car."

"He didn't even try to stop."

"He didn't have time to stop. Besides, he didn't."

"Didn't what?"

"Kill you."

"Has he ever introduced you to any of his friends?"

"Jack, this is none of your business. None of your business whatsoever. I only called because—"

"He hasn't, has he? You've never met any of his friends. That's because he doesn't have any and he doesn't have any for the simple reason that he doesn't exist."

Susan hated the smugness in Jack's voice. Susan was glad that what she said next was true.

"He's invited me to have dinner tonight—"

"Don't accept."

"—at the home of the Cuban consul."

Susan waited for a response from Jack. None came. Good, she thought, that shut him up.

"He said," Susan went on, "that I had never met any of his friends, and it was time I did. He said he wanted to make up for yesterday's accident."

"See? He admits it was his fault."

"No, he didn't admit any such thing. It's just that I once told him that it upsets me to see people run down in the street. And it does—even when it's you."

Why was it that Jack always made her say such things? Why did a simple telephone call to ask, "How do you feel?" turn into a tedious barrage of insults?

She'd felt bad for Jack the day before. Never mind that it was an impossibly stupid thing to have done—run out into the traffic of Fifth Avenue in order to save the life of a stray mongrel dog that would probably have made it to the other side of the street without mishap. Never mind that the whole thing wouldn't have happened at all if he hadn't showed up, unasked, unwanted, and totally out of line with vague and unwarranted accusations against Rodolfo. Never mind that Jack had been positively rude to Rodolfo at the door of the apartment building, refusing Rodolfo's help up to his flat. Never mind that Jack never ever failed to say something or do something that immediately annoyed her when they were together for more than five minutes. Nevertheless Susan had felt sorry for Jack when she pried him loose from the hood of Rodolfo's car.

Now she was glad she had called him. He was as impossible as ever. His narrow brush with death hadn't improved him. He was very very annoying, and she didn't need to feel sorry for him anymore.

"Good-bye, Jack," she said suddenly. "Look both ways before crossing." Then she hung up the telephone, sat down, and rubbed her feet for a couple of minutes before she went out to meet tour group number 4 (the Age of Pericles).

While she sat there she thought about Jack some more. In the four years since she'd last seen him, she had often considered what it would be like to run into him again, but she had always envisaged that event taking place in an environmental vacuum with nothing to distract from the actual drama of the encounter.

It hadn't happened that way the night before last. Immediately after she'd insulted him at the bar of Mr. Vance's, she'd seen Jack do a wonderful and brave thing. He had protected Libby's life at the risk of his own. The following day he had risked his life again, to save a dog from being run down in the street.

He'd never done that for her.

She remembered the bitterness of their parting—or rather, she remembered that she had felt bitter at the time.

No trace of that was left.

But if that really was so, then why had she been so unpleasant toward him for two days running?

She didn't like her own answer to that question. She had been unpleasant because she had feared that he still would be bitter toward her and that his animosity would be undiminished, and she would have to show him that she could match him.

But now, she was forced to admit, he seemed to harbor no such resentment. But did it really matter?

The previous day, after taking Jack home, Rodolfo had driven Susan directly to Washington Square. Rodolfo had parked and walked her to the door of her building. At the entrance, Rodolfo had kissed her.

His lips were hard and dry, his beard was coarse.

CHAPTER SEVEN

JACK STOOD NAKED in front of the full-length mirror on the back of his closet door and looked at his body. Actually, he looked at the bruises on his body. The bruises that were on his left leg—all up and down it. The bruises to his rib cage. He probed them with his fingers and they were tender. There was a long scrape from his neck to his solar plexus—the windshield wiper had done that. He turned around and looked over his shoulder. More bruises on his back, particularly on the left side. It felt like his joints creaked. Woolf came over and licked him where it tickled.

"Go away, Woolf."

He was too sore even to bend over and push the dog away. He went into the bathroom and stared at the tub, wishing it were possible for him to lie in it at full length. Jack's apartment building was newly converted, which meant that the apartments in it were newly small and newly inconvenient. Jack's apartment and two others had been made out of what had been one decent-sized flat. A living room, a bedroom, a bath with a tub that was only big enough for people less than five feet tall, a kitchen that was more suggestive of a dent in the living room wall than a place in which to prepare meals, and what the realtor had called "a winter closet." Jack had no idea what that meant, since there wasn't a summer closet to match it. There was only one tiny clothes closet, in fact. The view was not much to speak of either: both windows in the apartment overlooked a small echoing courtyard where the superintendent's children played incessantly. Nevertheless, Jack was pleased with the place. He was a bachelor, and bachelors don't need a lot of room. The apartment was furnished with a dozen fine pieces of furniture rescued from the wreck of his mother's fortune. It was old, and the upholstery was worn and faded, but it was comfortable and bore some old-fashioned charm and lent the flat a kind of gentility.

Jack turned the water on hot and stood in the shower, turning his bruises to the needles of steaming water. He came out wrinkled and tired and glad that it was Saturday and he wasn't expected at work.

He made coffee, and thought about Susan's call that had awakened him. He was glad she had called. He liked hearing her voice. He liked to think she cared whether he lived or died.

Woolf had made known his desire to go out by scratching at—thereby removing a fair portion of paint from—the door of the winter closet, evidently thinking that this was the way out of the apartment.

Jack put on loose clothing that would brush against his bruises as little as possible, improvised a leash out of an old rope that was tied around his fishing-rod case at the back of the closet, attached the three-foot length of cord to Woolf's collar, and sallied forth.

Woolf was a strong dog, and the leash was short and none too sturdy. Woolf pulled so hard that the bruises on

Jack's arm felt as if they were being stretched into areas of discomfort darker and larger than before. Woolf dragged Jack forward along Sixty-first Street in the direction of Second Avenue, which fortunately was exactly where Jack had intended to go. Woolf wouldn't allow Jack to stop at the first shop they came to, or the second. At the third, the dog consented to be tied to a parking meter while Jack went inside. Jack bought a box of Pep whole wheat cereal, three boxes of Birds Eye frozen vegetables, two bottles of Canada Dry club soda, and a box of Clix dog candy.

Not only the leash, but Woolf himself was wrapped tightly about the parking meter by the time Jack came out again. Jack carefully put down the groceries and untangled Woolf, who was in danger of choking himself and breaking both forelegs with his energetic movements against the rope.

"If I don't use the leash," Jack said to the dog, "will you promise to run away?"

"Woolf," shouted Woolf.

But Woolf did not run away. In fact, he trotted along at Jack's heels so close to Jack that several times Jack stumbled and nearly fell face forward onto the sidewalk.

Jack was thinking about Libby now, and the fact that in one week—bruises or no bruises—Libby was expecting him to ask for her hand in marriage. His thoughts were rambling. Libby had a huge pantry. Libby even had people who went out and bought groceries for her. Jack wondered if Libby would mind a dog with so little pedigree as Woolf. Jack wondered—

He wondered what the hell he was going to do, married to Libby Mather, the nationally known margarine heiress. He didn't really *need* all that money, and despite Libby's objections, he liked this apartment well enough.

Besides, he told himself, he liked being a bachelor.

Actually, what he liked was holding himself open in case Susan Bright ever decided she wanted to have something to do with him again. Jack didn't like to admit such things, even to himself, but his bruises hurt—every one of them—and it felt like Woolf was pulling Jack's arm out of its socket. A man admitted things under physical duress he wouldn't own up to otherwise.

The elevator man didn't approve of Woolf; pets were against the rules of the building. Jack named seven tenants of the building who owned dogs, and two more who owned more than one dog. "Number seventeen, I've been told," Jack said to the elevator man, "has a room that is completely given over to parakeets. They fly free," he added darkly. He gave the elevator man a five-dollar bill, and the elevator man conceded, "This dog's better behaved than most."

Jack's kitchen consisted of a cupboard that was the size of a medicine chest and a single multipurpose appliance—a Hess combination refrigerator, freezer, sink, oven, and gas range with three burners—all in a white enamel housing the size of a small steamer trunk. Jack put away his groceries, fed Woolf a half-dozen bone-shaped dog candies, and then lay down on the sofa and tried to go to sleep again. If he were asleep he wouldn't feel his bruises, and he wouldn't have to think about the fact that one of the five richest women in America wanted to become his wife.

His mother's sofa was normal sized, which meant that Jack, at his height, did not fit on it. Before long, he had not only bruises, but a sore neck and feet with impaired circulation. But he was asleep. He hadn't actually realized he was asleep, however, until the door buzzer awakened him out of that uncomfortable slumber.

He got up automatically and went toward the door, but his feet didn't work properly, and he stumbled and fell. He might have injured himself had his fall not been broken by Woolf who was barking energetically at the door of the winter closet, still convinced that was the way to the hallway.

The buzzer sounded again.

Jack pulled himself up off Woolf, and moved much more slowly this time. He had no idea who might be on the other side of the door.

It was Rodolfo García-Cifuentes.

Invalids, Jack thought, should not be subjected to unpleasant surprises, which retarded their healing.

Jack said nothing. Did not smile. Did not invite the man inside. There was something about this visit that offended Jack deeply. He tried to think of the last time anyone had showed up uninvited at the door of his apartment. Never.

"I was passing," said Rodolfo, "and I dropped by to see if you were well."

"I've got bruises all over my damned body," said Jack.

"May I come inside?" said Rodolfo, gently pushing away Woolf, who was industriously licking his brushed-leather shoes. The man dressed perfectly, even on a Saturday afternoon. Wearing an oatmeal-colored sport jacket and light brown flannel trousers. His oxford shirt was perfectly complemented by a brown silk tie. The ideal outfit to intimidate a rival in love. In his tousled hair, bare feet, wrinkled shirt, and his too-short trousers, Jack felt grubby.

"Have you recovered yourself?" Rodolfo asked, dropping into a chair with perfect ease, without invitation.

"I'll be fine," said Jack, taking a seat on the couch. "Someday."

Rodolfo smiled. The smile seemed genuine. "I am glad you were not injured."

"Lucky for me—and lucky for you as well," Jack agreed. "Foreign nationals running down native pedestrians is not looked on with favor here." He considered offering Rodolfo something to drink, then decided against it.

Rodolfo smiled again. "Shoo!" he said quietly to Woolf, now licking the cuffs of his trousers.

Jack remained offended by Rodolfo's presence. Whatever his motive in coming was, it was sure to be underhanded, sneaky, unworthy of a man. Jack had decided that one thing about Rodolfo was effeminate: not his appearance, not his carriage, or mannerisms, but his mode of treachery. Jack didn't know what Rodolfo intended to say or do this Saturday afternoon, but he was certain this visit constituted some sort of attack. He may not have had his arm raised high above his head, and there was no knife visible, but it was an attack all the same.

"Susan was very worried," said Rodolfo after a moment of silence.

"She telephoned a while ago."

"Did she?"

"Yes," said Jack.

"She said she intended to. I'm glad she did," said Rodolfo. "She also said you two were once in love."

Jack remained silent, but he could feel what must have been an entire pint of blood surging up out of his heart to suffuse his face with color. Rodolfo smiled. The smile enraged Jack. But he still refrained from speech. The last time he'd gotten into one of these bewildering conversations, he'd asked questions, and he'd ended up engaged—or, rather, engaged to be engaged.

"I am glad," said Rodolfo. Still Jack did not speak. He tried to will the blush to fade. Blood began to flow downward through the veins in his neck. He was beginning to look less like a beet, he hoped. "I do not like to be the first man that a woman has loved," Rodolfo went on. "A woman, when she loves for the first time, does not see clearly love. She does not love, she only imagines that it would be sweet to be in love. It is not she who loves, it is her heart. But the second time..."

The sensation was peculiar—to sit in his own apartment, attending to a Cuban making a disquisition on love.

It made Jack squirm. "The second time?" Jack prompted, and then wished he hadn't.

"...the second time, a woman loves not only with her heart. But with her soul. And with her mind. It is the second love that is the stronger."

"Would you like a drink?" Jack said, getting up and heading for the kitchen.

"No thank you," said Rodolfo politely.

Good, thought Jack, *that leaves more for me*. He poured three fingers of scotch into a glass.

Jack didn't talk about such things as love, neither aloud nor silently to himself. That was why it had taken him so long to realize that he still cared for Susan Bright. That was why he had gotten so entangled with Libby Mather. And now here was Rodolfo, employing love as a theme, and Jack had no idea how to respond.

"Miss Mather is very beautiful," said Rodolfo, when Jack had returned to the couch.

"Pardon?" asked Jack in surprise.

"Susan says she is also very rich." Jack didn't answer. "Very beautiful and very rich. Not all men are so fortunate as to marry a woman like that."

Rodolfo smiled blandly at Jack.

The blood that had been draining slowly through his neck suddenly reversed direction and sped back up into Jack's face. More came up from his heart. He feared his feet would go numb again because it felt like so much blood was rushing upward to fill his cheeks and make his forehead bead with sweat. Sodium pentathal. Lie detectors. The rack and screw. None of those could get the truth out of Jack Beaumont as quickly and as undeniably as his own blushes.

If Rodolfo had been guessing, then he now knew that he had guessed correctly. Jack felt cornered in his own house—as if he'd asked the Spanish Inquisition over for tea or opened the door to Hitler's storm troops.

It also occurred to Jack that Libby, despite her promise of discretion, might have placed an engagement announcement in the paper. The morning *Times* lay on the floor next to the couch. Jack stifled an urge to leap up, grab the paper, and search out the appropriate page to see if his name were publicly linked there with that of Elizabeth St. John Mather.

Instead, he took another swallow of scotch.

"It is an interesting question," said Rodolfo.

"What question?" said Jack.

"Who gets to the altar first." Rodolfo smiled. A smile that said, *I am a romantic Cuban, and my outlook on life is essentially romantic. You are a reserved American man, and do not show your feelings. Ah, well! At heart, you're no less romantic than I...*

Jack didn't buy a bit of it. Rodolfo had come here on a fishing expedition, to find out whether Jack still cared for Susan and to find out if Jack had any intentions toward Libby. By Jack's blushes, Rodolfo had got answers to both questions: Jack was still in love with Susan—whether or not he admitted it to himself. And Jack stood in danger of being married to Libby Mather—whether or not the actual proposal had been made.

Jack blushed again, for himself, and the contradiction in those two statements.

Then Rodolfo said: "I am glad that things have worked out this way."

"What way?" said Jack.

"That you are in love with Miss Mather as I am in love with Susan. So easy. So convenient. We do not step on one another's feet."

Jack said nothing.

"Love..." began Rodolfo, and then shrugged with a smile.

"Love what?" said Jack.

"Love will make a man do what he would not do under another circumstance. Not here, perhaps, but in Cuba," said Rodolfo, "a man may die for love."

"Is that so?" said Jack, idly noticing that his drink was more than half gone already. He pondered the question of whether he should ask Rodolfo to leave politely or ask him to leave in some other fashion—with a threat of instant death if he did not, for instance.

"A Cuban man may even kill for love," Rodolfo added blandly.

That was definitely a threat.

Good, thought Jack, *that's something I can deal with.* But Jack made no immediate response. He wanted to hear how far the Cuban would go.

No further, as it turned out.

"I must leave, and allow you to recover," said Rodolfo. "I would not like Miss Mather to think that I had delivered up her bridegroom as damaged goods."

Jack smiled a smile he hoped was as false as Rodolfo's. Jack saw Rodolfo to the door, and had to grab Woolf by the scruff of the neck to keep him from blithely following after Susan Bright's Cuban suitor.

CHAPTER EIGHT

SUSAN BRIGHT WORKED every Sunday morning, and sometimes evenings as well, quite alone in her small apartment, translating Russian pamphlets, documents, and letters supplied her by the U.S. Army. Even at the best, this was tedious work, but Susan was quick at it and accurate, and so the army used her even though it had a flock of its own specialists. Money earned this way bought Susan hats, the prices of which were in reverse proportion to their size—and hats this year were very small indeed. The work kept her atomizer filled with Duchess of York perfume. And once every two weeks, the translations paid for a trip to the hairdresser's.

She'd already made an appointment for late Saturday afternoon at Monsieur Marcel's—a new shop on East Forty-eighth Street—when Rodolfo asked her to accompany him on Saturday night to dinner at the Cuban consulate. Susan had been to the United Nations and had seen diplomats, but she had never sat down to table with a consul. She decided that she would ask Marcel to cut her hair in whatever was the newest fashion, no matter how peculiar it looked.

She cut her last tour short so that she could get to her appointment on time. The group of fifteen—from the Midwest, mostly—never realized that they had missed two large galleries of Florence and Siena...

Marcel's, from the street, consisted of a tiny door and a tiny window with two bewigged wooden heads staring sullenly out—as if the blades they were advertising were guillotines rather than scissors. Directly inside the door was a small reception area occupied by a red-haired receptionist, a young dragon-in-the-making, who was a martinet about tardiness and *never* let in anyone who hadn't had an appointment. It was rumored that the dragon was in frantic and useless love with Monsieur Marcel.

The layout of Marcel's shop was distinctive; it got bigger as you went farther back. And the place went so far back, that by the time you ever got to see Monsieur Marcel himself you had the feeling you'd already crossed Forty-seventh Street and were burrowing on toward Forty-sixth. First there came two long corridors of changing rooms, where smiling women with cold hands took your coat or your jacket and whatever else you were carrying, gave you a check for them, and then helped you into a large, loose, green smock with large green buttons down the front. (It had been recently reported that these green smocks had now been seen at Palm Beach, as quaint cover-ups for bathing costumes.) The corridors widened into a large room filled with sinks and hair dryers and the sound of rushing water and the thunder of blowing hot air and women talking, talking, talking. A dozen ill-paid female assistants with pruned fingers massaged the scalps of a dozen women in smocks while a dozen more women sat beneath dryers reading about Mamie Eisenhower's plans for redecorating the White House and other such articles of absorbing interest.

Then finally, behind absurdly large double doors of oak, was the inner sanctum of Monsieur Marcel himself. A half-dozen tall raised comfortable chairs were arranged in a circle, facing outward—like some sitting-room Stonehenge— and a half-dozen women, staring at themselves in the mirror-lined walls, were all taken care of simultaneously by Monsieur Marcel and a single assistant. (Monsieur Marcel was a tall man and didn't like to stoop when he was designing. Designing was Monsieur Marcel's own word for what he did.) Monsieur Marcel wore black trousers, a white shirt, and a black silk tie. His skin was very white, and his hair was black and slick. Monsieur Marcel looked like a black-and-white photograph. Monsieur Marcel's assistant looked as if he might be a younger, adoring brother, who tried his best to look and act exactly like his elder sibling. The assistant had red cheeks, however, which gave him an air of health, but spoiled the resemblance.

Susan arrived half an hour before her appointed time. The dragon eyed her suspiciously, checked the appointment book twice, answered the telephone and tried to make it appear that Susan herself was the object of the conversation, and finally allowed Susan to pass through the narrow door behind her desk.

Susan smiled at the young woman who helped her into a smock, picked out a recent issue of *Collier's*, and then stepped into the shampooing room.

The place was always a madhouse of laughter, chattering voices, and running water. The odor of perfume, shampoo, and lotions seemed to take up what little space wasn't occupied by the noise.

On the worst days, a shampoo, cut, and set could take five hours. Four of that was waiting. One girl employed by Monsieur Marcel did nothing but make coffee all day long.

Susan read all the articles in *Collier's*, then picked up a discarded copy of *Vogue*, paying particular attention to the ads. She asked herself what she would buy if she had a million dollars to spare. Not much.

Only two and a half hours of waiting. Not bad.

Her hair was shampooed by a girl whose nails were too long and who went after Susan's scalp very much after the fashion of a cat attacking a scratching post. With a light green towel turbaned on her head, she was led into the inner sanctum. There she waited another ten minutes for an empty chair.

Monsieur Marcel's chaos was organized. When one of the six women in the ring was finished, she got down from her perch and sailed majestically out—the pinnacle of coiffured fashion. Susan climbed into a chair as yet another woman came through the door, to wait *her* ten minutes till a chair was free.

"Susan!"

She didn't even have to turn, she knew the voice. And in the mirrored wall she could see the reflected visage of Elizabeth St. John Mather.

Susan, pretending she hadn't seen or heard, did not immediately respond. Then she arranged herself comfortably in her smock, prepared a tight little smile, looked up again, and said, "Hello Libby. What a coincidence."

Before the two young women could engage in any further conversation, Monsieur Marcel was behind Susan, asking wearily, "Which do you want? The Botticelli, the Bellini, or the Michelangelo?"

The fashion of the day was Italian cuts. A shaggy sculpture of curls, with deep waves on the crown, and spit curls to frame the face. While waiting in the shampoo room, Susan had seen eight women walk out with the same hairdo.

"What's the difference?" asked Susan.

"Well," said Monsieur Marcel, "the Botticelli and the Bellini are exactly the same. The Michelangelo comes with silver streaks."

"Then the Bellini," said Susan.

Monsieur Marcel peered at Susan's face in the mirror. "Turn," he said, and she gave him her profile. "It will look very good on you," he announced. He held out his left hand and from one side of the chair his assistant placed in his grasp a comb. He held out his right hand and the assistant came around the other side to place in his hand a pair of scissors. The assistant melted away. Monsieur Marcel began cutting. Monsieur Marcel didn't converse with his customers; Susan didn't mind.

"Monsieur Marcel," said Libby, having risen from her chair and now standing in front of Susan, braving the hairdresser's iciest, most forbidding smile. "Do you mind if I talk to my friend while you design?"

"Very much," said Monsieur Marcel politely.

Crushed, Libby backed away.

"Thank you," Susan said quietly to Monsieur Marcel. Susan had never seen Libby obsequious before, but really thought that she preferred Libby brash.

In five minutes, Monsieur Marcel had finished. Susan liked what she saw in the mirror; the Bellini suited her.

"Now," said Monsieur Marcel, "we'll let it rest for a moment or two and then we'll come back to you for a final shaping."

Then, as luck would have it, when Monsieur Marcel had finished with the woman in the next chair and sent her packing, Libby Mather took her place.

"I'm *dying* to talk to you," Libby whispered as she climbed up onto the perch. "Poodle," she instructed Monsieur Marcel, "basic poodle."

Monsieur Marcel unwrapped Libby's turban, tossed it at his assistant, and went to work on Libby's head. Italian haircuts didn't suit blondes, and Libby had the sense to know it.

In ten minutes Monsieur Marcel had finished temporarily with Libby and moved on. Libby immediately leaned over toward Susan, and caught Susan's eyes in the mirror.

"I couldn't believe what happened to Jack yesterday, *I couldn't believe it*. And you were there, you saw the whole thing. I was so upset when I heard—*so upset*." Libby was whispering, because Monsieur Marcel didn't approve of conversation in the inner sanctum. It distracted him from design.

"Jack was lucky," said Susan quietly. "Next time he runs out into the middle of a busy street he might get killed."

"What a terrible thing," said Libby sadly, shaking her head. "Do you think Jack is mad at your friend?"

"My friend?"

"Mr. Havana."

"Rodolfo?"

Libby nodded vigorously.

"I don't know if Jack is mad at him or not. How would I know what Jack thinks about anything?"

"You used to be so close," said Libby. "And it's funny—isn't it—how all of a sudden you've come right back into his life after four years? Where have you been hiding all this time?"

"I haven't been hiding anywhere, Libby. I guess we just haven't been traveling in the same circles."

"But now we're running into each other *everywhere*," said Libby.

"Things happen that way," Susan replied vaguely.

"Well," said Libby, "if Jack isn't mad at Rodolfo then I want to invite you and Rodolfo over to my place next Saturday night."

Susan looked at Libby curiously. "I'm not sure it would be a good idea, Libby—the four of us..."

"Oh," said Libby with a careless wave of her hand, "the four of us and about four hundred others. If Jack and Mr. Havana don't want to talk to each other, they won't have to."

"You're having a party for four hundred people?" Susan asked, trying to calculate the cost, even assuming that Libby was exaggerating by a factor of four. Four was Libby's usual standard for exaggeration, Susan remembered.

"Well, about a hundred really. My closest and nearest and dearest friends, they all have to be there. And I want you, too," she added, as if Susan didn't quite fit into the category of closest and nearest and dearest. "And Mr. Havana," as if Rodolfo were quite beyond the pale. "*Everybody* has to be there..."

"They do?"

"Of course," said Libby. "When I announce my engagement."

Susan opened her mouth to reply, but before she had a chance to say anything Monsieur Marcel interrupted their whispered tête-à-tête with a weary, "Ladies...please...*my designs are suffering.*"

❀ ❀ ❀

It was an unfortunate coincidence that the Cuban consulate was on East Sixty-sixth Street. It was nearer Fifth Avenue than Jack Beaumont's apartment, but the address made Susan think of Jack when she did not wish to do so.

There were seventeen at dinner, and Susan was universally admired. For once, with Monsieur Marcel's Italian haircut, Susan had managed to mount the crest of tasteful fashion. She wore her best black dress, and her most translucent pearls. With her white skin and inky black hair she was a feminine version of the austerely black-and-white Monsieur Marcel. Susan Bright, moreover, spoke excellent Spanish, and foreign diplomats are very impressed to meet an American who knows some language besides English.

In turn, Susan was impressed. The Cuban consul treated Rodolfo intimately, drawing him aside several times before dinner, and disappearing with him into a study for half an hour after dinner. Susan herself was treated like—there was no other way to describe it—like a prospective daughter-in-law.

The consul's wife was a handsome, middle-aged woman, who dressed very much as Susan's mother used to dress when Susan was a young girl. Susan liked her for that. While Rodolfo was closeted with the consul, the consul's wife stood with Susan in the bowed window of the drawing room. They drank cups of black coffee laced with rum. Beyond the lace curtains was Sixty-sixth Street, and from where Susan stood, she could see a little bit of Central Park. The consul's wife said to Susan, "We are very fond of Rodolfo. I hope he is good to you, for you are a very nice girl. I have met your uncle in Havana. He is a kind man and he spoke to me of you. He said that one day, you will inherit all his estates. Then, Miss Bright, you will be extremely rich indeed."

CHAPTER NINE

JACK'S BRUISES PROGRESSED through a spectrum of color in the course of the weekend. He watched the changes in his mirror. He grew to be great friends with Woolf because Woolf was always there beside him as he gazed at his damaged reflection. He tried to get Susan on the telephone, but she was either never at home or not answering. Libby commiserated fulsomely on the phone with Jack's pain, but she did not visit him. She was busy planning the party for the following Saturday night, and anyway *nothing* could persuade her to visit that dreadful apartment on that terribly uninteresting street. Jack went out with Woolf on Sunday morning and bought all the papers that he could find and took them back to his apartment and read them through. Woolf amused himself by tearing to shreds each section of newspaper as soon as Jack finished it. When Jack had finished reading the papers it was dark out and the room was covered with shredded newsprint, and Jack had nothing to do except think about the fact that in one week he would be engaged to Elizabeth St. John Mather, the fifth richest single woman in America, while he was still in love with Susan Bright, who had no money.

Jack made himself a pitcher of Clammy Marys— clam juice, vodka, and tomato juice, with a dash of Worcestershire sauce—and sat in the darkness and tried to figure out what was best to do, what was possible to do, and what he would probably end up doing after nothing else worked.

Jack went to work Monday morning with strict instructions for Woolf not to do anything awful in his absence. It was fortunate that most of Jack's bruises—now a rich shade of aubergine—were hidden beneath his suit. He was unable to hide the stiffness of his gait, however, and he told everyone at the office he had fallen out of a window over the weekend.

Jack tried to get hold of Libby as soon as he got to his desk—not to tell her over the telephone that he had no intention of marrying her, but to set up a dinner, over which he would tell her that he had no intention of marrying her. Libby wasn't home.

Late Monday afternoon, Jack telephoned Susan, not to tell her he was still in love with her, but to set up a dinner, over which he would tell her he still loved her. Susan wasn't home.

Very late Monday afternoon, Jack's boss came in and instructed Jack that he was to go to Boston for a few days on business. An ex-governor of Massachusetts had just died, and the governor's family was kicking up a row about the investments that had been made in his name by Jack's predecessor in the firm—a man who had been fired for making bad investments. Jack couldn't refuse, though he did point out that he had just fallen out a window and couldn't be expected to be at his best.

"Miss Mather has invited me to her home on Saturday night," said Jack's boss. "She said we were to expect an important announcement. I'm very happy for you and Miss Mather. It is a coup. But it was an expected coup, my boy."

Suddenly, getting out of town for a few days didn't seem such a bad idea.

Why was it that when something particularly awful was happening in one's life, one's body was never in top condition? How could Jack think about being in love with S.B. and getting married to E.M. when he had trouble raising his arm to shoulder height?

Woolf's farewell to Jack at the expensive kennel on Second Avenue was a reproachful snarl. The snarl was contemptuously repeated when Jack promised that he would be back for Woolf on Friday at the latest.

Jack took the train to Boston on Monday night. He met with the ex-governor's children early on Tuesday morning, and with difficulty persuaded them that his firm was not a band of incorporated thieves, and that the investments—though peculiar, and not of the usual sort—were basically sound. Some of their inherited holdings even gave promise of surprisingly energetic rises if the Shah of Iran could remain on the throne for a few years. With many long-distance calls to his home office, and daily meetings with the governor's family—meetings that were complicated by the fact that since leaving office, the governor had been married three times, and that his third wife was younger than the children of his first marriage—Jack passed the time in Boston.

Jack Beaumont was a hard worker, and always dedicated himself to the task at hand. Now he was straightening out the tangled strands of the lives of a dozen people he had never met—and didn't particularly like now that he had—while his own life threatened to crash down around his head on Saturday night.

It was one thing that he should marry imprudently—if marrying a woman whose net worth was written with nine figures on the left side of the decimal could ever be called imprudent—and quite another for Susan Bright to do something of the same sort.

Jack ate alone in the evening, and he went to movies at the University Theater. He saw *Lili* twice, because when he squinted his eyes, Leslie Caron reminded him of Susan. He closed his eyes altogether when Zsa Zsa Gabor came on as the aerialist, because she reminded him much too much of Libby Mather.

Jack finished up his work in Boston late on Thursday night. He took the early morning train back to New York on Friday arriving in time to have a bad lunch around the corner from his apartment. He went into work for a few hours, made his report on the pacification of the heirs, then fetched Woolf from the kennel.

As punishment for abandonment, Woolf pretended not to remember who Jack was. Jack took Woolf home, mixed a Rob Roy for himself, and got on the telephone.

Neither Libby nor Susan was at home—or at least neither of them answered.

Feeling very sorry for himself—and very much alone—Jack made the dinner he always made (and *only* made) when he was depressed: an entire plateful of hot dogs covered with mayonnaise.

Woolf shared Jack's enthusiasm for the menu.

After dinner, Jack sat on his couch and watched television. He kept the telephone in his lap, and at every commercial break he called Susan and Libby. No one ever answered.

Jack fell asleep about midnight, with a reconciled dog already dozing with his weary head on Jack's lap.

Susan wasn't home on Saturday either.

Jack wondered if she might not simply have packed up and moved away. To Cuba, maybe.

Libby was at home, but wouldn't talk to him; she was too busy, she said. But Libby called him five times to tell him that she loved him even though she hadn't time to speak five words to him. She had missed him dreadfully, she said—but that was only after Jack informed her that he'd spent the week in Boston.

She asked him to come over to her apartment as soon after five as possible.

"Bring your clothes," she instructed him, "you can change here."

"What about my dog?" he asked. "I left him for four days. If I go away all evening, he'll think I've abandoned him again. He's already eaten my telephone directories."

"You have a dog?"

"Yes," said Jack.

"Bring him. You might as well, the rest of the world is coming."

Jack arrived at Libby's apartment at a quarter after five. When the elevator doors opened, Jack thought he was in the wrong place. He stepped back into the elevator. The elevator man shook his head. "This is it," he said with a shrug.

Gone was the Middle East. Banished were the spangled pillows. Fled were the brass filigree lamps, and the hanging materials, and all the atmosphere of a caravansary.

The apartment was flooded with light. Again, it was possible to see just how enormous it was. Windows seemed to be everywhere, and French doors led out onto terraces that surrounded the place. It seemed as if a tawdrily decorated shoebox had exploded into Buckingham Palace.

Caterers and decorators and temporary servants thronged the place. The decorators were still putting finishing touches on the vaguely eighteenth-century English style that was fairly comfortable looking. The caterers were setting up tables for the evening. The servants were gazing at everything with a conniving interest that suggested that they were deciding now what could be easily carted away at the end of the evening. Jack could count more than two dozen persons who had been hired—at outrageous expense he was sure—to construct the festivities around the announcement of an engagement he was about to quash.

Libby was nowhere to be seen and Woolf tugged valiantly at his leash and barked ferociously at the decorators—two grimly smiling young men who wore matching diamond rings on the littlest fingers of their right hands.

Jack asked one of the decorators where Libby was.

"Miss Mather is in her boudoir, I believe," said the decorator, moving away from Woolf's slathering advances.

"She is ensconced with the representative from Tiffany's," remarked his companion in the same lilting accent.

Jack headed in the direction, he hoped, of Libby's bedroom. A servant he recognized as a regular member of the household staff pointed a confirming finger down the hallway that led to Libby's bedroom.

Libby's bedroom, with its own private terrace, would have enjoyed a splendid view of the East River, had it not been for the buildings in between. Big, soft, and cluttered, it was decorated in blue and yellow. Libby sat at a large vanity that was covered with bottles and jars and the contents of cast-aside handbags. She was staring at herself in the mirror.

Her hair was rolled in small steel curlers, and she was wrapped tightly in a blue kimono. A black-haired gentleman wearing a blue suit, a white shirt, and a red tie stood behind her, and was wedging a moderately sized diamond tiara down among the curlers.

"In honor of the coronation next month," said Libby to Jack in the mirror without preamble. Then she saw

Woolf, panting happily. "Is that what you meant when you said a dog?"

"He's friendly," said Jack. "His name is Woolf."

"Go home, Woolf," said Libby amiably. "Are you late, or are you early?"

"I'm on time," said Jack. "But on time for what?"

"To help me plan," said Libby.

"We'd get a much better idea of the effect of the tiara," said the man with the red tie, "if we could take a few of the curlers out."

"The curlers come out in half an hour," she told the Tiffany man. "Find some champagne. Go to the kitchen, will you please, and tell somebody we need a bottle of champagne."

The man stared at Libby in the mirror as if she'd just asked him to scrub the bathroom floor. Representatives of Tiffany's did not make champagne runs to the kitchen. Not even for clients as rich and as spendthrift as Elizabeth St. John Mather.

"Miss Mather..." he said with forced politeness.

"Yes?"

His hair was dyed, Jack decided. Jack reflected that if he married Libby, a lot of his life would be occupied by men with dyed hair who wore red ties. It was a depressing thought.

"Miss Mather, I believe the tiara will look splendid."

"I think so too," said Libby briskly. "Put it on my bill."

The man smiled faintly, nodded to Jack, picked up his case, and departed.

"Do you think his hair was dyed?" Libby asked.

"I've no idea," said Jack. "Libby, I need to talk to you about tonight."

"Fine," said Libby. "We'll talk about tonight tomorrow. I can't think of anything right now except this party. Is it a madhouse out there?" She pointed vaguely in the direction of the rest of the apartment.

"Yes," said Jack.

"It's been like that all week. Since everything else was going to be confused this week, I thought I might as well have the apartment redecorated while I was at it, and I was looking at *Town & Country* and I saw an article about Princess Elizabeth's coronation, and I thought, 'I won't do it Marie Antoinette, I'll do it Queen Elizabeth,' so I called up the two Henrys, and I said—" She had been regarding Jack in the mirror all the while she spoke, but suddenly she leaped up and threw her arms around Jack's neck. "You were gone! You were gone! And I missed you so much!"

One of the steel curlers gouged his neck.

"Libby, you didn't even know I was gone till I told you on the phone this morning."

"I didn't see you," she said, logically enough, "and I missed you. What does it matter whether you were in Boston or right here in New York? If I didn't get to see you every minute of the day, I missed you."

Jack pried himself loose from Libby.

He had never figured out why women said things like that, when they obviously didn't mean them. Libby did a thousand things during the day that would have been spoiled for her if Jack had been around. Libby had one set of female friends with whom she lunched, another set with whom she shopped, another set with whom she gossiped over cocktails, another set who called her early the next morning before she was even out of bed and told vicious stories about all the others. Libby had very little use for a man, except perhaps very late at night, when all her female friends had gone home to their husbands.

Perhaps she did love Jack—probably she did care for him a bit—but Jack also knew that Libby would chafe if she had to see him for more than a few hours every day. So why did she say those things?

None of that mattered, Jack suddenly realized. Not when he didn't intend to marry her. Not when he intended to marry Susan Bright, if Susan would give up that Cuban who had no connections that would stand up to scrutiny. If Susan would—

"I talked to Susan this afternoon," said Libby, as if she divined his thoughts. She slumped languidly down on the vanity seat again, and once more she talked not to Jack but to his reflection in her mirror. "She'll be here tonight," said Libby, pushing Woolf away.

"Libby—"

"With that man," Libby went on. The way she looked Jack in the eye made Jack think that Libby knew something, and that she was trying to tell him that she knew something, and that Jack had better listen closely while she told him.

"Rodolfo?" asked Jack.

"Yes," said Libby quietly, her voice now slow and soft. "That interesting, handsome Cuban. He took her to dinner at the Cuban consul's home last Saturday night, and she enjoyed herself immensely. This week he took her to the theater twice. They saw *The Seven Year Itch* and hated it. They saw *Picnic* and loved it. Last night he took her to dinner to La Caravelle—and he proposed to her over coffee."

Libby smiled, dropped her eyes, and overturned a small box of face powder on Woolf's head. The dog howled away into a corner, shaking and sneezing.

"And," demanded Jack. "*And?*"

"What else does a girl do when the man she loves proposes marriage?" shrugged Libby. "She did what I did. She accepted."

Libby raised her eyes again, and looked into Jack's. "What was it you wanted to say to me about tonight?"

Jack blinked.

Woolf had jumped up onto the middle of Libby's enormous blue and yellow canopied bed, and was sneezing continuously.

Jack said, "Nothing, Libby. It wasn't important. It'll wait till tomorrow."

"And now please find me some champagne," Libby said, smiling as Judith must have smiled, emerging from the tent with the head of Holofernes. "It's almost time for my curlers to come out."

CHAPTER TEN

THE NEWS OF HER inheritance—though it might be many years distant—came as a distinct shock to Susan.

Her first thought—even before the Cuban consul's wife had finished speaking to her at the window overlooking Sixty-sixth Street—was, *She's a silly old woman, and she's making up gossip she never even heard.*

But the consul's wife was not a silly old woman. She was intelligent and good-hearted. She was fat, but mere bulk wouldn't impugn her reliability.

Susan's second thought was, *How much does he have?*

Her uncle owned a great deal of land in Cuba, and grew a great deal of sugarcane and tobacco; he lived in a big house and had lots of servants. All that may have been true, but it didn't necessarily mean a great deal of wealth by New York standards. On the other hand, her uncle might be very wealthy indeed. Or his estate might be so encumbered with debt that anything he might leave Susan would be eaten up by taxes and legal fees.

Her third thought was, *I don't want him to die.*

Susan could be described as an orphan. Susan was an only child, and both her parents had died seven years before, and neither of them had been members of large families. Therefore she had few relatives, and she didn't like to think of their dying. She'd gotten along on her own for years now, but the knowledge that she had an uncle on her father's side in Cuba, and another uncle on her mother's side in San Francisco, had been a sort of comfort; even though she wrote them only on their birthdays and major holidays, and even though she'd seen neither of them in more than ten years.

Knowing herself to be James Bright's only surviving relative, she wasn't totally surprised to think that he would leave his fortune to her.

The thought of that possible inheritance succeeded, for the rest of the evening, in driving out of her mind the thought that Jack Beaumont was engaged—or almost engaged—to be married to Libby Mather.

Libby moved in so many circles of friends and acquaintances that it was impossible to tell exactly who anyone was at one of her parties. Susan could assign only a few of the guests to one or another of the contingents she knew to be present. There were executives of Libby's margarine company. There were the executives and subalterns of the firms that provided her lawyers, accountants, and whatever other professionals someone as rich as Elizabeth St. John Mather required. There were friends from school and their husbands; the remnants of New York café society that Libby had been a part of two years ago (and would be still if she hadn't managed to alienate most of them, one by one). There were a few famous musicians; a few actors and actresses; a former

Miss America who was now making a living pointing at the insides of household appliances on television; a former governor who was going to run again if his heart, his wife, and his accountant allowed him; and a gorgeous young woman whose photograph had appeared on the front page of the *New York Post* the morning after her unexpected acquittal. About seventy-five persons fell into one or another of these categories, but about twenty-five more didn't seem to belong to any particular group at all. Susan—and possibly Libby herself—had no idea why they were there.

A small jazz combo played on a tiny triangular stage that had been installed in a corner of the living room. The dining room table was loaded with food, and more food was set out in the library. Two bars had been set up inside the apartment, and, taking advantage of the exceptional warmth of the evening, a third had been set up out on the living room terrace.

Libby wore a gown from the apex of fashion—in Paris, at any rate. A bodice of red-and-white spangled lace flared out into a skirt built up of layers of red-and-white tulle. When Libby was still, the dress looked marvelous in the way that a new and outré fashion always does. But the skirt was so wide and so stiff that Libby had to move through doors sideways, and that made dramatic entrances impossible.

Libby touched her long white gloves to the back of Susan's hand. "Pretty dress," she said. "So pretty."

Libby somehow gave the impression when she said "pretty" that what she really meant was that it looked to her as if Susan had constructed her dress herself out of old dimity flour sacks.

Susan's dress, in considerable contrast to Libby's, was simple. A swath of ivory silk crossed her breast diagonally. The long wrap-around skirt was of the same material, fringed in silver. It gave Susan a silhouette as narrow and classical as Libby's was wide and modish. It had set her back three hundred hard-earned dollars. She wore white gloves so short they seemed barely to reach her wrist, and a tiny white sequined rocker hat that was like a smudge of white paint on her intensely black hair.

"Hello," said Libby to Rodolfo. "I'm so glad you could come."

Rodolfo bowed, lightly touching the fingers of Libby's gloved hand to his lips.

"Susan," said Libby immediately, "I really must talk to you. Privately, do you mind?" she said to Rodolfo. "And then I'd like to have a word or two with you."

Susan glanced back at Rodolfo as Libby led her away. What could Libby possibly have to say to him? She hadn't even called him by name. And if she was making a point of her indifference to him, why should she...

Whatever Libby had to say to Susan, she was making it seem important. As they crossed the crowded room, everyone they passed tried to speak to Libby. But the hostess, with Susan's gloved wrist in a vise grip, pushed through them all with smiling indifference, like a steamroller with a broad grin painted on the front.

Libby's bedroom was being used as a powder room; coats and wraps were thrown across the pink-and-yellow bed and the air smelled like the first floor of Bloomingdale's with the mixture of the scents of a hundred different atomizers. Women were gossiping in the corners and out on Libby's private terrace. Others were fighting for mirror space, queueing up for the bathroom, and all of them—with more or less pretense at indifference—learning all they could about Libby herself by a close examination of whatever objects lay at hand.

Libby smiled at the crowd of women with a scarcely apologetic, "Oh I'll talk to everybody later. Susan and I have—"

She didn't finish the sentence because by that time she had pulled Susan into one of her clothes closets and pulled the door closed behind her.

"Shhh!" said Libby.

It was disorienting. With the door shut the closet was very dark. The closet wasn't very large, and it was filled with clothes. Susan felt a welter of fabrics brushing her arms and scraping her face. A rackful of shoes tumbled down over Susan's feet. Libby must have been very close for Susan could feel her breath and smell her perfume stronger than she could her own.

"Is there a light?" asked Susan.

A light came on—a single bright bulb in a ceramic fixture on the ceiling of the closet. Libby's hand was on the chain. Libby's face looked garish in the harsh light, as if she'd been made up as a clown—the sort of clown that frightened children rather than amused them. Her dress seemed to fill the closet, and the rustle of the stiff skirt sounded like rats in the wainscoting.

"Are you going to do it?" demanded Libby in a sharp, low whisper.

"Do what?" returned Susan, mystified—and wondering what the women on the other side of the closed closet door were thinking.

"Steal my thunder," said Libby.

"I have no idea what you're talking about."

"You know why I'm having this party. You know why I'm spending all this money. You know why I've gathered together all the people I dislike most in the world."

"You tell me why," said. Susan.

"To announce my engagement," said Libby. "My engagement to Jack." After a moment, she added, as an afterthought, "I love him very, very much."

"Libby, what do you mean, steal your thunder?"

"By announcing your own engagement, of course."

"My engagement to whom?"

"To—you know." Even behind closed closet doors, Libby wouldn't admit that she remembered his name.

"Rodolfo?"

Libby nodded.

"He hasn't asked me to marry him yet," said Susan, and then regretted she'd said *yet*. She wasn't exactly sure why she regretted saying it, but she did. "And even if he had asked me, and even if I had said yes, why would I announce it at *your* party? Libby, I don't think I know more than four or five people out there. And them I don't like."

"Who does?" said Libby. "And I'd very much appreciate it if you wouldn't throw yourself at Jack tonight."

"Libby, I don't throw myself at anybody. Ever."

"Well, I know it would make Jack very uncomfortable if you—"

"If I what?"

"If you talked to him about...things."

"Libby, I have never known you to beat around the bush like this. You dragged me into this closet, and you're holding me prisoner here"—Libby was standing with her back to the door, and Susan couldn't have gotten out unless she'd pushed Libby down and trampled over her and her new Paris dress—"so say what you've got to say and stop playing games. It's stifling in here, and I'm going to pass out from breathing your perfume if you don't."

"All right," said Libby. "I'll say what I have to say. I'm trying to protect Jack."

"Protect him?"

"From you. Jack thinks that you're still in love with him." Susan's eyes widened. "He thinks you're carrying a torch. He thinks that you never really got over him, and he's embarrassed. He's so sweet and he hates to think that he's hurting you, and if you go up and talk to him he'll just start to blush. And you know how he is when he starts to blush. He gets dizzy. And I don't want Jack to get dizzy on the night I'm going to announce our engagement so I don't want you to talk to him."

"Libby, if you didn't want me to talk to Jack tonight, why on earth did you invite me to this party?"

Libby looked startled by the question, and she responded in all apparent innocence, "Because I like you. Because you're the only real friend I have in the world."

It was Susan's turn to be startled. To think that Libby Mather, rich as she was, known by so many people, and traveling in the circles she traveled in, should call Susan her best friend was almost beyond Susan's comprehension. But Susan looked into Libby's eyes and saw no conniving about this statement. About the other notion, though, she had strong doubts. There was some reason that Libby didn't want her to talk to Jack. Susan decided right then and there, in the closet, being attacked by Libby's dresses and breathing Libby's perfume, that she was going to speak to Jack as soon as possible.

CHAPTER ELEVEN

"OH, I PLEADED with her," cried Libby. "Just pleaded and pleaded."

"Pleaded with her to do what?" said Jack. He was standing in a corner of the terrace overlooking the intersection of Park Avenue and Sixty-first Street far below. He was trying to persuade Woolf, whom he could see through the open window of one of the maids' rooms where Libby had exiled him for safekeeping during the party, that it would not be a good idea to jump from the window across to the terrace, even though it was only a matter of a few feet. Jack had without success been trying to toss hors d'oeuvres through the window onto the bed on which Woolf was stationed, preparing for the leap. A number of other guests on the balcony were watching this proceeding with interest, and one gentleman had even tried to bet the bartender twenty dollars that the dog would jump.

"I pleaded with her to talk to you," said Libby. "I said 'Let bygones be bygones, Susan.' That's what I said to her, Jack. I said, 'I'm marrying Jack and you're marrying Rodolfo and we're all going to live happily ever after.'"

In a slightly strangled voice, Jack asked, "And...and what did she say to that?"

"She didn't want to talk about it, she didn't want to talk about it at all. What did you do to make her so angry?"

"Nothing. In fact, I—"

"You made those terrible accusations about Rodolfo, didn't you?"

"I made a few accusations," said Jack, coloring and now sorry he had told Libby about his suspicions. "They weren't so awful."

"You told her he didn't exist."

"He doesn't."

"You don't tell a woman that the man she loves doesn't exist," said Libby sententiously. "It's not polite. Especially not coming from someone she used to...used to be acquainted with, if you know what I mean. Jack, is that dog going to commit suicide?" she asked suddenly, catching sight of Woolf with his forelegs perched on the sill of the maid's room's window just beyond the edge of the balcony.

Jack reached across the twenty-three story abyss with black caviar spread on a yellow cracker.

Woolf lapped it up out of Jack's palm and retreated a few inches into the room.

"He's lonely, that's all," said Jack. "And he has no fear of heights."

"If you think he's going to jump, why don't you just go close the window in the maid's room?"

"Because every time I start to walk away, Woolf climbs even farther out," Jack said simply. "Would you mind...?"

"I have guests to attend to," said Libby curtly. "And if he does decide to jump, I want *you* to deal with whatever or whoever he hits down there. You understand? *You* take care of it."

Jack nodded, then gently suggested that Libby's other guests were probably anxious to speak to her.

She nodded. "It's ten o'clock now. I'm making the announcement at eleven." Quite suddenly and unexpectedly then, she reached up, threw her arms around him, and kissed him. "I love you very very much," she said quickly and loudly. "And remember, Susan really doesn't want to talk to you. So leave her alone, please. Just for tonight." With that she was gone.

There had been something pointed and peculiar about Libby's injunction. It was clear she didn't want him to talk to Susan before she made the announcement about their engagement. Which had the effect of making Jack desperate to speak to Susan. He had approximately fifty-eight minutes to find her in the crush of the party, separate her from Rodolfo, convince her that the engagement was all Libby's idea, persuade her that he loved her desperately after all these years, and that nothing remained but for her to agree to marry him.

Temporarily sated with caviar and crackers, Woolf retreated from the window of the maid's room. Relieved of his mission to preserve the dog's existence, Jack quickly went up to the bar.

He needed a drink even if getting up to the bartender's table on the terrace used up a few of the precious minutes. He waited impatiently behind a man who wanted a Rob Roy, two salty dogs, an apricot cassis, and a rye with Canada water.

Jack asked for scotch on the rocks—a triple.

The bartender handed Jack the liquor and then paused, staring curiously at Jack.

When Jack tasted the drink, he understood why. His mouth was daubed with Libby's bright red lipstick. This, of course, was the precise moment that Susan walked through the glass doors onto the terrace, saving him the trouble of searching her out in the crowd.

"Hello, Susan," Jack said, wiping Libby's lipstick from his mouth with a handkerchief.

"Congratulations," she replied.

"On what?" he asked, swallowing half his drink.

"On convincing Libby to marry you."

Sweat beaded out across his large forehead. He wiped it away with the handkerchief, smearing Libby's lipstick across his brow in the process.

"I..."

"You what?" she prompted.

"I tried to call you this week," he said.

"I tried to call you," she replied, a little puzzled.

"About this engagement..." Jack began.

Libby and Rodolfo suddenly appeared in the French doors nearby. Libby gave Jack and Susan a quick, hard glance. Then she smiled, took Rodolfo's hand and patted it indulgently.

"Rodolfo and I have been having the most interesting conversation," said Libby. "Every word of it in English. Susan, Rodolfo has something to show you."

Susan looked at Libby, then at Rodolfo.

"Yes?"

"Inside," said Libby. "He'll show you the way."

Then, as quickly as she had come, Susan was gone. Jack had said none of the things to her that he had meant to say, and in forty-three minutes, Libby was going to announce their engagement.

"What do you have to show me?" Susan asked.

Rodolfo was leading her down a mostly empty corridor. No guests here, only servants rushing back and forth with trays.

He tried the knob of one of the doors, but it opened onto a closet.

"No," he muttered, "not the third door, the fourth."

They went in through the next door in the corridor and found themselves in a small bedroom. It was evidently an unoccupied maid's room. Its only furnishings were a dresser, a couple of straight-backed chairs, a rush rug, and near the window an iron bedstead. On the bed was a red blanket, and on it lay a large dog, peacefully shredding a Manhattan telephone book.

"Woolf?" said Susan.

Woolf leaped to his feet and began barking, showering the blanket with bits of torn paper.

"What is that dog doing here?" Rodolfo demanded with displeasure.

"He's a good dog," said Susan. She sat down on the bed and, taking off her gloves, caressed Woolf and tried to keep him from licking her three-hundred-dollar dress. She glanced out the window and saw that the terrace of Libby's penthouse began not more than three or four feet away. She could hear the murmur of conversation and the clink of the bartender's bottles. "What did you want to show me?"

"*Mía amante,*" said Rodolfo.

"Please," said Susan uncomfortably, "let's speak in English. Do you mind?"

"I love you," he said simply, and convincingly. "And I want you to marry me. *Will* you marry me?"

Susan smiled briefly—at Woolf. She couldn't think what to say. "Why are you proposing to me in a maid's room?"

"Because I could not wait. Tonight I saw how happy they were—"

"They?"

"Miss Mather and Mr. Beaumont—and I could not wait. Please, Susan. Please say—"

Susan held up her hand. "Let me think."

"No!" Rodolfo cried, kneeling at her feet. He spoke in a rapid voice that tumbled headlong in Spanish and

English. *"No es posible* to let you think—*porque* you might say no to me. I could not bear that. I love you, Susan. With my *corazón*—all my heart. There is nothing else to say. You have to marry me because I love you the way I do."

Susan was astonished. She'd known Rodolfo for months, but if he'd been courting her every evening, she would still not have been prepared for the passion of this outburst.

He covered her hand with kisses.

He rubbed his forehead against her knee, and he wept, spilling salty tears on her dress.

A slight movement out of the corner of her eye caused her to turn her head, even while Rodolfo still knelt before her with bowed head. She leaned slightly back and looked out the window.

There was Jack, on the balcony a few feet away, leaning forward over the parapet and gesticulating wildly.

"I have to talk to you!" he hissed. She didn't actually hear him, but those were the words his lips formed: *"I have to talk to you!"*

Rodolfo looked up into Susan's face. Rodolfo's voice was choked when he spoke. Out of the corner of her eye Susan could still see Jack's frenzied gyrations.

"Say it," Rodolfo whispered. "Say you will marry me. Say you will be my wife and love me the way I love you. Say you will allow me to care for you. Say you will be mine forever from this day forward. Say anything to me so long as you do not say to me, no. Say—"

"No!"

But it wasn't Susan who said no. That was someone behind her.

It was Jack, poking his head and shoulders through the window.

Susan whirled around, and Rodolfo was on his feet, brushing away his manly tears and stalking forward.

Susan could see that Jack was actually trying to climb in through the window. He'd evidently leaned out over the balcony—twenty-three floors above the street—and caught at the window ledge.

And now he was pulling himself through.

"Don't say yes!" Jack cried. "Don't marry him!"

"You—" began Rodolfo, with clenched fists.

"Don't!" cried Susan in alarm, fearful that Rodolfo would somehow cause Jack to lose his grip and fall to his death.

But then the unexpected happened. Woolf bounded from the bed right at the window and at Jack.

Surprised at this sudden movement, Jack's mouth flew open and his fingers lost their grip on the windowsill.

Jack Beaumont spilled through the air, straight down.

Then there was just Woolf, on his hind legs, panting happily in the window, waiting for more hors d'oeuvres.

CHAPTER TWELVE

JACK'S FALL WAS broken by an awning of the apartment terrace two floors below Libby's. Jack's collision with the awning knocked the breath out of him. He slid down the slanted coarse striped fabric and was nearly pitched out into the air again, had he not, at the last moment, caught at the scalloped edge of the awning. It tore off with a loud ripping noise, but Jack swung 'round and managed to drop to the stone floor of the terrace.

"Thank G—" he whispered, but didn't finish the involuntary thanksgiving because when he fell, he landed on his head.

Susan stared down out the window of the maid's room. She didn't scream. She brushed Rodolfo out of the way and rushed to find Libby, who was surrounded by people in the middle of the living room.

"Who lives in the apartment with the striped awning a few floors below you?" Susan demanded, jerking on Libby's arm.

"A perfectly awful couple," replied Libby. "Truly ghastly—actually, they're right here," she interrupted herself, tapping the shoulders of a man who looked like a banker and a woman who was holding on to him very tightly as if afraid he was going to run away with one of the maids.

The banker and his wife turned. The banker stared at Susan as if he thought she were about to ask for a cash loan, without collateral, of a hundred thousand dollars. The wife stared as if she thought Susan were having an affair with her husband and was about to demand his release from the bonds of marriage on account of youth and love. Libby looked at Susan as if she believed both these things at once and wasn't a bit surprised at it.

Susan took a breath, and in the course of that breath she wondered how to begin. It wasn't, she decided, the sort of situation that required—or needed—a whole lot of leading up to, so Susan plunged right in: "Libby's fiancé just fell out the window of the maid's room and he landed on your terrace."

Libby screamed. Not once, but three times. She spilled her drink onto the wide bosom of the banker's wife and probably would have slipped down to the floor in the extremity of her emotion had not her skirts kept her upright.

The banker took Susan and Rodolfo down to his apartment by way of the elevator. While the banker turned on lights and the elevator man telephoned for an ambulance, Susan and Rodolfo rushed through toward the terrace doors. They pushed them open and went out. They heard the traffic from the street below them, and the confused murmur of Libby's party from above. Jack lay unconscious on the concrete. His left arm was bent crazily beneath his body.

Susan looked up through the ragged awning. Woolf was leaning precariously out of the maid's room window, barking happily into the night.

Rodolfo said to Susan softly, "You never answered my question..."

With an entirely new set of bruises, Jack lay propped up in the hospital bed. His left arm, in a plaster cast, was caught up in a sling, and a wide white bandage was wrapped around his head. It was Sunday morning. Jack had been taken to Roosevelt Hospital on the West Side, an institution that had come to specialize in what were known as "Saturday night accidents." It was said that the news photographer Weegee was an habitué of Roosevelt's emergency room.

Libby stalked around his bed, complaining. On top of everything else that had happened, she was unhappy about the necessity of going over to the West Side to visit Jack. Libby visited Florida more often than she did the west side of Manhattan.

"After that I couldn't, I just *couldn't* make the announcement. How could I say, 'Ladies and gentlemen, I would like to announce my engagement to Mr. John Beaumont, Esq. I'm sorry Mr. Beaumont isn't here to receive your congratulations, but he just jumped out of the window.' How do you suppose that would have sounded? I mean, as it is, your little escapade got into the papers today. Did you see Walter Winchell?"

"The nurses showed it to me," said Jack faintly. "Winchell didn't imply that it was a suicide."

"When a man jumps—"

"Falls—"

"—*falls* out of a twenty-third story window on the night of his supposed engagement," said Libby severely, "people talk. People have a *right* to talk when something like that happens. And what am I supposed to do with that dog? The caterers called to complain today. That dog got into the caviar, and it upset the ice sculpture and now there is a water stain to end all water stains on the new carpets I just got last week. When Henry and Henry saw that carpet they just about jumped out the window after you. What am I supposed to do with that dog?"

"Take him to a kennel. There's one on Second Avenue I used for him last week. But you have to take his papers with you or they won't accept him. The papers are on the top of my dresser, I think."

"I'm not going to do all that. I'm just going to let him loose," said Libby.

"Please don't do that. Just take him to the kennel. Please, Libby. I'm in pain…"

"*I'm* the one who's in pain," returned Libby sharply. "I'm the one who *really* wanted to die last night, after what happened happened." She continued to stalk and fume. "Do you know who saved me last night?" she demanded suddenly.

"Saved *you*? I was the one who nearly fell to his death."

She paid no attention. "Rodolfo, that's who. He was a gem. He got you into the ambulance, came right back up, and saved my life. He and Susan both. I love those two. What a happy couple they'll make. He loves her like"— Libby paused for a comparison, and then found one that appeared, in her mind at least, to apply directly to Jack— "Rodolfo loves Susan the way a man *ought* to love the woman he's going to marry. Anyway he and Susan were wonderful. Rodolfo calmed everyone down—he has a fine speaking voice, and not one person laughed at his accent. I guess everybody's so used to Cuban accents now with Ricky and Lucy—and Susan dealt with the caterers. I was prostrate, Jack, I can't tell you how prostrate I was. With humiliation. Thank goodness my mother and father are not alive. My mother would have died from humiliation, and my father would have gone downstairs and tossed you off that terrace, that's what he would have done. I bet if I had asked Rodolfo to toss you off the balcony, he would have done it."

"I bet he would have," Jack agreed.

Libby continued to fret in silence.

Jack watched her. She was wearing an outfit he'd never seen before. A bright red jersey dress with narrow mink cuffs, a large gold safety pin over her left breast, short red gloves and a narrow bracelet of rubies. Jack supposed it was an *ensemble* she reserved for high dudgeon days.

Jack was not completely sorry for the fall. It hurt, of course, and it hurt still, but it had given him a reprieve. He wasn't engaged to Libby.

Of course whether he was or not would make little difference if Susan Bright had become engaged to Rodolfo García-Cifuentes. If Susan married Rodolfo, he thought, then he might just as well go on and marry Libby, reflecting that some forms of suicide are less painful than others.

"I'm *not* giving another party," said Libby definitely. "No, I'm not, so don't ask me. I'm simply going to have the engagement announced in Sunday's *Times*. Something nice and discreet, with just my picture. Luckily for us, Jack, the *Times* has a policy against printing stories about prospective bridegrooms leaping to their deaths out of twenty-third-story windows."

"Libby—"

"Don't you *dare*," she cried.

"Dare what?"

"Try to say anything to me after the humiliation you put me through last night. The severe humiliation. Just tell me what place on earth you hate most of all in the world."

He didn't give it a second thought. "Havana," he replied.

"Good," said Libby. "Then that's where you're taking me on our honeymoon."

CHAPTER THIRTEEN

DESPITE THE INAPPROPRIATENESS of the moment, single-minded Rodolfo pressed Susan for an answer. As they were riding down on the service elevator of Libby's building with the two ambulance attendants and Jack on a stretcher between them, Rodolfo again asked—in Spanish—if she would marry him.

After they saw Jack safely into the ambulance, Rodolfo persuaded Susan to return to the party with him. "Miss Mather would be very upset to discover that you had accompanied her fiancé to the hospital."

"Will you marry me?" he asked her, once more, when they were helping to calm and disperse the guests.

"I can't think about it right now," she replied.

Actually, she was thinking more about her three-hundred-dollar dress. The fringe had caught on something in the banker's dark apartment, unraveling a whole length of its waist attachment. She had smeared grease on the right sleeve in the service elevator, and her white gloves were streaked with black.

But she was also thinking about Rodolfo's proposal. And about Jack's ill-fated but interesting interruption.

It certainly seemed as though he had been sincere. For him to have pulled himself across an abyss that was twenty-three stories up showed a certain spirit. But *why* had he interfered? That was the question.

Susan knew Jack didn't trust Rodolfo. He didn't want her to marry the Cuban, that much was clear. But was he a disinterested third party, or did he want her for himself?

The latter seemed unlikely, since all this had taken place at the party to announce Jack's engagement to Libby.

The doubt in Susan's mind was sufficient for her to put Rodolfo off for a little while. The only reason for haste in this matter was courtesy to Rodolfo. Much more, however, was at stake.

At the door of her apartment building, he asked her, in both English and Spanish, if she would marry him. He loved her with his soul, he said. His entire soul. He was damned and dead without her.

But she put him off.

He asked to see her in the morning.

Her Sunday mornings—as he well knew—were spent in translating Soviet agricultural documents.

Could he watch her while she did her translating?

She couldn't concentrate when someone was watching her.

Could he see her in the afternoon?

She hesitated, then conceded, "If I finish my work..."

He kissed her violently. His beard still scratched her face, and his lips remained hard and dry.

Susan got up early the next morning and began work; she didn't want to put herself into the position of having lied to Rodolfo.

At eight o'clock she went out and got the Sunday papers. She began looking through the *Times,* starting with the engagements. Jack and Libby weren't there, she was relieved to see. She cursed herself for not having asked the ambulance attendants which hospital they were taking Jack to. She debated calling Libby, then finally decided to call. She dialed the number, but then hung up before anyone answered.

She got out the Manhattan Yellow Pages, and began calling the hospitals on the East Side—assuming that surely Jack would have been taken to one that was as close as possible to Libby's flat.

Jack wasn't on the patient register of any of them.

Perhaps he's already been released, she thought with relief.

Maybe his arm hadn't been broken after all, or it had already been put into a sling; if the concussion had been light, it was possible that he had already been sent home to recuperate.

She started to dial his number, but then thought that if his phone were not near the bed then he would be forced to get up to answer it. She didn't want that. If he were asleep, she didn't want to disturb him. If he was being hounded by Libby or a reporter he wouldn't answer the telephone at all.

Susan wanted to *see* Jack, she didn't want to talk to him over the telephone. So she looked at herself in the mirror, decided she ought to change. She put on another dress, looked at herself in the mirror again, regretted the change, but didn't go back to the first outfit. She next donned a large all-over print silk dress with a pattern of enormous pink and red peonies against a cream background. The skirt was wide and stiff, the back was bloused out, and when she looked at herself, she thought she looked like a stick puppet got up in a pair of old draperies. At least the colors were bright and springlike, and perhaps they'd help to raise Jack's spirits. She picked up her pocketbook and went down to the street, startled by the number of people out at what was still—by Greenwich Village standards— an early hour of the morning. Then she realized that the Village Art Show days around Washington Square were on, and that hundreds of artists were gathering to display their latest work, to gossip with one another, and perhaps even to sell a Pollock-like canvas or a Klee-like gouache or an Ernst-like collage to tourists entranced with the idea of taking home a genuine piece of Manhattan culture.

She hurried up Fifth Avenue until she was free of the crowds and then caught a taxi. She got out at the corner of Sixty-sixth and Third, then walked down the block slowly. She was trying to calm herself. She'd decided, on the ride uptown, that she'd tell Jack the truth—that she felt no animosity toward him, that in fact...

The door of Jack's building was locked. She peered through the vestibule doors, and saw the elevator door propped open with a broomstick.

She hesitated just a moment, and then pushed the button of the apartment marked BEAUMONT, J.

Susan waited with suspense.

After a few moments, the speaker crackled to life— but there was no voice.

Susan spoke into it, "Jack, it's Susan Bright. May I come up for a few minutes?"

There was a moment of hesitation—Susan imagined Jack with his finger on the release, wondering what this visit meant—and then the buzzer sounded on the door catch.

Susan grabbed the handle and pushed inside the building.

She stepped into the elevator and waited. The elevator man did not appear. She looked at the mechanism, and thought she could work it on her own, if necessary, but she continued to wait.

After a few minutes, an old woman with a small Pomeranian used a key to enter the building, then joined

Susan in the elevator. The woman stared at Susan's dress in a disapproving manner; Susan knew then that the choice of outfits *had* been a mistake.

Eventually, the elevator man appeared and stared into the elevator as if Susan and the old woman with the Pomeranian had been visitors from Hades. He shook his head, came inside, and said, "Floors, please."

Susan got out on the fifth floor, looked around and saw half a dozen doors.

"Beaumont," she said to the elevator operator, and he pointed.

The elevator doors shut and Susan proceeded to the indicated door and knocked.

Susan had never been to Jack's apartment, but hoped it was nicer than the place he'd kept in Boston. She remembered that place well enough. It—

The door of Jack's apartment opened.

Libby Mather stood there wrapped in a sheet and holding a bottle of green Prell shampoo. She was smiling.

"Hello, Susan," she said.

Woolf bounded up to the open doorway and tried to get at Susan, but Libby blocked the way. Woolf jumped up on the margarine heiress, who cried, "Ooop!" and let go of the sheet.

She was naked underneath.

Libby swooped down and grabbed the sheet, as Woolf leaped by her to get at Susan.

"Hello, Woolf," said Susan in a voice so strangled that she barely recognized it as her own.

"Jack's taking a shower," said Libby. Inside the apartment Susan could see that the bathroom door was open and she could hear running water. "He has a hard time reaching his back, so I was just..." Libby smiled a knowing smile.

Susan backed away, farther out into the hallway. Woolf was still with her.

"How is he?" Susan asked weakly. "I just came to—"

"He's fine now. The doctor said all he needed was bed rest, and I'm going to see that he gets it. Don't you want to stay and—"

"No, no," said Susan. "I—"

"Oh yes," Libby said, "Jack was going to call you today."

"He was?"

"To ask you if you would mind taking care of his dog for a few days, till he gets better."

"No, I don't mind," said Susan. "I'll—"

"Fine," said Libby, and she shut the door in Susan Bright's face.

Susan was mortified beyond the words to tell it. In a daze she pushed the elevator button. When she got down to the lobby she looked around as if she'd been transported there suddenly from the far side of the moon. Then, dragging Woolf by his collar, she climbed into another taxi and rode back down to Washington Square.

Over and over in her mind she replayed the conversation with Libby. As she did it, her own distress increased, her defeat grew more grinding and cruel, and Libby's triumph higher and greater. By the middle of the afternoon, Susan felt like crawling into the closet among her old shoes and gathering dust for a few years.

And she just might have if Woolf had not been so anxious for a walk.

Susan was intensely embarrassed. Intensely chagrined. Intensely depressed. How could she have so misread a situation? How could she have talked herself into a totally groundless hope that Jack was still in love with her? How could she have showed up at his apartment, unannounced, expecting—what? A kind word? A reconciliation? A proposal of marriage?

Of course, Woolf was the final insult. That Jack Beaumont considered her a kind of kennel, her Washington Square apartment a place to park his dog while he got a little bed rest—with Libby Mather.

She walked Woolf around and around Washington Square Park half a dozen times, until the dog was panting from thirst and stopping every twenty yards to rest. She was alternately shivering with embarrassment, quaking with anger, and shaking with her own great disappointment.

Finally, she had worn herself out. She returned to her apartment, took the telephone off the hook in case Rodolfo called, and then fell asleep on the sofa with her head pushed as far down between the cushions and the upholstered back as it would go. Woolf snored on the floor at her side.

She awoke sometime in the middle of the night, cried for a little while, took off her clothes, crawled into bed, and slept till morning.

The first thing she did when she got up was to telephone Rodolfo, apologize for not seeing him the day before, and ask if he would be so good as to take her out to dinner that evening.

CHAPTER FOURTEEN

JACK'S BED IN Roosevelt Hospital was too short, though the nurses insisted that he was merely too tall and that people tended to shrink the longer they remained in bed. They told him that by the time he was well he'd fit into the bed without difficulty.

Nobody visited Jack in the hospital. He'd shared his room with a fat man for the first couple of days, and the fat man was cheerful and always awoke in the middle of the night to smoke a forbidden cigar. Both of these things, the cheerfulness and the smoking, annoyed Jack intensely. Finally the fat man was taken away for an operation and didn't come back. This made Jack feel guilty that he had resented the cheerfulness and the cigars so much. The fat man's twin daughters, also fat, dropped by and asked Jack what the fat man had been like in his last days, and Jack thought, *How do I get into these situations...?*

"He was very cheerful, right up to the last," said Jack. The fat man's family wept to hear it.

Jack had tried several times to get hold of Libby, but after her visit to him the previous Sunday morning, he'd neither seen her nor heard from her. The servants in her home took his calls, said merely that Miss Mather was out, that they didn't know what time she'd return, and that they'd give her the message that he'd called.

Libby never called back.

Susan Bright never answered her telephone at all.

If he'd had a telephone in his room, he would have dialed Libby and Susan incessantly, but the only telephone for the use of patients was a pay phone down the hall. It was frequently in use, and the nurses seldom allowed him to leave his bed. Besides, he was always running out of nickels, since there was always some servant around Libby's place to answer. Also, it was a tricky physical matter for a man with a broken arm to operate a telephone.

Jack felt hopeless, cut off.

But it wasn't quite true that nobody visited Jack; Maddy, his secretary, came. She brought work. He tried to put her off.

"I can't do any work," he said. "I fell out of a window."

"You've used that excuse before," said his secretary darkly. Maddy, a bottle blonde who had worn leopard prints long before they came into fashion the previous winter, was a bitter person. If Maddy took any joy in life, Jack wasn't sure what form it took, and he wasn't even sure he wanted to find out. She had eyes the color of new steel, and skin the color of boiled chicken, and her hair was the color of corn in the ad for Nucoa margarine. Maddy gave new dimension to the concept of tightness in dress. Her job, before coming to Jack's firm, had been as a receptionist at an advertising agency whose principal client was a manufacturer of ladies' foundation wear. In her tenure there, she'd gotten a lot of free samples. Maddy always looked trussed-up beneath her clothes. She had also been one of the first women in Manhattan—and perhaps the world— to have created a wardrobe made entirely from synthetic fabrics: rayon, nylon, Dacron, Orlon, and Fibrolane. All of Maddy's clothes seemed to *whine* whenever she sat down. Though Maddy looked as if she should be a manicurist and she was frequently extremely impertinent, she could take an astonishing two hundred words a minute in dictation, and was very efficient.

"Maddy," pleaded Jack, "write my letters for me. Pretend I'm giving you dictation, then just type them up and send them off."

"I have to have your signature," said Maddy reproachfully, as if he'd just asked her to find him a gun with which to assassinate the mayor. Maddy's voice was high-pitched and breathless, which wasn't surprising considering the tightness of her underpinnings.

"Forge my signature," said Jack. "You have for years anyway."

Maddy wasn't having any of it. Maddy visited him every morning, made Jack look over the previous day's correspondence, took down his dictation, and then made him sign the letters he'd dictated the day before.

"Maddy," Jack asked on Thursday as he was mechanically signing a sheaf of documents with no memory of having dictated them, "have there been any messages for me at the office?"

Maddy was perched on a little aluminum chair, with her head bent down between her knees, brushing out her peroxided locks. Maddy was a fabulous secretary in her way, but her habits of personal grooming knew neither appropriate season nor place.

"I bring you all your messages," said Maddy, with sullen rebuke, and still bent over.

"I mean have there been any personal messages?"

"I bring you *all* your messages," she repeated, lifting her head, and staring at him. She held her hairbrush aloft as if threatening to hurl it at him if he asked another question.

"Well," said Jack, chancing the injury, which would have been slight compared to what he'd already suffered, "have there been any people to call up and say, 'Is Jack there?' and when you say no, they don't leave a message, they just say they'll call back later? Has there been a *woman* calling up? Has there—"

Maddy was growing exasperated. She put away her brush and pulled a mirror and a box of Lady Esther face powder out of her alligator bag—it was more like a small trunk—and began critically to examine her face.

Jack rambled on for a few moments. "—been anybody who maybe called up and asked what hospital I was in, or—"

"No," said Maddy, patting the sides of her face with the powder puff, so that the room was instantly suffused with the scent of Lady Esther. It was different in odor but not in intensity from the smoke of the deceased fat man's cigar.

"No," she repeated, "no one's called. No one's left a message. No one wants to know how you are or where you are and whether you're going to live or die. Mr. Estess says to tell you that you have five more days of sick leave but then they turn into vacation days and you only have two of those, so you'd better get well quick."

Mr. Estess was director of personnel. Mr. Estess, for some reason, was interested in Maddy. Maddy tolerated Mr. Estess because Mr. Estess provided gossip and on frequent occasions juggled his books to give her an extra sick or vacation day.

"I can't believe this," said Jack. "I can't believe that *nobody* has come to visit me."

"Nobody's asked about you either," said Maddy, rummaging in her purse. She came up with a small bottle of Mum Mist spray deodorant and Jack fervently hoped she wasn't going to apply it in his presence. Maddy regarded it for a few moments, and then dropped it back inside her bag. "Would you like me to call up somebody for you?" Maddy asked vaguely, with some remote semblance of polite concern.

"My fiancée hasn't even called," said Jack miserably.

"The one whose apartment you jumped out of the window from?" said Maddy.

"I didn't jump out the window because of her. I jumped—wait a minute. I didn't jump at all, Maddy. I fell. It was not a suicide attempt. It was a stupid accident, and I'm lucky to be alive. I just wish somebody cared. Libby hasn't called?"

"Her lawyer called. This morning."

"I thought you said *nobody* called."

"I didn't count him because he didn't leave a message. People who don't leave messages don't count."

"What did he want?" demanded Jack impatiently.

Maddy, still peering at herself in the mirror, asked, "Is one side of my face darker than the other, Mr. Beaumont?"

"What did Libby's lawyer say?"

"Nothing!" Maddy screamed back. "He didn't say anything! He said, 'Is Mr. Beaumont there?' I said, 'Mr. Beaumont is in the hospital.' He said, 'Do you think he's still going to be there on Sunday?' And I said, 'I'm not his doctor so I wouldn't know.' He said, 'Thank you.' I said, 'You're welcome.' He said, 'Good-bye.' I said, 'Good-bye.' Satisfied?"

"Why would Libby's lawyer want to know if I'm still going to be in the hospital on Sunday?"

"Maybe he wasn't a lawyer at all. Maybe he was a thief who wants to break into your apartment on Sunday morning and doesn't want to get caught."

Jack considered Maddy's suggestion and rejected it. He felt sure that the man on the telephone had indeed been Libby's lawyer, wanting to know whether Jack was going to be out of the hospital by Sunday or not. But *why*?

Jack begged the doctor to tell him when he'd be able to leave.

The doctor examined him, consulted his record, thought for a moment, and then replied, "Your arm has begun to heal, and as long as you keep it in that cast, you'll be fine. Your head is as right as it's ever going to be, and you appear to have gotten a little rest. I think there should be no problem if I let you out"—he thought for a moment—"say on Sunday morning. In time to see if Juliet's going to die."

"Juliet?"

"'The Heart of Juliet Jones,'" said the doctor in surprise, staring at the bandages on Jack's head, as if he'd suddenly decided that perhaps Jack wasn't fully recovered after all. "She thought she just had the mumps, but this morning Dr. Chet Davis told Juliet's sister the truth."

When Maddy came the next morning she looked as if she'd finally laced herself in too tightly. Her steel blue eyes wandered a little, and beneath the layers of powder and paint her face seemed more pallid than usual.

She wasn't even carrying her alligator bag.

"Good morning, Mr. Beaumont," she said in a tentative, breathy whisper, and seated herself on the edge of the aluminum chair. Her pink rayon skirt whined in protest. "How do you feel?"

"Pretty terrible, to tell the truth. You didn't bring another briefcase-load of work for me to look at?"

She shook her head.

"You didn't bring the letters I dictated to you yesterday?"

She shook her head again. The rayon skirt—and Maddy inside of it—slid backward on the chair.

She looked forlorn. Jack was worried. Maybe someone in her family had died.

"No messages for me?"

"Just one," she said hesitantly.

"From..."

"From Mr. Estess," she said, with a sudden eagerness to get this over with, whatever it was.

"Yes?" Jack prompted.

"You're fired."

CHAPTER FIFTEEN

SUSAN BRIGHT WAS calmer after she had asked Rodolfo to take her to dinner. Calmer, but much more angry. Angry with Libby for the smug satisfaction she'd shown Susan at the door of Jack's apartment. Angry with Jack for leading her on the way he had—interrupting a proposal of marriage by flinging yourself in through a window argued a certain continued interest in the lady concerned. Angry with herself for letting Libby get the best of her, and for ever believing that Jack Beaumont would turn out to be something other than what he was today and always had been—a total cad.

She fairly vibrated with animosity toward Jack as she passed Sixty-sixth Street on the Madison Avenue bus on her way to work.

The club women on her guided tours that day at the Metropolitan came away from the galleries with the unfortunate impression—engendered by Susan's tone of voice, and sharp commands—that the Golden Age of Athens must have been something similar to Hitler's Third Reich.

After work Susan went straight home and climbed into a hot bath. When it grew cold, she ran hot water again, and soaked some more. Woolf whined and scratched at the bathroom door. When that didn't gain him entrance, he tried barking. When that didn't work, he pulled all the covers from Susan's bed, dragged them into the kitchen, and went to sleep on the soft pile. In the tub, Susan tried not to think of anything, but she could not blot out what had happened the day before.

She wore gloves that evening because her fingers were so water-wrinkled.

Rodolfo took her uptown to La Caravelle for dinner. That made her feel good, even though the restaurant was only ten blocks south of Jack's apartment, and four avenues over.

Rodolfo was wearing a new suit, a light-colored tropical-looking linen suit. Susan didn't like it. It wasn't quite the season yet; it was still a few weeks till the time Manhattan men allowed themselves lighter colors. And the suit somehow made Rodolfo look more Cuban. Extraordinarily handsome still, of course—but handsome in a, well, Cuban sort of way. She said nothing about the suit, however, though she flushed when she saw the maître d' eyeing it with what she took to be disapproval. As if a too-light suit were more ridiculous than the bow-tied mink stole worn by the floozy who was escorted in right after them.

Two martinis, a bottle of wine, and La Caravelle's fine food began to restore Susan's equanimity. It was a relief also that Rodolfo had not renewed his proposal of marriage, though she expected it to come before the end of the evening. That put her in mind of another engagement. The thought occurred to her again and again, until it was like a chant in her mind, that Libby and Jack were both fools and deserved each other.

...*deserved each other*...

...deserved each other...
...deserved each other...

Rodolfo reached inside the pocket of his linen jacket and withdrew a long, oversized white envelope. He placed it on the table between them.

Susan looked at it and him quizzically.

"Open it, please," he said.

She took up the envelope and held it to her breast a moment as the waiter took away some of their dishes. When the waiter was gone, she took out the papers that were inside.

The alcohol was making Susan's head swim. The romantic lighting in the restaurant was dim and it was hard to read the small lettering.

"They're tickets," she said finally, and pushed them back into the envelope. "Tickets on the Italian Line. Tickets for where?" she asked, forming her words carefully, trying not to sound as tipsy as she felt.

"Two first-class cabins on the *Andrea Doria*. Sailing for Cuba a week from tomorrow."

Susan stared, not quite sure what to say. Nothing came to mind. She opened her mouth, and what came out was "To Cuba..."

"My home. You must meet my family—and your uncle, of course. I have already written him, and I have had a letter from him today. He says we must stay with him for a few weeks. He says that he feels very ashamed— he has neglected his favorite niece for far too long."

"I am his *only* niece," Susan pointed out.

"He says that he will build us a house to live in. I will run his plantation and you will make him laugh."

Susan smiled, though she knew that a smile at this juncture might get her into trouble. "He says my letters make him laugh," she said to Rodolfo. "I don't make anybody else laugh. I make most people uncomfortable."

"That is because you tell the truth."

Susan looked away, thinking about Jack and Libby. She hadn't told either of them the truth.

...deserved each other...

If she had told Jack that there was still some possibility of love between them, instead of insulting him every time she ran into him, then perhaps he wouldn't now be in the clutches of Libby Mather.

If she had told Libby that she wasn't done with Jack Beaumont yet and that she—Libby—was to stay way the hell away until Susan *was* done with Jack Beaumont then maybe Libby wouldn't be wearing that dreadfully ostentatious diamond on her finger. Libby wouldn't say it was an engagement ring, but she denied it in such a way that it was no denial at all.

If Susan had spoken up and told the truth, she wouldn't be practically engaged to this handsome Cuban sitting across the table from her.

She hadn't told the truth; and now she must pay the consequences.

He was speaking to her in Spanish. And probably had been for some time, but her mind had been wandering, and it was befuddled with the martinis and the wine. Now a second bottle of wine had been brought to the table, and Susan was replying to him in Spanish. It really wasn't a very good idea, though she didn't know exactly why that should be so.

"Do you prefer to be married here or in Cuba?" Rodolfo asked.

Susan sipped at the wine he'd poured her, and thought, *How do I get into these situations...?*

"If we get married here in New York," Rodolfo went on, "the wedding will be held in the home of the Cuban consul and we will need only one cabin on the *Andrea Doria*. And if we get married in Cuba, the wedding will be held in the home of your uncle."

Susan continued to sip her wine. She smiled, though a smile was now more dangerous than ever. She thought about it all, and to her surprise, she didn't have any difficulty imagining it happening. It was certainly no stranger than imagining the wedding of Jack and Libby. She knew that she ought also to consider what life with Rodolfo would be like *after* the ceremony, but she was tired, and she'd been through a lot. Her imagination at this interesting point seemed to give out.

"Which will it be?" Rodolfo persisted. "New York or Cuba?"

Susan took another sip of wine.

"Cuba," she said.

Susan was hung over the next day. She decided to take the day off, and she called in sick.

"Did I do the right thing?" she asked Woolf over breakfast.

Woolf hesitated, as if waiting for her to explain, *about what?*

"About Rodolfo," said Susan.

Woolf wagged his tail rapidly. Evidently he felt that she had.

The telephone rang. She was certain it was Rodolfo.

A little perversely, she felt that her acceptance of his proposal of marriage should be enough; he shouldn't pester her with telephone calls. She placed a pillow over the telephone, which muffled the ring until Woolf pulled the pillow off in order to play with it as if it were a dead animal.

Susan took Woolf out with her about eleven o'clock. She walked around Washington Square, then set off west, along Christopher Street toward the Hudson River. She bought herself and Woolf hot dogs from a vendor, not forgetting that Woolf liked ketchup and relish. She decided to try to call Jack—to tell him that he really was going to have to take his dog back as she was going to Cuba in order to get married and she had no intention of taking Woolf along with her on the *Andrea Doria*, not because she wasn't fond of Woolf, but because there wasn't time even to apply for a quarantine exemption. She dialed his number from a pay phone, but he wasn't at home.

Susan stood at the end of Christopher Street and watched the Cunard Line ship *Caronia* pass downstream. It was headed toward the Battery, toward the Statue of Liberty, and out to sea toward some other country. She could see the passengers, with champagne and balloons, leaning over the deck rails and waving. A week from today, a week from this very moment, she'd be on another ship, headed toward Cuba. Depressed for some reason, she bought Woolf another hot dog, and spilled ketchup on her shoes.

When she returned home, there was a telegram waiting for her.

There were four folded sheets inside the envelope. Her landlady on the first floor had tipped the delivery boy fifteen cents, and demanded that she be reimbursed.

Susan gave the woman three nickels, explained that Woolf wasn't there permanently but was only visiting for the afternoon, and then—having got rid of the landlady and locked Woolf in the bathroom—she sat down and read the telegram.

It was in bad German, and it bore no signature.

She read it through again.

She stared out the window at the brick wall.

Woolf was barking in the bathroom. She got up and let him out. He bounded through the apartment with all the apparent joy of someone who's been unjustly locked up for years seeing unbarred sunlight for the first time again.

Susan read through the telegram a third time. It no longer seemed so strange to Susan that the telegram had been composed in German.

She crumpled up the four yellow pages into a ball and placed them on a saucer and set a match to them. The burning fired a black circle on the surface of the china, but Susan didn't care. She was somber, and her hangover was gone.

Accepting Rodolfo's invitation to travel to Cuba aboard the *Andrea Doria* now appeared to have been a very wise thing to do.

Susan swung into action. She packed two small bags with clothing, and set them beside the door.

She grabbed her purse and went down to the street, then headed toward Seventh Avenue. On the way she stopped in at a delicatessen and purchased half a dozen cans of Red Heart dog food. On Seventh Avenue she walked downtown until she came to the Hertz Driv-Ur-Self System outlet, where she rented herself a forest green Nash Airflyte Ambassador with power steering.

She drove back to Washington Square, parked illegally by a fire hydrant, ran upstairs, and fetched her bags and Woolf in a single trip. She got in the car and headed uptown. At a Western Union office on Second Avenue and Fifty-fifth Street—only eleven blocks from Jack's apartment—she sent a telegram to Rodolfo.

It read:

HAVE GONE TO TELL MY AUNT ANNE THE GOOD NEWS STOP BACK IN TOWN SATURDAY STOP NO NEWSPAPER ANNOUNCEMENTS PLEASE STOP (SIGNED) SUSAN

She turned east and zoomed over the Queensborough Bridge. She drove fast, as if someone were chasing her. All the way out to the end of Long Island Woolf sat next to her on the front seat with his head lolling out of the window, staring teary-eyed into the warm spring wind.

CHAPTER SIXTEEN

JACK QUIZZED MADDY relentlessly. What had Mr. Estess meant when he said that Jack was fired?

"He meant that you don't work for the firm anymore," said Maddy.

Jack was in a daze. Had Mr. Estess meant to imply that Jack was not to come to work anymore, that he was not to receive any more employee benefits—such as health insurance, use of the executive cafeteria, and a biweekly paycheck?

Maddy nodded miserably. Tears began to dig tiny trenches through the layers of makeup on her cheek, just as the Colorado River had worn through seven thousand feet of geological strata to create the Grand Canyon. "Do you know who they're giving me to?" Maddy wailed in the midst of her erosion. "They're giving me to Mr. Hamilton. Mr. Hamilton is a pansy, Mr. Beaumont. Mr. Hamilton will never even look at me!"

Jack was embarrassed. In the first place it had never occurred to him that Mr. Hamilton was a pansy; he'd thought him no more than a meticulous dresser—and rather envied him that. In the second place Jack never knew that Maddy put so much stock in being admired; he knew how infrequently he had complimented her in the past two years. Jack blushed violently on both counts.

But then the color drained from his face with the realization—coming to him with full force—that he had actually been fired.

"Did Mr. Estess give a reason?" Jack asked, wiping the perspiration from his brow. "I can't believe it, Maddy."

"I can't believe it either, Mr. Beaumont. He didn't know the reason. I asked him twice, Mr. Beaumont. I said, 'Mr. Estess, is there a reason?' And he said, 'Maybe somebody knows, Maddy, but I don't.' And I said, 'Mr. Estess, there *has* to be a reason,' and he said, 'I'm sure there is, Maddy, but I have no idea what it could be.'" Maddy had a tendency to repeat conversations verbatim, as if she mistrusted her ability to provide a faultless synopsis of even the most insignificant exchange. At the same time, she tried to recapture the precise flavor of the conversation by imitating the different voices. She was generally a good mimic, but when it came to reproducing her own voice and mannerisms, she was a master.

"Maddy, I'll call Mr. Estess, and then I'll call Mr. Young, and we'll see what's what."

"It's true," said Maddy dismally. "I know it's true, because they told me I'm supposed to start for Mr. Hamilton this afternoon. Mr. Hamilton keeps body building magazines in the lower left-hand drawer of his desk. He says his baby brother is a boxer, but nobody believes *that*." Maddy was rambling, somewhat irrelevantly.

"I wish I could help you, Maddy, but since I don't work there anymore..."

"Mr. Beaumont," said Maddy, staring in a tiny

mirror cupped in her hand, and dabbing at her tears one by one with a blue handkerchief, "you'll find a job, I know you will. And when you do, will you send for me? Will you say you can't get along without me? Because wherever you go, I'll go, Mr. Beaumont. For you, I'd even go—" Maddy took a deep breath—"I'd even go to Elizabeth, New Jersey."

Greater love hath no secretary than this, Jack thought.

When Maddy had gone Jack started on a new round of telephone calls, all these directed to his office.

He talked to Mr. Estess. Basically, he had the same conversation with the director of personnel Maddy had had with him.

Jack telephoned Mr. Young, his immediate superior. Mr. Young wouldn't speak to him, but Mr. Young's secretary said that Mr. Beaumont would be receiving a letter providing reasons for his sudden termination. Then Mr. Young's secretary spoke to Jack in a hurried, low voice, evidently not to be overheard, "I don't know what it is yet, Mr. Beaumont, because Mr. Young hasn't dictated the letter to me yet. But as soon as he does, I'll call Maddy and tell her and she'll tell you. Everybody is very upset, because everybody likes you, and it won't be the same place without you. Maddy cried all through lunch. She's very upset. I do know that Mr. Young didn't like to have to do it. He drank bourbon at lunch and when he drinks bourbon it's because he has to do something he doesn't like to do."

"Thank you," said Jack. He had to leave it at that for now. He waited for a telephone call from Maddy all Friday afternoon, but none came.

If there was a more miserable man in Manhattan on Saturday, Jack wished somebody would bring him over to

Roosevelt Hospital so they could jump out of the window together.

But then, about noon, he suddenly felt better about the loss of the job. It was the sudden realization that he was—ostensibly—engaged to be married to the fifth richest single woman in America. He wasn't going to lack spare change to buy Woolf dog biscuits, at any rate.

This proved comfort to him for about five minutes. Then Jack grew depressed again—at the actual prospect of getting married to the fifth richest single woman in America.

Jack was released from Roosevelt Hospital late Sunday morning. Hospital attendants saw him downstairs in a wheelchair, and paused long enough for him to purchase a *Times* in the lobby gift shop. He wanted particularly to find out if there was an announcement of the engagement of Elizabeth St. John Mather to Mr. John Beaumont, Esq. A nurse stepped outside and hailed a taxi for him, then helped him into the cab with his two small bags and his briefcase. She shut the door, waved, and called out that she hoped everything would turn out all right. Jack could only reflect bitterly how unlikely a hope *that* was.

In fact, everything was not turning out all right already. The nurse had left his *Times* on the seat of the wheelchair. Jack would have asked the driver of the taxi to stop so that he could buy another *Times* but all he had in his pocket were three twenty-dollar bills, and he knew that no vendor in New York City would sell a newspaper—even a Sunday *Times*—to a man holding a twenty-dollar bill. He sat back and sighed, and then began to wonder about Woolf. He hoped the dog was well and that Libby had taken him to the kennel as he'd asked and not simply let him loose on the street. Then he hoped for a few blocks that no one had broken into his apartment in his absence. Then for a few more blocks he hoped that perhaps the doorman had a message for him from Susan Bright, along the lines of, *Everything has obviously been a long series of silly misunderstandings, let's you and I get married...*

Then he was home. With his arm in the sling, and the driver, fuming over the twenty-dollar bill and ill-inclined to assist him, Jack took a good bit of time in getting his bags and briefcase up to the door.

The elevator man was as usual nowhere in sight. Jack got the outside door open, kicked his bags inside. He fumbled with his keys, got the inner door open, again kicked his bags inside. One by one he then got his bags into the elevator, and kicked out the broomstick that held the door open.

Predictably, at that moment, the elevator man made his appearance, tearing around the corner of the lobby, crying, "Wait, wait!"

Jack pulled the lever that opened the door again, and glowered at the elevator man.

"Glad to have you back," the elevator man said as they rose upward. The elevator man was lazy and nosy and smelled of schnapps. His wife was lazier and nosier than he was, and filled the basement, the stairwells, and the elevator shaft with the fumes of cooking cabbage.

"Any messages for me?" Jack asked.

"Just one. About an hour ago. This girl came by—"

"What girl?" Jack had a sudden hope that everything that had gone wrong in the past few weeks was about to be set right. Susan *had* come by, she had come by to see him and they—"Did she have dark hair?" Jack demanded feverishly, interrupting his own very interesting and hopeful thought. And then he realized with a sinking: *Oh, maybe it was Libby.* "Or was she a blonde? Was she—"

"I couldn't tell what color her hair was," said the elevator man. "She was wearing a veil."

"A veil?"

"You know—a wedding veil."

"What was the message?" demanded Jack. In the extremity of his suspense, he swung this way and that in the elevator, a motion assisted, not hindered, by the unusual weight of the cast on his arm.

"She said you should come to the wedding this afternoon. One o'clock."

"The *wedding?"*

The doors of the elevator opened on the fifth floor. Jack didn't get out.

"'This afternoon, one o'clock,' she said."

Susan was marrying Rodolfo, and as a final kick in Jack's teeth, she'd dropped by on the way to the church and invited him to the wedding—as an afterthought. *Oh, the wedding limousine was driving by and I saw the sign for Sixty-sixth Street and I said to myself, I've forgotten to invite Jack. For old times' sake.* She—

"What church?" Jack demanded suddenly, realizing it was well past noon.

"The one at the corner of Fifth and Fifty-fifth. Or -sixth. Or -seventh. Numbers and me, you know, we don't get along so good."

"Go back down," said Jack.

"What?"

"Take the elevator down again."

The elevator man stared. "Here," said Jack, reaching in his pocket and giving the man all the change he'd got from the taxi. "Please take my bags and put them in my apartment."

They rode down without speaking, but Jack noisily tapped his foot. He beat his hand against the side of the elevator. He hissed through his teeth. He allowed his whole body to fall and jar against the back wall of the elevator until the slowest piece of machinery on the island of Manhattan at last ground to a halt on the lobby floor.

"What time is it?" Jack demanded of the elevator man,

as he pulled open the door of the elevator. Jack's watch had been smashed in the fall the week before.

"Ten minutes to one," said the elevator man. "You'd better hurry."

Jack fled into the bright spring sunshine. He'd have to hurry indeed if he was going to stop Susan's wedding.

CHAPTER SEVENTEEN

JACK FOUND A taxi at the corner of Third Avenue and Sixty-fourth Street. An elderly couple wanted it, but Jack told them that his wife was having a baby in the hospital at that very moment and he had to get to her.

"But he stopped for us," said the old woman.

Politeness being of no avail, Jack simply leaped in front of them and got into the taxi. He said, "Fifty-sixth and Fifth."

"That wasn't nice, mister," said the taxi driver. "And there ain't no hospital where I'm taking you."

"It's a private hospital," said Jack. "It just opened. I had my arm put into a cast there."

The taxi driver glanced mistrustfully in the rear-view mirror, but he took Jack where he wanted to go.

"I might have known," he grumbled when they arrived, "that somebody like you would try to pawn off a double sawbuck on me."

"A dollar tip," pleaded Jack, who was looking around for a sign of Susan Bright in a wedding dress. Not only was there no Susan Bright, there wasn't even a church.

Knowing that there was no church at the corner of Fifty-seventh Street, Jack ran down Fifth Avenue toward Fifty-fifth. His run was loping, but off-balance because of the cast. With every step the broken bones of his left arm jarred painfully.

There was a church at the corner of Fifty-fifth Street. Maybe his luck was changing. He clambered up the shallow stone steps to a pair of red doors. The door he jerked on first was locked, though he pulled so hard he nearly incapacitated his right arm as well.

In order to get to the other pair of red doors, he tried to climb over the wrought-iron railing that ascended the steps right up to the doors, but it was too high. He didn't get over, merely succeeded in ripping a hole in his right trouser leg, crotch to knee.

He also pulled a muscle in his right calf. This new pain seemed in some way to balance his broken left arm.

He limped down to the sidewalk, and then up the other side. The red doors there swung open easily.

He found himself in a shallow dark vestibule with a high vaulted ceiling and marble floor. He stood still, thinking, *Wrong church...*

He then became aware of a murmuring from the sanctuary, on the other side of a pair of wide mahogany doors inset with yellow and green stained glass.

Damn...

He pushed open the door to the sanctuary.

The vestibule had been so narrow and tight that Jack wasn't at all prepared for the size of the church. It seemed to stretch all the way to Sixth Avenue inside, and was so high that the hazy dust motes at the ceiling appeared to be about to coalesce into wisps of cloud. The long ranks of polished oak pews looked like a neatly felled forest, and the altar was hazy and soft in the distance.

And there at the front, before the altar, stood Rodolfo García-Cifuentes and his bride. A minister as tall as Jack was officiating. Only a dozen guests had gathered in the pews to the left and the right of the wide center aisle, down which Jack rushed till he was nearly halfway to the front.

"I—" cried Jack.

Rodolfo turned and smiled faintly.

The bride turned, but her gaze was concealed by her veil. Jack could easily imagine Susan's grim smile, her whispered, "I'm not a bit surprised..."

The guests in the sanctuary turned and stared at Jack in astonishment, and put their heads together and murmured.

Jack blushed violently, but he stood his ground.

The preacher grimaced at Jack as he spoke the words, "I now pronounce you man and wife."

Jack turned and fled from the church like a man possessed.

He spent the afternoon in an Irish bar near Times Square on Seventh Avenue. It was a dim, smoky place, and the ratty decorations left over from St. Patrick's Day jostled with the even rattier decorations left over from Valentine's Day. Jack had captured a booth all to himself, and wouldn't give it up even to the parties of six who came in and stared at him balefully and made loud comments about people who were even more selfish on Sunday than they were weekdays. The management wouldn't move Jack because he was drinking enough for six.

Jack spent on bourbon the change from the taxi that had taken him to the church where Rodolfo García-Cifuentes had married the woman he loved. That left him a single twenty-dollar bill in his pocket. He thought maybe he should eat and asked the bartender if the kitchen would prepare him a plate of wieners smothered with mayonnaise.

The kitchen wouldn't like it, the bartender told him, but the kitchen would do it. A kitchen in a bar in Times Square got a lot of unappetizing requests.

As he consumed one white and slippery weiner after another, Jack wondered what he should do with the rest of his life now that Susan Bright was out of it.

The first thing he should do, he thought morosely, was to pick a fight with somebody and get his other arm broken.

He amended that plan to: get drunker first, and *then* pick a fight and get your other arm broken.

He was halfway through his last twenty-dollar bill when he ordered a second plate of weiners smothered with mayonnaise. He washed them down with bourbon. Jack could take up a whole booth by himself, he was so lanky and tall, and as he got drunker he seemed to stretch. With a torn trouser leg, his arm in a cast, his eyes bloodshot, his clothing rumpled and bourbon-stained, he looked very much the barfly.

He carefully preserved the two dollars that would get him home in a taxi. He staggered out of the bar at seven-thirty in the evening, but no taxi would pick him up.

He would have to walk home.

This will sober me, he thought, not wanting to be sober.

He could easily have avoided Times Square, but that didn't suit his mood. He wanted to appear as he was—an unemployed tramp.

Fate, which hadn't been very kind to Jack recently, decided to go along with his mood for once.

It put acquaintances in his path. Passing the theater where *The King and I* was playing, he saw a couple he recognized as friends of Libby. They stared at him with horror as he approached them.

"Where's Libby?" Jack demanded, grabbing the man by a lapel. "She's gonna be my wife. Where is she? She won't answer the phone. She's gonna make me the husband of the fifth richest woman in America..."

The man pushed Jack away with a startled expression. "It *is* you. Helen and I couldn't believe..."

Jack thought he was going to throw up, and he thought it best not to throw up on Libby's friends.

He staggered off.

Rosalind Russell was playing in *Wonderful Town*, and Mr. Hamilton—Maddy's new pansy boss—was waiting to see it with several of his friends.

All of Mr. Hamilton's friends were meticulous dressers. Jack counted five—no, six; no, just five—of them waiting outside the theater.

Mr. Hamilton knew it was Jack. The cast on his arm, the torn trousers, the drunken limp, the bleary eyes—none of that fooled Mr. Hamilton for an instant. Mr. Hamilton turned abruptly away with a blush so violent it nearly could have matched one of Jack's own.

Jack grabbed Mr. Hamilton's shoulder and spun him around.

Mr. Hamilton's friends were alternately petrified, scandalized, and indignant. Mr. Hamilton himself was very nearly tearful—to be humiliated this way in front of his peers and a crowd of strangers. What good did careful attention to one's appearance do when one was subjected to incidents like this? *Pawed* by a drunk in the street.

"Tell Maddy she's beautiful!" Jack shouted right in Mr. Hamilton's face. "I don't care what you think about her, tell her she's beau-ti-ti-ful!"

Then Jack staggered on, leaving Mr. Hamilton to find whatever meager enjoyment he could get out of Rosalind Russell's performance this evening.

Twice Jack fell off the curb, scraping his knees and doing more damage to his trousers. First he hit the pavement of Park Avenue, and later the sidewalk near Sixty-third Street.

From time to time he would make an attempt at hailing a cab, and finally one did stop for him, and Jack climbed in. "Sixty-sixth between Second and Third," Jack said, slumped in the seat.

But because they were only a block and a half away from that destination, the driver threw him out again.

Jack hadn't lost his keys, though he might as well have, because he couldn't get them into the lock. He fumbled and swore until the night elevator man noticed his plight and opened the door for him. Jack stumbled into the lobby and winced against the forty-watt bulb in the ceiling fixture, which shone bright as the sun.

"Some party, hunh?" said the elevator man, pulling Jack toward the elevator.

Jack got into the elevator, but then he began to give out. His legs started to crumple under him, and he sank all the way to the floor and fell asleep.

The elevator man awakened him on the fifth floor.

"Here you are, Mr. Beaumont. Give me your keys."

Jack shook his head. "I can do it," he said groggily.

Then he fell asleep again on the floor of the elevator.

The elevator man fished in his pocket for the keys, picked him up off the floor—with a little help from Jack himself—and then led him to the door of his apartment.

Jack heard violent barking from inside.

He turned to the man and said wistfully, "Somebody still loves me..."

The elevator man turned the key and pushed open the door.

"You be all right?" he asked.

Woolf jumped out and knocked Jack against the wall of the narrow corridor.

"No dogs allowed," said the elevator man mildly. "I'm going to have to report you. Good-night."

"Good-night," said Jack, giving the elevator man the two dollars he'd so carefully saved for the taxi.

Woolf licked Jack's face, cast, and any other place he could find with bourbon stains.

Jack sat in the corridor for a while and allowed himself to be licked. His apartment, through the open doorway, seemed about three miles away. He was just dozing off again when he felt someone's gaze on him. He looked up groggily, and then was unsure whether he was dreaming or not.

There in the open door of his apartment stood Susan Bright, looking down at him with a grimace of disgust. She was not wearing her wedding gown.

"I'm not a bit surprised," she said.

CHAPTER EIGHTEEN

"I CAN'T FACE him right now," Jack pleaded, his head pressed against the swirled pink plaster of the corridor wall. "Later. Not now. Tell him to go away. Please. Just do that for me, Susan."

Jack hugged Woolf close.

"Who are you talking about?" asked Susan. "You're drunk. I can't believe how drunk you are. You stink, you're dirty, and look at that hole in your trousers. I can see your underwear."

A door opened down the hall and an old woman peered out.

"Somebody get rid of that dog!" she called out.

Woolf barked vehemently at the woman.

"You're drawing attention," said Susan darkly. "At least come inside. It's your own apartment, after all."

"Then he's not inside?" Jack asked weakly.

"Who?" said Susan.

"Rodolfo."

"Unless he's been hiding in the closet for the past five hours, Rodolfo is *not* in your apartment. Five hours—that's how long I've been waiting for you."

"You came here right from the church then," said Jack as he struggled to his feet. Or attempted to. His balance was not good and Woolf had evidently decided that smack between Jack's legs was the only place in the world to be. Nowhere else would do.

Susan gave him a helping hand.

"You're not making any sense," she said. "Do you know that? Do you know how little sense you're making? I'm going to make some coffee, and you're going to take a cold shower."

"I'm not allowed to take showers," Jack mumbled. "Not with my cast."

"Then you're going to take a cold bath. Right now," she said.

He obeyed docilely...

A quarter of an hour later, Jack had come to the conclusion that there was, in the entire range of human experience, only one sensation that was worse than a cold bath when you're drunk, and that was a cold bath when you're drunk with a dog licking the side of your face every time you started to fall asleep.

"Cover yourself," called Susan from outside the bathroom door. "I'm bringing in a cup of coffee."

Jack jerked the shower curtain halfway closed. In its cast, his left arm dangled to the tile floor away from the water. Unfortunately, the opaque white shower curtain was decorated with an undersea scene with sunfish and mermaids, and was just suggestive enough of the sea to make Jack's stomach queasy.

"Are you a little less drunk?" said Susan.

"A little. What's your husband going to say when he finds you in the bathroom with a naked man?" said Jack morosely. The coffee smelled good as Susan handed him the cup.

"Don't worry," said Susan, calmly putting down the toilet seat and arranging herself comfortably on it. "In the first place, you're hardly in a condition to attack me. In the second place, I'm not married."

Jack halted the cup at his lips. He sniffed at the coffee, then took a sip. He thought about what Susan had just said.

"You're not married?" he asked, trying not to slur his words. He thought that he ought to get this part straight, even if he understood nothing else.

Susan shook her head. "*Definitely* not married. Did you have a particular reason for thinking I might be?"

Jack nodded, staring at the water and continuing to sip his coffee.

Woolf took the corner of the shower curtain in his teeth and dragged it open again.

Susan, politely averting her eyes, readjusted it.

"When can I get out of this cold water?" he asked. "It's horrible in here."

"When you're sober," said Susan. "Why did you think I was married?"

"Circumstantial evidence," said Jack, even though those were difficult words for him to articulate. "I went to the church this afternoon and I saw you and Rodolfo standing in front of the altar and I heard the preacher say, 'I now pronounce you man and wife.'"

Susan stared. Jack continued to sip his coffee.

"'I now pronounce you man and wife,'" Jack repeated.

"Rodolfo got married today?" asked Susan after a moment.

Jack nodded.

"Who was the bride?" she asked.

Jack smiled. A smirky, bitter little smile.

"What time was this wedding?"

"One o'clock. I was a few minutes late."

"At one o'clock I was passing through Hicksville, Long Island. I had to stop for gas."

"You don't have a car."

"Rented."

"At one o'clock?" said Jack, swallowing the last of the coffee and automatically holding out the cup for more.

Susan had brought the pot along, and had it right outside the bathroom door on a pot holder. She fetched it and poured another cup for Jack.

"Yes," she said, "at one o'clock, I was at a Standard Oil station in Hicksville, Long Island. I remember seeing a clock."

"Then who was the bride?" said Jack.

"You didn't see her face?"

"Brides wear veils."

Both of them pondered for a few moments. Jack ran a little more cold water and thought he'd die, but he was getting sober very quickly, and an idea was forming in his brain. He was beginning to make certain connections in his mind. *Item 1*: Susan Bright did not marry Rodolfo García-Cifuentes. *Item 2*: Susan Bright was now in his apartment and had been, she said, for some time. *Item 3*: What was item 3? It was the most important of all, Jack knew, but he wasn't sufficiently recovered to have figured out just what it was. That was why he'd just run a little more cold water, even though it made him want to commit suicide.

Susan was thinking hard, too.

"You're sure it was Rodolfo?" she asked.

"Positive."

"How did you know about the wedding? Were you invited?"

Jack nodded. "More or less. The bride came by this morning and left a message with the elevator man. I thought it was you."

"This morning I was in the Hamptons," said Susan. "Visiting an old family friend—my father's law partner in fact. I needed a little advice of a legal nature." Her tone discouraged curious probing on the subject, and anyway,

Jack was in no condition to solve two sets of mysterious circumstances.

"Well, it *was* the bride who was here. The elevator man said she was wearing a wedding veil, and she—"

"Which means that you know the bride," said Susan, with a leap of reasoning utterly beyond Jack.

"Yes," he said after a moment, "I guess you're right."

"So who is it?"

Jack thought a moment. Then he looked at Susan, and Susan looked at him, and they both knew the answer, and they stared at each other, and then Susan began to giggle.

In another hour, Jack was nearly sober, though he had a headache that felt like the entire North Korean Army was marching across the inside of his forehead. He still had not figured out what *Item 3* was.

"Are you hungry?" he asked Susan. She was sitting in his living room, curled up on the sofa, watching the "Schlitz Playhouse of Stars."

"I'm famished," she said.

"There's a spaghetti joint around the corner. If you can rip up one of my shirts so that the cast fits through the arm, I'll take you."

Susan pondered a moment, as if deciding between Jack and Irene Dunne. Miss Dunne had just promised Susan a splendid hour's entertainment, but Jack's offer won. "Let's see what we can do..."

They found a sport shirt in Jack's dresser, and with a pair of kitchen shears Susan slit the left sleeve, and helped Jack wriggle into it.

Woolf was already excited. Any sort of movement in the apartment suggested to Woolf that he was about to be taken for a walk.

"Not tonight," said Susan warningly to the dog.

"Maybe later," said Jack.

Sullen Woolf laid himself down across the threshold of the front door, so that when they left it was necessary for Susan to pick up the dog and move him aside.

The restaurant, called Simeone's, was somewhere in the neighborhood, though Jack couldn't remember exactly where. Sixty-seventh or -eighth or -ninth or maybe even Seventieth; between Second and Third avenues, or maybe between Third and Lexington.

It turned out to be on Seventy-first between Second and First, which Susan discovered by looking in a book in a telephone booth.

Simeone's had red-and-white checked tablecloths, guttering candles in old wine bottles, Agfa-Color photographs of Naples and the Isle of Capri on the wall, and a gypsy violinist who wouldn't go away for less than a dollar.

"No wine for you tonight," said Susan, peering at the menu.

"Do you have Orange Crush?" Jack asked the waiter.

The waiter shook his head.

"Nehi? Royal Crown? Yoo-Hoo? Squirt? Coke?"

"No soft," said the waiter carefully—it was evidently a memorized speech in a foreign tongue. "Only wine."

"One glass for you," Susan said.

The waiter went away and came back with a bottle. They ordered spaghetti and ravioli.

Jack poured for them both.

They raised their glasses, as if to toast, and then—simultaneously—they put their glasses down, and looked away, embarrassed.

After a moment, Jack looked at Susan. "How did you get in my apartment today?"

"The elevator man let me in. He recognized Woolf."

Jack considered this.

"Why did you come?"

"I was returning Woolf."

"Why did you have him? I told Libby to take him to the kennel."

Susan looked at Jack closely. Then she said slowly, "I came to see you last week. You were in the shower, and Libby—"

"What do you mean, the shower? I just got out of the hospital this morning," said Jack.

Susan blinked. "You mean that Libby..."

"Libby what?"

Susan didn't answer the question. She changed the subject. She said: "You were right about Rodolfo."

"Well, you didn't marry him."

"He asked me."

"But you said no."

"Actually," said Susan, "I said yes. But I didn't do it."

"Why did you say yes?"

"It seemed like a good idea—or at any rate it didn't seem like a bad idea."

"I think he might even be dangerous."

"He was. That's one of the most attractive things about him. Besides, being around Rodolfo couldn't possibly have been as dangerous as being around you," she said, glancing at his broken arm.

"He would have made you very unhappy."

"Probably," admitted Susan.

"I was fired," said Jack suddenly. He'd just remembered that.

"What?"

"I was fired. On Friday. Maddy came by the hospital and told me I was fired. I don't know why."

Susan pondered this. "I know why," she said.

Jack stared.

"Libby had you fired."

"Why? Why would she do that?"

Susan shrugged. "She was probably mad at you for something. For trying to commit suicide on the night you were supposed to announce your engagement."

"You know I didn't try to commit suicide. You of *all* people know—"

"I know," said Susan, "but Walter Winchell said it was an attempted suicide."

"I have never even met Walter Winchell. I wish people like Walter Winchell—"

"I think that Libby was upset—so upset that she ran off and married Rodolfo. Therefore I wouldn't be a bit surprised if she was upset enough to show up at the office of the president of your firm, and say, 'Jack Beaumont has mismanaged my finances. I want him fired.' I think it might well have happened that way."

Jack's eyes were wide. "I think maybe you're right. I don't see any other way it *could* have happened. But how do you think those two got together? Libby and Rodolfo. Libby was always pretending she couldn't even remember his name."

Susan looked troubled. "I don't know exactly. But something happened between last Monday night—when Rodolfo asked me to marry him—and this afternoon, when he and Libby got married."

"We're not really sure it *was* Libby," said Jack. "I didn't see her face, after all."

"I'm pretty sure," said Susan. "And I'm not happy about it either. The more I think about it, those two—" She took a long sip of wine.

"Those two what?"

"—Don't deserve each other," she concluded.

"Rodolfo doesn't deserve Libby? Or Libby doesn't deserve Rodolfo?" Jack couldn't help grinning, but he didn't get to hear Susan's opinion, because just then the waiter brought their food. In the few moments he took in putting down the dishes in the wrong place and getting them right again, Jack figured out exactly what item 3 was.

Item 3: If Susan Bright was not married to Rodolfo García-Cifuentes, then she was ostensibly free to marry Jack.

"So will you?" he said aloud, forgetting that Susan had not been privy to his sudden happy enlightenment.

"Will I what?" asked Susan, blushing.

"That's the first time I've ever seen you do that—blush," said Jack. "Will you marry me?"

CHAPTER NINETEEN

"ON ONE CONDITION," said Susan.

"All right," said Jack. He didn't care what the condition was; he'd accept anything so long as Susan agreed to marry him. His mind was still a bit fuzzy, but he knew one thing with absolute certainty: the only truly important thing in the world was that as soon as possible he and Susan Bright stand up in front of a preacher and say the words, "I do."

"Aren't you going to ask what the condition is?"

"No," said Jack. "I don't care." She looked so disappointed that he asked, "What's the condition?"

"That we go on a honeymoon and I choose the place."

"Anywhere," he said, then after a moment added, "except Cuba. Where do you want to go?"

She didn't answer, but looked at him with misgiving.

"Cuba?" he asked.

She took a sip of wine and nodded.

"Then of course we'll go to Cuba on our honeymoon," Jack said briskly. Despite his word, in his mind he saw the face of Rodolfo García-Cifuentes, and wondered if there was a connection. "Now wasn't that easy? So when?"

"When what?"

"When do we get married?"

"As soon as possible," Susan said, and then added, peculiarly, "I'm very anxious for us to get down to Cuba."

Jack ate a little ravioli, wondering if he really had heard somewhere that Italian food cleared the brain or whether he had just made that up, and then said, "I think there's something you're not telling me, Susan. And since we're going to be married—or at least I *think* you said you'd marry me—"

Susan nodded vigorously. "Oh yes, I have every intention—"

"—Well, since we *are* going to be married, maybe you should tell me why you're so interested in our going to Cuba."

Susan put her hand over her mouth, and glanced about the restaurant as if making sure she could speak freely. There weren't more than half a dozen other couples in the place, plus the owner's loud, fat family at an enormous round table in the corner, and the slender gypsy violinist sitting alone with a plate of spaghetti in another corner. No one was paying attention to them. "Are you all here?" Susan asked. "I mean, you're sober enough to hear what I have to say, aren't you?"

"Yes of course I am," he said, trying not to be offended.

"Please don't be hurt," she said, "but this is important. You were wrong about Rodolfo—"

Jack was right. All of this Cuba business *did* have something to do with Rodolfo García-Cifuentes. While it may have been true that Susan wasn't going to marry the Cuban, Rodolfo was still in the picture. That was annoying.

"Wrong how?"

"He *does exist,* no matter what you may think, and he's exactly who he says he is. My uncle's letter of introduction was genuine, although I think my uncle made a mistake in writing it. In general, you were right about Rodolfo."

"Right how?"

"That he was up to no good. He asked me to marry him—"

"So I heard," said Jack dryly, holding up his broken arm. "If you'll remember, I was there."

"Oh yes, the window business." She smiled as if at the memory of a charming drawing room escapade. Then her face darkened. "He asked me to marry him because he thought I was an heiress."

Jack blinked. Though Susan had never confided to him the details of her trust fund, he had a pretty good idea of what her bank statements and savings books looked like. Solvent, but not impressive. Beautiful, but no heiress.

"Why would he think that?" said Jack. "You've never really made any secret about..." He trailed off diplomatically.

"About the fact that I have to work for a living? No, I've certainly never denied that, but the fact is, I *am* an heiress. Or I will be, when my uncle dies."

Jack looked at her sharply. One eye was a fiancé's, the other eye that of a financial analyst. "I didn't know this," he said.

"No, neither did I. I don't think I was supposed to, but someone let it slip. I wrote my uncle recently, and he confirmed it. He also said..."

"Said what?" Jack prompted when Susan hesitated.

"—He also said that someone was trying to kill him."

Jack didn't drink any more wine that evening. Susan saw him back to his apartment, and there was an awkward moment when it was apparent that out of politeness and happiness, despite his fatigue, he wanted to ask her to stay the night. It was equally obvious that she, out of circumspection and dignity, should refuse the invitation.

All that was a bit odd, of course, since it was to Jack that Susan had lost her virginity six years before. What Susan remembered most about that first experience was that it hurt—not because of what Jack did to her, or any roughness on his part, but because they did it in the bottom of a small boat tethered to the dock of the boat house used by the Harvard rowing team one rainy spring night.

Despite that and three other experiences with him, Susan now decided that she wanted to wait. Just in case.

Just in case what? she asked herself, but it was a question she couldn't answer except to repeat, *just in case.* If there ever came a time, Susan reflected ruefully, when a woman didn't have to worry about pregnancy every time she was in a room alone with a man, if the pleasure of making love were not always attended by the possibility of trouble and humiliation in only nine months' time, *then* you were going to see a few changes. It might even be that women would pursue men with the ardor with which they were now pursued. But until that time, women were going to pull back, shake off the embrace, readjust their straps—and ride home alone in a taxi.

"Tell me about your uncle," said Jack, barely able to keep his eyes open. "Who's trying to kill him?"

"Tomorrow," said Susan. "I'll tell you everything tomorrow."

Susan stood with her hand on the door as Jack, unmindful of anything but the desire to go to sleep, was already pulling off his shirt. Woolf looked from one to the other, as if wondering whether he was to go with Susan or stay with Jack.

"Take care of Jack," Susan said to the dog softly, and then was gone.

Susan could hardly sleep that night for excitement and nervous pleasure. When she'd thought through her happiness a few dozen times, she began to turn over in her mind the question of whether she should have stayed the night in Jack's apartment. After an hour or so of serious meditation on the topic, she concluded that she would be spending the rest of her life with this man, and that one night more or less wouldn't make any difference. There was also the notion that he would respect her more for having gone home alone in a taxi. Of course, a pleasure denied was a pleasure that could never be recouped, so despite all the arguments in favor of not sleeping with Jack before the wedding, she was now sorry that she hadn't. Despite her certainty that Jack had been fast asleep by the time she reached the lobby of his building, it was still possible that before morning he might meet someone else and fall madly in love with her. She herself might contract a rare disease and die in bed before morning. Some large, unforeseeable obstacle might place itself in their path just as they were walking down the aisle—certainly the last weeks had been a series of misadventures, and perhaps their bad luck wasn't over yet. She thought about all that for another hour. Then, as dawn filled the small air shaft outside her windows, Susan worried for a while about her uncle, who felt himself to be in mortal danger.

She'd just fallen asleep when the telephone rang. It was Jack. "I couldn't sleep," he said. "Well, I guess I did for a while, but I dreamed of you. Are you still going to marry me?"

"Um-hmmm," she murmured, trying to pry open her eyes.

"When?" he asked.

She peered at the clock. It was a few minutes before seven.

"Ten o'clock?" she suggested.

Ten o'clock wasn't possible, of course; there were certain formalities. So they went together to get blood tests at a little public health office over on Ninth Avenue, where for three-quarters of an hour they obliviously shared a waiting room lined with prostitutes and men with social diseases.

Jack got the license that afternoon. After the waiting period, they would be able to get married on Wednesday.

"But the boat sails tomorrow," Susan protested. They were walking arm-in-arm through Washington Square Park, he still a bit hung over and she pale from not enough sleep, but happiness still showed through.

"What boat?"

"The *Andrea Doria*," she replied. "We have first-class tickets."

Jack stopped in his tracks and stared at her. "Did you—"

"Rodolfo bought them—part of his plan to pressure me into marrying him. I see no reason not to use them."

"I see half a dozen reasons at least. One, they're not ours. Two, Rodolfo can claim them stolen. Three, he might have canceled them. Four, he and Libby might show up on the boat. Five, he—"

She interrupted him hastily. "Rodolfo proposed to me, I said yes, and then a week later he runs off and marries someone else. These tickets are merely recompense for alienation of affection—inadequate recompense, at that. Besides, now that you have no job, how did you intend to pay for this little Caribbean jaunt you're taking me on? Libby lost you that job, so it's only fair that her new husband pay for the honeymoon you can no longer afford. Isn't that logical?"

"No, it's not logical. Because we don't know for sure it was Libby that Rodolfo married."

"Did you read the *Times* this morning?"

Jack shook his head.

"'Señor and Mrs. Rodolfo García-Cifuentes, the former Elizabeth St. John Mather, departed this morning for an extended honeymoon vacation in Cuba and the other Caribbean islands.'"

"They flew?"

"Evidently," said Susan. "And I called the Italian Line. The tickets are still good. And if the license is in order, the captain will marry us. Now, what were objections five and six?"

"I can't remember five," said Jack. "Six was: What do we do with Woolf? Last time I left him, he forgot who I was after three days."

"There's no quarantine on dogs to Cuba. I checked."

"Then tomorrow it is," said Jack. "On the *Andrea Doria*."

CHAPTER TWENTY

THE ITALIAN LINE ship *Andrea Doria* had been commissioned six months before and had made its maiden voyage from Leghorn to Southampton and Bremen. Its second voyage had been to New York, and then a return to Leghorn via Le Havre, Lisbon, and Nice. Its third voyage was to New York again, and it was on the first leg of the return journey, via the Caribbean, that Rodolfo García-Cifuentes had bought tickets for two single A-deck cabins.

The Italian Line had a policy in regard to unmarried couples traveling together. They couldn't be allowed accommodation in a single cabin, but they could obtain rooms next to one another with a connecting door that was tightly secured by the steward. However, with Latin enlightenment the gentleman of the twosome was always given a key, "in case of emergencies."

On boarding, Susan explained to the purser that the name on the ticket, "Rodolfo G. Cifuentes" was simply an egregious misspelling of "John Beaumont." The purser was skeptical at first, but a little added thickness to his wallet convinced him that such a mistake made by misunderstandings between secretaries in the Italian Line office and Mr. Beaumont's was the kind of thing that happened all the time.

Jack tried to use the key to open the door between their cabins, but couldn't get it to turn in the lock.

He went out into the corridor, knocked on Susan's door, and asked if she minded coming over and trying the key. She had a knack with such things, he remembered.

"Who are the candy and flowers and champagne for?" she asked, as she turned the key in the lock and pulled open the door.

"You," he said, following her into her own cabin, where she had been in the midst of unpacking the clothes she thought she'd wear on the leisurely two-day voyage.

"Well, then," she said, briskly snapping shut a suitcase, "open the champagne!"

They gazed out the porthole of her cabin and toasted the Statue of Liberty as the *Andrea Doria* sailed past her.

Rodolfo had been generous in obtaining first-class cabins, but even so Jack was too tall for them. He sat at one end of Susan's tiny sofa with his head pressed against the lampshade on the small end table and his feet stretched almost to the doorway to his room. Susan sat on the other end of the couch, her legs drawn up beneath her and her head resting on Jack's shoulder. Jack's legs went to sleep.

"I wanted to stay at your apartment last night," said Susan quietly.

"I wanted you to stay," said Jack.

They were quiet for a few moments, and Jack felt the arm inside his cast go to sleep. The confined cabin smelled of flowers and the sea.

"We're getting married tomorrow," said Susan quietly, "and we should probably wait." She reached over past him, putting her elbow against his breastbone as she did so, and took a sip from her champagne glass. She sank back into place, relieving the pressure on his chest. "But I don't want to wait."

"I don't either," said Jack.

"Nothing can happen between tonight and tomorrow, can it?" said Susan. "To keep us from getting married, I mean? So it doesn't matter if we wait till tomorrow or not, does it?"

Jack shook his head. "Nothing can happen that will prevent me from marrying you tomorrow."

She reached across him once more, put down her glass, and turned out the light.

"Then let's not wait."

Jack and Susan weren't the most alert or most cheerful bride and groom that ever got married on shipboard. They'd had no sleep the night before, the ship was sailing through rougher waters than were ever suggested by the smiling advertisements for the Italian Line, and Jack wasn't even sure he'd recovered from Sunday's binge.

If they didn't exactly feel married when they returned to the cabin late Wednesday morning, they certainly did when a general announcement was made at luncheon. Half a dozen bottles of champagne were delivered to their table in congratulations, half a dozen jovial husbands stopped to offer facetious condolences to Jack, half a dozen wives smiled with genuine good feeling on Susan, and the purser himself came to unlock the connecting door that had, in fact, stood wide open all the night before.

The sea calmed down as they steamed south, and for the rest of the afternoon, Jack and Susan drank champagne, ate ravenously, and confined themselves to their now officially enlarged cabin. There, in astounding detail, they recounted every thought, feeling, misapprehension, fear, and yearning they'd experienced since running into each other at Charles' French Restaurant in Greenwich Village. They shuddered at how nearly they'd come to marrying others, and they wondered again and again at the strange fate that had brought them together—and nearly kept them apart. They were, in short, deliriously happy with each other, with life, and with every single thing that had led up to these two wonderful days they were spending in the tiny first-class cabins of the *Andrea Doria*.

That evening Jack and Susan Beaumont were seated at the captain's table in honor of their wedding aboard ship. A lady seated across from them, in diamonds and a white fox fur, said to Jack, "Didn't I read about you in Walter Winchell? Aren't you supposed to be dead?"

The way that her husband reacted, with a harrumphing cough, and a vague, "My dear, this newly wedded couple have no interest in Mr. Winchell, I'm sure..." suggested to the newly married couple that their story was known in more detail than they had suspected.

"Let's get out of here," said Jack in a low voice, swallowing his coffee in one long gulp.

"No," replied Susan out of the corner of her mouth, which was smiling at some further inanity of the woman in white fox and diamonds. "As a single woman, I did not run away. I don't intend to start now, just because I'm married."

"I was only thinking of you," said Jack under his breath.

"I'm not the one who threw myself out of a twenty-third story window," Susan pointed out.

"And I'm not the one who accepted first-class boat tickets from my fiancé and then went off with another man entirely," returned Jack.

Suddenly the music started up, and to show everyone that they didn't care what was known or suspected about them, Jack and Susan danced through the night.

Rodolfo had taught Susan the cha-cha, and now she taught it to Jack.

The *Andrea Doria* was to dock in Havana about one o'clock on Thursday afternoon. The morning dawned fair, and Jack and Susan breakfasted, endured what they hoped would be the last of a series of wearisome honeymoon jokes, visited Woolf in the hold, and returned to their cabins to pack. Leaving their bags to be taken ashore by the steward, they went up on deck and watched for Cuba to come into view.

Already many tiny fishing boats were visible. The fishermen waved to Jack and Susan, and Jack and Susan waved dutifully back.

A number of passengers crowded on deck, scanning the fishing boats in hope of seeing the great bearded man in the wide hat, scribbling on a pad. The great bearded man never waved back to the tourists who screamed at him, but as the captain pointed out, it was an honor just to see so great a writer at work.

"What are you thinking about?" asked Jack, noticing that Susan looked pensive.

"My uncle."

"I wish you'd saved that telegram."

"I told you what was in it," said Susan. "Someone's been trying to kill him. He thought the poison and the gunshot were just accidents—that sort of thing is evidently fairly common around here. Food going bad. Clumsy servants dropping firearms. But the exploding Jeep evidently convinced him that someone was trying to kill him."

"Why *did* you burn the telegram?"

"I didn't want it around. I didn't want there to be any possibility of Rodolfo coming across it."

"Was Rodolfo in the habit of prowling about your apartment, reading your telegraphic correspondence?" asked Jack dryly.

"No," said Susan, "but better safe than sorry. I suppose I was overly cautious."

"But the telegram didn't implicate Rodolfo, did it?" said Jack.

Susan shook her head, and pointed toward the south. The island had just come into view, a nubby line of brown floating on the blue water. "No, but he did speak of Rodolfo's family—"

"But anything specific?"

"No. My uncle is a great one for hints and for dramatizing things. I don't even know if any of this is true—it's not clear yet that he actually *is* in danger. And there's certainly no motive that he can make out. I have the only motive, he says, because I'm the one who's going to inherit everything."

"In the meantime," said Jack, "do you think he can find me a job?"

❀ ❀ ❀

In another hour the ship had docked. Susan and Jack stayed out of the way of the crush on the deck, not only because they didn't want to be mangled in the crowd, but also to avoid the final barrage of honeymoon jokes.

The afternoon was hot and bright. Jack and Susan wore light clothing and wide-brimmed hats and sunglasses, and kept in the shade as much as possible. Susan scanned the crowd on the dock below looking for her uncle, whom she'd telegraphed of her arrival.

"I don't see him," she said.

The gangplank was lowered, secured, and the passengers began to debark. The *Andrea Doria* was to be in Havana for two days, but all the passengers seemed to be taking the opportunity of going ashore immediately. Susan still searched for her uncle in the quayside crowd. "He's fat and he always wears white. He has a white moustache, blue eyes, and carries a cane and usually he has about three little boys along with him to run errands—at least that's what I remember from ten years ago. And people like my uncle don't tend to change much—they just get more so."

"I don't see anyone like that at all," said Jack. "Are you sure he's—"

"Of course I'm sure," said Susan. "He said he will use *any* excuse to come to Havana for a few days."

When the stream of disembarking passengers had thinned a bit, the newlyweds made their way down the gangplank. They finally located James Bright—far away from the crowd. He was on an adjoining pier, his enormous weight delicately perched on a piling. The pier itself was old and filthy, but James Bright appeared fresh and cool. His eyebrows and moustache were a glistening white, as white as the three-piece linen suit he wore. His skin was nearly as pink as the linen tie about his neck. He wore tiny round glasses with emerald green lenses, and was delicately spooning a yellow ice out of a tiny paper cup.

"I was avoiding the crush," he said to them, without apparently looking up.

"Hello, James," said Susan.

"Susan darling, I am so glad you've finally come to visit me again," James Bright replied, still not looking up at her. "Not only are you no longer fifteen years old, but you also seem to have acquired an entourage. I approve of entourages, and yours makes up in good looks what it lacks in numbers. Is this a hired chaperone? Or Prince Charming perhaps—who broke his arm wielding a sword in your defense? Or is this a chance acquaintance made on the deck of the *Andrea Doria*? Is this a man who would be willing to accept my meager hospitality on this strange little island?"

"I'm married, James. To Prince Charming here."

"I'm pleased to meet you."

James Bright extended his left hand—the one with the paper cup in it—out to the side, and a little dark-skinned boy ran up out of nowhere, snatched it away, and fled with it.

Then James Bright held out his right hand, and shook Jack's.

"Jack Beaumont," said Jack. "Susan and I were married on board the ship."

"How romantic." At last he seemed to look up at them. He smiled a fragile, melancholy smile. He shoved his glasses down a bit on his nose and squinted up at them in the harsh sunlight. "Susan darling, *do* you forgive me for an unforgivable decade of callous neglect?"

His eyes were sad, Jack thought. Weary.

"Of course, I forgive you," said Susan quickly. "I told Jack what you told me in the telegram. Your German is atrocious."

"But perhaps necessary," James Bright said, turning his sad, weary eyes full upon Jack. "I have been watched."

Jack believed him, and thought how odd it was—to have so suddenly married Susan, and been plunged into a delirious happiness that had been totally unanticipated, and now here they were suddenly plucked out of it all again. It was like a fast-moving merry-go-round that's halted with a wrench, the calliope music giving way to the scream of someone who was injured. That's what it felt like, standing on this decaying pier in the massive shadow of the *Andrea Doria* talking to this fat, pastel, courtly gentleman with the sad, weary eyes.

He glanced at Susan and knew that she was feeling the same thing. She probably felt the difference even more keenly, for James Bright was a relative for whom she had maintained a real—if distant—affection for many years.

"I've reserved us rooms at the Internacional," said James Bright. "Though now I think we ought to see if the presidential suite is available—for the happy couple. Susan, I hope—"

"No, no, don't say a word." Susan seemed to anticipate her uncle's apology. "Jack and I came down here to help you in any way we can—didn't we, Jack?"

Jack nodded yes, of course.

"As long as you need us, we'll be here."

"That's right," affirmed Jack.

"Jack was fired from his job last Friday—"

"I'm sorry," said James Bright politely.

"—and I quit my job on Tuesday, so we are as poor as churchmice, and for the time being we're going to make you support us."

Jack was about to protest, but James Bright's smile of pleasure at this declaration was so manifestly sincere, that he contented himself with, "Susan and I *would* like to help you, Mr. Bright, if we can."

"And I'm sure that with you two here, everything will be right as rain," said James. He started to raise himself from the piling, but it wasn't a real attempt—he merely seemed to lift his shoulders and torso a few inches before settling himself back down again. It was an indication of a desire to get up, rather than anything more substantial.

Susan looked around the pier.

"Where are your boys?" she asked.

James whistled once, surprisingly shrilly, with two manicured fingers placed delicately behind his lower lip.

Immediately, five small boys—including the one who had run off with the empty cup a few minutes before—converged on the man. Like an ancient Roman emperor beyond the responsibility even of moving himself about on the earth over which he reigned, James Bright was raised up with the coordinated efforts of the five small boys.

"Five," said James Bright looking around, as he was being arranged for movement, it was to be supposed, in the direction of the Hotel Internacional. "There are five of you. Why?"

He looked around at the children, who seemed to move faster and faster, and counted them off, "Manuel One. Manuel Two. Felicio. Roberto. Then who are—"

He stared with alarmed curiosity at number five. He was a bit older than the others—about nine, perhaps, and wore short yellow trousers and a dirty white shirt with all the buttons gone.

In an instant, the older boy took a knife out of his trousers, jumped up into the air, and slashed it across the throat of Susan's uncle. James Bright gave a startled gurgle as his emerald green glasses slipped off his perspiring nose and his enormous bulk sank to the planks of the pier.

Jack and Susan rushed forward—Susan to help her uncle, Jack to grab the tiny assassin with his good arm.

Manuels One and Two, Felicio and Roberto had drawn back in stunned horror at what had happened. Then with one movement they ran off down the pier, setting up a little thunder of bare feet on the planks, leaving their employer behind, and incidentally, crashing into Jack. Jack was knocked over, not only landing on his cast-bound arm, but also losing the grasp that he had gotten on the shirt of the knife-wielding child.

The boy flung the knife into the water and took off toward the quay, his short legs pumping like pistons.

Jack struggled to his feet, and found that the massive bulk of James Bright, with shining red blood covering his white suit, was hanging over the side of the dock. Susan, who weighed no more than a third as much as her uncle, was holding onto his trouser legs, valiantly attempting to prevent his slipping away completely.

Jack threw himself forward and grasped the man's arm, and also struggled to pull him back.

James Bright's face, upside down about a dozen feet from the water, was red with the blood that was flowing through the wound in his neck. Jack's hand was about

James Bright's wrist tightly and he felt no pulse. Also the blood had ceased to spurt out of his neck. It flowed out sluggishly now, with no living rhythm. The man was suspended over the water like a piece of hung game.

"He's dead," said Jack.

Susan cried out—a hollow cry such as Jack had never heard before. Her grip was loosened for only a second on the white trouser legs, and then James Bright's corpse dropped headfirst into the murky waters of Havana harbor.

CHAPTER TWENTY-ONE

JACK STOOD ON the pier with his unbroken arm wrapped around his wife's shoulder. From above, crew members of the *Andrea Doria* looked down, pointing and murmuring from the various decks of the ship and from portholes. Tourists—some of them who had sat at table with Jack and Susan on the voyage down from New York—stood on the dock, twisted telephoto lenses onto their Leicas, and snapped photographs of the massive corpse of James Bright as it was hauled out of the oily water of Havana harbor.

The Havana police said they had an Aqualung and an experienced diver, but until the Aqualung and the officer were found and brought together to the pier, a half dozen near-naked youths were diving in hope of recovering the knife with which the rich American plantation owner had been killed.

Jack was glad that Susan's Spanish was fluent. He was even happier that Susan remained as calm and staunch under these trying circumstances as he could possibly have hoped she would. Her eyes were red, but she had stopped crying. She answered all the questions that the police put to them, and she spoke with the doctor who signed the certificate of death and asked his advice on what to do with the body.

Since any idiot could see that the man died as the result of the slash of a knife across the throat, no autopsy would be required. This was supposed to be a sort of consolation, Susan surmised. Three policemen took their names and New York addresses, and the name of her uncle and the name of his plantation on the coast in the province of Pinar del Río. At last, after the sodden body in its soiled suit had been unceremoniously wrapped in an olive-drab blanket and shoved across the back seat of a rickety police vehicle, Jack and Susan looked at one another, and wondered what they were going to do.

Woolf did not act as if there had been a death in the family. He leaped at the sides of his narrow container. He chewed at the wooden bars, and barked loudly. He stopped only when he realized that no one had brought him food. Liberation from the cage made up a little for that, but not entirely.

Eventually their luggage was absently gathered together and Jack and Susan climbed into a taxi and went to the Hotel Internacional. Susan spoke to the man at the desk in Spanish, and when he replied in English, she didn't even notice but continued to speak to him in the native tongue. Jack inscribed the register: MR. AND MRS. JOHN BEAUMONT, and stared at the signature in perplexity, as if it were some obscure biblical inscription.

Susan peered at the book, squeezed Jack's arm, and managed a weak smile.

Their room on the fifth floor overlooked the flower-bedecked plaza in front of the hotel. Woolf had been assigned to a small kennel in the basement of the hotel, which was darker than the ship's hold and where his cage was smaller. Flakes of rusted iron came off in his mouth when he chewed the bars.

Susan sat at the vanity, and looked at herself in the mirror.

Jack stood at the window and peered out at Havana. The city looked simultaneously bright, colorful, and dirty. All the cars were American—and dented. On the other side of the busy roadway was the Gulf of Mexico, beating relentlessly and remorselessly against a decaying, ancient seawall. The ocean water looked hot and dangerous.

"Have you ever before had to deal with death?" he asked her without turning around.

"Not quite at such close range," she replied. "And not someone as close to me as James. This makes me the last of the Brights."

"Actually, you're a Beaumont now. There are no more Brights at all."

"We're suspects, I bet," she said wearily. "The police will think we did it. Or at least they want culprits. We got down off the ship and slit the throat of the first overweight rich man we came across, and wasn't it a coincidence that it turned out to be my very own uncle?"

Jack was not entirely surprised. It was the sort of thing that every tourist dreaded when he crossed an international border, whether he admitted it to himself or not: a trial for murder, or any crime, conducted in a language he did not understand. "What do we do about that?"

"We hope they don't arrest us," said Susan. "I've heard jails are not very pleasant in Cuba. We should probably inform the embassy, maybe they can help. We should do that right now."

She made no move to rise, however, but continued to stare at herself in the mirror. Jack didn't press.

After a bit, Susan went on: "Then I should arrange for the funeral—I'm the only relative, and I'm already here. After that, we should see about the will." She glanced at Jack in the mirror. "After they see how much I've inherited, they will *really* think that we did it."

The next few days were peculiar and wearying. Nothing much happened on Friday, and in Cuba over the weekend even the police torturers went home, and investigations into senseless murders were put off till Monday, when they might well have sorted themselves out, and gained a motive, or a perpetrator, or a witness. Jack and Susan, feeling cut off and alone, took Woolf for long walks around Havana during the day, always on the lookout for a chance glimpse of the boy who had committed the murder. In the evening they ate dinner as early as possible in the hotel dining room in order to avoid contact with other tourists. Other tourists did not have favorite uncles being kept in a butcher's freezer around the corner.

Jack had suggested that since nothing was doing on the weekend, they might drive down to James Bright's plantation, but Susan did not feel it right to leave Havana before her uncle was buried and the investigation into his murder had been officially undertaken by the police. Susan, however, did think it a good idea to get in touch with the servants and other staff of her uncle's estate, if only to let them know of James Bright's death. And perhaps, she hoped aloud to Jack, they could provide some clue that would help to identify the child who had committed the dreadful act. Wrestling with the telephone system of Cuba required much patience and ingenuity, but all it produced was the operator's opinion that the telephone at the plantation was out of order.

Sunday night seemed impossibly hot and long, but early on Monday morning, Jack and Susan visited the undertaker and arranged for the funeral. It was to be quiet, as tasteful as any ritual taking place in Cuba could be, and James Bright was to be buried in the tiny Anglican cemetery on the edge of the suburb where most of the English lived. James Bright hadn't been English, and he'd been a jovial agnostic, but he was known to the English community in Havana. Susan bought a black dress and Jack a black suit. There were daily interviews with the police, and attempts to find James Bright's lawyer, who didn't seem to be in his office, in his home, or at any of the bars where he was known to spend his late mornings and early afternoons. Most of their time was consumed in waiting, in finding out where a functionary was to be found (never in his office), or discovering what was expected of them in the way of forms and fees. They spent hours in uncomfortable chairs, their feet scraping on filthy floors, learning the minute habits of doorkeepers, stewards, and receptionists. Jack began to pick up a few words of the language.

Results with undertakers, lawyers, police lieutenants, and what passed for detectives in Havana, were depressingly inconclusive. Many promises and a quantity of inaction that would have stalled a juggernaut on a downhill run.

Even the inquest into the matter of James Bright's death was somehow casual and off the mark. In a cramped noisy courtroom with a jury that had apparently been impaneled with the expectation of hearing some other case, two policemen testified. Neither of them had been present when the body was recovered. Jack was called next as a witness, and a quarter of an hour was spent in establishing the fact that he could not speak Spanish. Susan was not called at all, though the judge stared at her for a considerable amount of time. The verdict, it was announced, would be announced later.

The only thing that did proceed with any speed was the funeral of James Bright. The sun hurried that along;

burials in Havana tended to be quick affairs. There was no church service, only a burial at the Anglican cemetery. The graveyard attendant pressed a bottle of smelling salts into Susan's hand as she and Jack entered through the creaking iron gate. When she shook her head no, the attendant replied in a quiet voice that the salts would come in handy to mask certain unpleasant odors.

But there were no unpleasant odors, because James Bright's casket was mounded with flowers. The tradesmen with whom he had dealt lavishly in Havana, his friends in the English community, several lower-echelon members of the American embassy, and even the elusive lawyer had sent wreaths and drapes of cut blooms.

The only persons to attend were Jack and Susan; a weedy Englishman with a red nose and the careful gait of the noontime drunkard; a man who was very evidently a policeman in plainclothes—plainclothes being in this case red trousers and a stiff black shirt patterned with large yellow roses; and a little short dark-skinned man in a shiny black suit who looked as if he had attended many funerals in his time.

The ceremony was short and dignified. As the coffin was lowered into the ground, Susan flung a handful of earth onto the top of it and then turned away.

The weedy Englishman came up to her and spoke a few incoherent words of sympathy, handed her a little dog-eared card with his name and address on it, and she thanked him. With a sense of quiet malice that Susan felt her uncle would have appreciated, she grabbed the plain-clothesman before he could slink away, shook his hand heartily and told him, in Spanish, that she was glad he had come because her uncle had often spoken of him in the highest terms of praise.

The small dark man in the black suit alone remained, eyeing the detective, then Jack, and at last sidled up to Susan. The sense and drama of his movements might have been appropriate for an evil-smelling dark alley in the middle of the night, but this was one o'clock in the afternoon, the cemetery was open and dazzlingly bright. The only noise was that of the gravediggers' shovels.

Susan did not offer to shake this man's hand, but the man approached her and said, "My deepest sympathies." His English was unaccented.

"Thank you," said Susan. "Who are you?"

"Richard Bollow. My assistant tells me..." Mr. Bollow trailed off. Bollow had been James Bright's lawyer, and the last four days, Mr. Bollow had not been available for consultation.

"Thank you for coming," said Susan. "My husband and I—"

Richard Bollow smiled a tight smile at Jack, and there was a hesitant, awkward shaking of hands.

"—We've been looking for you," said Jack. "High and low, in fact."

"Dreadful accident," said the lawyer, glancing toward the grave. "May we go somewhere else please?"

Near the lawyer's office was a bar called McGinty's. Jack and Susan had been there twice in search of Richard Bollow, but they had never sat down in the place; not that it was perceptibly dirtier than any other Havana bar. Bollow led them through a maze of empty tables and unoccupied chairs toward a remote corner of the place, where neither sun nor breeze of ceiling fans ever reached. Bollow took a seat with his back to the corner of the bar, leaning his head against the smoke-stained wall with a small smile of satisfaction—as if now assured of his protection from attack from behind. He ordered a daiquiri, glanced at Jack and Susan, who nodded. He held up three fingers, and after a few minutes, the bartender maneuvered through the empty tables and chairs with a tray of drinks.

Bollow glanced at Jack, and Jack paid.

When the waiter went away, Susan said, "It was *not* an accident. My uncle was murdered."

"Oh yes," said Bollow blandly. "A terrible murder."

"It would have been very helpful," said Jack evenly, "if we had had your assistance in the past few days. After all, we're strangers here in Cuba, and you were acquainted with Mr. Bright's affairs. We had no way of finding you."

"I was away," said Bollow. "On business for your uncle, in fact. When I heard..."

He finished his daiquiri, but not his sentence. Richard Bollow was obviously a man who did not like to give too much of himself away at first encounter.

Jack and Susan had not touched their drinks. Bollow eyed the filled glasses. Susan pushed hers closer to him, and he smiled a small smile of gratitude.

"We could have used your assistance with the police, for one thing," said Susan.

"They haven't arrested you," Bollow pointed out. "That would have been dreadful. Don't get arrested here," he added, as if he were giving a piece of excellent and totally unheard-of advice. "In fact, the best thing you could do would be to return to New York immediately."

"How do you know we came from New York?" Jack asked.

"Mr. Bright often spoke of his charming niece," said Bollow smoothly. "Besides, it is no secret how you got here. Am I wrong in so assuming?"

"No," said Susan. "We came from New York—and we would like to return, as soon as possible. But I want to stay until I'm certain that my uncle's things are in order."

"Yes," said Bollow. "I would certainly advise that."

Bollow glanced at Jack's daiquiri.

"Go ahead," said Jack. "I don't like to drink in this heat."

Bollow smiled, and pulled Jack's glass toward him. He raised it to his lips and touched his tongue to it as if he didn't know quite what taste to expect.

"When had you planned for the reading of the will?" Jack asked.

Bollow glanced up over the rim of the glass.

"What will are you speaking of?" he asked.

CHAPTER TWENTY-TWO

"M Y UNCLE'S WILL," said Susan slowly.

"There's no will that I know of," said Bollow. "Maybe your uncle had a will, but he did a lot of things without consulting me or requesting my assistance. He may very well have written a will, had it witnessed properly, and hid it somewhere. I have never seen such a document, however," said Bollow. He finished off Jack's daiquiri, his third.

The newlyweds glanced at each other.

"Let's have another round," said Jack. "Let's have two rounds—I think I'll have one myself."

Susan nodded, and Jack caught the bartender's eye and ordered.

"He told me he had made out his will," said Susan, looking at the small-boned, dark-skinned lawyer with a mistrust that she didn't bother to disguise.

"Then I'm sure you are right," said the lawyer, "and if you have reason to believe that you would benefit by it,

then I would suggest that you try to get hold of it. Have
you been out to The Pillars?"

The Pillars was the very un-Spanish name that
James Bright had given his house on the coast, and
the name that, by extension, was accorded the entire
estate.

"No," said Susan, "we were hoping to get things
settled here before we went down."

The drinks were brought. Both Susan and Jack now
took swallows of the daiquiris.

"I'd advise making a trip out there," said Bollow. "If
the will exists, then the will is there."

"What happens," asked Jack, "if we don't find the
will? Doesn't the money go to the next of kin?"

The lawyer looked around the room for a few
moments.

"In theory, yes," he said at last.

"Meaning?" Jack prompted.

"Did you know that your uncle had given up his
American citizenship?" said Bollow.

"No," said Susan, surprised. "Why on earth would
he have done that?"

"Some little misunderstanding with the powers that
be," said Bollow, with the air of having said less than he
might on *that* subject. "He became a Cuban eight years
ago. I handled the business myself—though I must tell
you, I did advise against it."

"And this means...?"

"This means that if you do not find a will, the estate
will be thrown into the Cuban courts. And, I must warn
you, that it is harder to get out of a Cuban court than it
is to get out of a Cuban jail. Sometimes estates disap-
pear very much the way that people do. They are...
absorbed."

"Then there's only one thing to do," said Jack.

The lawyer glanced up.

"We have to find the will," said Susan simply.

Bollow said he would do what he could in Havana: trace the bank accounts, search out the investments, go through his files and documents, start the process through the legal system with the assumption that the will would be located, do all that he could for them. He suggested that Jack and Susan remain one more day in Havana, consulting with him the following afternoon, and then drive out to The Pillars. He'd even take care of renting a vehicle for them, mark maps, telegraph the servants at The Pillars.

In short, Mr. Bollow suggested that he would do the things a good lawyer would do in such a case.

Susan was certain this was a screen. She didn't trust him. She wasn't even certain, she confided to Jack on their way back to the hotel, that he *was* her uncle's lawyer.

"I don't trust him either," said Jack. "Do you think that he has the will and is suppressing it?"

"I don't know," said Susan. "There would be no one to suppress the will in favor *of*."

"No one except Batista," Jack suggested quietly.

Jack was right, Susan realized. President Fulgencio Batista had been in power in Cuba for almost all of the past twenty years, and the government had an endless capacity for corruption. Perhaps that was what Bollow had meant when he said that estates that fell into the court system were "absorbed." Absorbed by judges, government lawyers, clerks of the court, and Batista's relatives—and perhaps the president himself.

They talked about it over dinner in the hotel restaurant. Just as at McGinty's, they were seated in a distant corner, protected from eavesdropping by a sea of empty tables and chairs.

"This is not the regime to get on the wrong side of," Susan pointed out.

"We could go back to New York. Just pack up and go. Put Woolf on a leash, buy him a seat on the airplane, and take off. Abandon all this."

"Is that the advice of Mr. Beaumont the financial consultant, Jack the concerned husband, or little Johnny who's afraid that somebody might grab him at the entrance of a dark alley?"

"It's not my advice at all. In fact, I would advise taking the truly stupid course of action."

"Which is?"

"To stay right here in Cuba and try to find out, not only where the will is, but who murdered your uncle. The police are looking for a nine-year-old boy, not so well-dressed, who murders rich foreigners in broad daylight without motive. I don't think that they're going to get very far with that line of investigation. Which means that it is up to us to find the persons responsible for your uncle's death and at least to deposit them on justice's doorstep."

"And the will?"

"Your uncle left you that money and he wanted you to have it. Even if this fellow we talked to this afternoon really is Richard Bollow, and even if Richard Bollow really was your uncle's lawyer, I don't think that your uncle would have wanted his entire fortune to go to *him*—and I certainly don't think your uncle would have wanted his money to line the pockets of the Batista regime. So I think that you have an obligation to find the will, and claim the fortune. Besides," he added with a small shrug, "if you don't, we're pretty much broke."

"Yes," agreed Susan, "that is stupid advice—but I think I'll take it. All we need now is to get charged with the murder ourselves. I can't imagine why the police haven't done that yet."

"One more thing to consider," said Jack seriously. "Whoever killed your uncle may now come after you."

"I had considered that," said Susan. "And have therefore resolved to keep Woolf by my side from this moment on."

They took coffee, and made a plan of action. That evening Jack would write a long letter asking the advice and counsel of one of his old Harvard roommates, who was a lawyer in Philadelphia now. In the morning, after registering their presence, telling their story, and detailing their plans to the American embassy, they'd get in touch with the Englishman who'd attended James Bright's funeral and ask him what he knew about the dead man's affairs. Specifically, they'd try to find out if the Englishman had recognized Bollow as Susan's uncle's lawyer. It was fortunate, Susan told Jack, that the man had presented her with his card.

Whether or not they'd ascertained anything, they would meet Bollow in the afternoon, insisting that it be at the lawyer's office—not in a bar or other public place. That would give them a better idea of the man. Then, if nothing intervened, they'd start out for The Pillars on Friday morning, a little over a week after their arrival in Cuba.

They returned to their room, and Jack immediately sat down and wrote the letter to his lawyer. Susan helped. They read it over, made several changes, and then Jack wrote it out again. At the hotel desk they purchased airmail stamps, and decided that they'd take it to the post office themselves in the morning. It was odd how this business had generated in them a sort of general distrust of everyone and everything, for it had even occurred to them as a possibility that their mail might be stolen, opened, read, and destroyed.

By ten o'clock they were finished. Susan felt invigorated by the sense, at last, of having *done* something. Jack lay on the bed, and Susan gently massaged his wrist that was aching from an unaccustomed bout of penmanship.

"Do you realize," she said, "that we've been here for five days and we haven't spent one evening out?"

"We've been in mourning for your uncle," Jack pointed out gently.

"Yes," said Susan, "and there have been other things as well..."

Jack smiled. It was surprising what one could do, even with one broken arm.

"And I still am in mourning," Susan went on, "but don't you think we could just put on some clothes and go out for just a little while?"

"Would you like to go to the casino?" Jack asked. Since the legalization of gambling the year before, all hotels in Havana had hastily opened casino rooms with roulette wheels and blackjack tables. Gambling had been widespread before in Cuba, but the governmental rake-off of the proceeds from illegal lotteries, gambling rooms, cockfights, and dog races had proved insufficient for the rapacity of the current regime, so these pastimes had been institutionalized for the more efficient collection of revenues.

"No," said Susan, "remember what happened last time we went to a casino? You nearly got killed."

"Libby nearly got killed."

"I don't like gambling," said Susan. "Let's waste our little stock of pesos on a nightclub instead."

The Internacional had a nightclub as well as a casino, but Jack and Susan decided that they'd spent enough time in the hotel. After Susan had bathed and dressed, she helped Jack slit the sleeve of his best jacket in order to accommodate his cast, and they sauntered out into the warm evening, walking the two blocks to the Hotel Nacional. The difference between the Nacional and the Internacional was not readily apparent, since both looked like Miami Beach hotels, and both were filled with American tourists who had come to drink and gawk and gamble.

Jack and Susan entered the nightclub, called the Varadero Room, between shows, and were seated at a minuscule table near the back from which they were able to see very little. They were served large, fruit-infested and expensive drinks, and were generally assaulted with a multitude of accented English that ranged from Midwest twang to New England quaver to Southern drawl.

The floor show, when it exploded out from behind a deep velvet curtain at the front of the room, was energetic, noisy, and brash. The women were all very tall, with enormous busts and hips, and they seemed to be wearing miles of crepe paper in colors that Susan had seen before only on cheap postcards. They pranced and chattered and sang songs that seemed—even to Susan's accustomed ears—to be composed principally of nonsense syllables strung together in an obscure but precise arrangement.

But after what they'd been through, the noise and the light and the prancing women and the shouting, guffawing, hysterical Americans seemed innocent and bright. Jack and Susan sipped at the vile drinks, and held hands beneath the table. For a little while they did not think about murdered relatives and stolen fortunes and dictatorships that persisted for decades.

They drank too much, but sometimes too much to drink is just what the doctor ordered. They sat through two shows, which were exactly alike, down to the last chattering nonsense syllable, and then rose uncertainly to make their way back to the Internacional. Susan even prepared a little smile for the couple that was waiting to take their place at the relinquished table.

Prepared a smile, but didn't use it, because the couple waiting to take their place was Rodolfo García-Cifuentes and his newlywed wife, Elizabeth St. John Mather García-Cifuentes.

CHAPTER TWENTY-THREE

THERE WAS AN understandable, to say the least, awkwardness in the encounter. And why was it, Jack wondered, that whenever something like this happened, he'd always had a little too much to drink?

The sheer momentum of having gotten to their feet after having sat so long at the table carried Jack and Susan past Rodolfo and Libby. But before they'd gotten very far, Jack and Susan glanced at each other, eyes wide, and swung back around in a single motion.

What had gone through their minds was this: James Bright's telegram to Susan in New York two weeks before had suggested that Rodolfo's family had somehow been behind the attempts to murder him. James Bright was now dead, his murder seemingly unmotivated, his killers unknown—and here was Rodolfo.

It wouldn't do to press the Cuban down into a chair, shine the forty-watt bulb from the tiny pink table lamp in his face, and say, "Spill it, Rodolfo." Jack and Susan would have to play a part, and hope that Rodolfo—if he knew anything—would somehow, in some manner, betray himself.

But what part? Jack and Susan both suddenly felt quite sober.

"What a *surprise!*" Susan gushed, not realizing how good an imitation she was making of Libby herself.

Jack smiled a smile that he hoped would pass for genuine in the dim light and held out a hand to Rodolfo. The Cuban took it with only a moment's hesitation.

"We *have* to find more chairs," said Susan, even before Libby could respond to her first greeting. "We have to hear *everything*," she added, deciding that the best thing she could do was take the offensive. Better to advance across unfamiliar ground than be forced to retreat across it. "Do you know what happened?" she said, placing her hand on Libby's arm. "Do you know what happened? Jack actually went into the church and saw you and Rodolfo getting married! You were wearing a veil, and he thought it was *me*, and he went right out and got drunk, but everything worked out fine—didn't it, darling?—and we got married... when, Jack? When was it you and I got married?"

"A week ago today," said Jack, finding an empty chair nearby and bringing it to the table with his one good arm. Rodolfo was getting another. In another moment the two couples were seated at the cramped table, peering into one another's faces over the dwarf pink lamp.

"Libby," exclaimed Susan, "I have never heard you so silent! And you have so much to tell us! Jack and I *still* have not been able to figure out just how you two got together, and decided so suddenly to get married."

"Yes," said Jack, taking his cue from Susan and looking directly into the eyes of his former fiancée, "I had the distinct impression that I was engaged to you, and Susan thought that she was engaged to Rodolfo."

"What are you two doing here?" said Libby in quiet bewilderment. "You're married? To each other?"

"Oh, yes," said Susan. "Married on shipboard. Wonderfully romantic. And now of course we're desperately happy. We fight constantly—we always did, you know—but we wouldn't fight with anyone else."

"Congratulations," said Rodolfo in a voice that showed little strain. "I am very happy for you."

"Oh, Rodolfo," said Susan, "you're the one who deserves congratulations. Marrying Libby. I'm so happy for both of you."

"We're on our honeymoon too," said Rodolfo.

Libby said nothing, but she didn't contradict her husband.

"How are the casinos?" said Susan. "Do they make you *very* happy, Libby?"

Libby nodded uncertainly.

"I remember," said Jack, "that you came to see me one day, Rodolfo."

"Yes..."

"And we made a little bet as to who would make it to the altar first. I guess you won. I'm sorry, by the way, that I couldn't stay for the reception. You were very kind to come by the building that morning and invite me, Libby."

Jack and Susan smiled happy, honeymoon smiles at each other across the table, as if whole universes of circumstance had whirred and wheeled to produce just this particular little quartet of marital happiness. But Jack and Susan's eyes also spoke to each other, saying, *Something is wrong here...*

Libby and Rodolfo were not looking at each other with honeymoon smiles. Libby was silent, and that was about like the Sphinx turning into a chatterbox. Rodolfo was quiet from an apparent desire to give nothing away.

Give nothing of *what* away?

"The show is tremendous," Jack said. "It should start again in a few minutes. There's this song that goes 'hum-de-la-de-hum-de-la-de'..."

"You forgot the words," said Susan. "It goes 'Ah-de-do-do-do-do-do-oh-ha-ma'..."

"I saw in the paper that your uncle was murdered," said Rodolfo suddenly. "I am very sorry."

Susan blinked and glanced at Libby. Libby's mouth was open.

"Yes," said Jack soberly. "We were actually talking to him when it happened. A small boy ran up and slashed his throat with a knife."

"Oh, Susan!" said Libby, looking at her with real compassion. Susan was suddenly ashamed of herself. Maybe there was more to Libby than Susan had ever given her credit for. But there was no help for it, and Susan knew she had to play out the role she had assumed. James Bright had expressed more than vague uneasiness to Susan about the motives and methods of the García-Cifuentes clan. It was now important that Jack and Susan appear—at least to Rodolfo—to be thoughtless and carefree.

"Yes," said Susan quickly, "it was terrible. But we were told—by the police, by everyone—that such things happen."

"A child did it?" said Libby.

"No doubt he was...what is the word?" suggested Rodolfo.

"Simple?" Jack suggested.

Rodolfo nodded. "Deranged."

"Yes," said Susan, "probably that was it. Just another mentally defective nine-year-old roaming the streets with a knife, slashing random throats on the piers of the harbor."

A few moments of silence passed awkwardly. A waiter appeared, and when Jack and Susan did not take this opportunity to say good-night, but asked for another round of what they'd had before, Rodolfo bit his lip.

Which means that he's not comfortable with us here, Jack thought.

Which means he'd like very much for us to go away, Susan decided.

For the next quarter-hour there was a little desultory talk of Havana and its nighttime splendors, and no more mention of interrupted weddings, jilted fiancés, or harborside murders.

The master of ceremonies waddled out and announced—in Spanish and English—that the third show of the evening would begin in just a few minutes. Jack and Susan exchanged glances—this sort of communication was getting easier for them—and they both rose to take their leave. It would be too noisy to continue any conversation. With a little nod of her head, Susan left it up to Jack to plan for another meeting between the two couples.

But there was no need, for Rodolfo said quickly, "Please. It has been such an unexpected pleasure to run into you both again. This is my city, as New York was yours. You both were very kind to me there, so please allow me to be kind to you here. In the morning, Libby and I will be attending the Gran Premio—the auto races. Please allow me to send two tickets over to your hotel. We would be so happy to see you both again."

He glanced at his wife—almost for the first time, it seemed to Susan.

"Oh, yes," said Libby absently, then adding with fervor, "Yes, Susan, please do come."

"What I want to know," said Jack, "is will you still love me when my arm has healed?"

He lay with his good arm encircling his wife's shoulder. His left arm in its cast was resting on the seat of a small chair that had been drawn up to the side of the bed.

"We won't know, till it does heal, will we? I imagine I will. Will you still love me if we don't ever find any of this mysterious fortune?"

"Possibly. Though, given the choice, I'd rather be married to an heiress of incalculable wealth than to a drudge who totally supports her injured husband."

"Just remember," said Susan, "if we go back to New York, I don't have a job either."

"I don't even know how we're going to pay for this room."

"I'm an heiress in name only," Susan sighed.

"Then what we're going to have to do," said Jack, "is track down the boy who killed your uncle, find the will, have it probated, cash an enormous check, and then pay the hotel bill."

"Yes," said Susan, "these things are actually quite simple once you attack them logically."

It was a difficult situation. They had little to go on.

There was one thing, however, that they hadn't talked about for awhile: the business of Rodolfo and Libby's marriage. It was clear to both Jack and Susan that Libby was the sort to run out and marry someone on the spur of the moment, but why had Rodolfo abandoned Susan? Susan, after all, had agreed, in so many words, to marry him. Rodolfo's defection was much more of a mystery than Libby's.

But what totally confused Jack and Susan, as they sweltered through the hot Cuban night, was whether the two questions were related—Libby and Rodolfo's marriage, and the murder of James Bright. It hardly seemed likely...

Despite their lack of sleep, Jack and Susan spent a busy morning. They rose, bathed, and breakfasted. Then, with Woolf straining at his leash, they walked to Richard Bollow's office, and found him not in. His assistant or secretary or whatever he was, was not in either. The door of the office was locked, and even the sign that had read RICHARD BOLLOW had been taken down. That certainly looked suspicious.

They went to the neighborhood police station and tried to get a little information about the lawyer, but the police were not helpful. No one there seemed even to have heard of Bollow. The police, in fact, seemed more interested in whether Woolf had had his full complement of shots, and whether his license was in order. Jack was sternly warned that if the dog bit anybody he'd be shot.

Even at ten o'clock in the morning, McGinty's bar was open, and the same bartender who had served them on their previous visit was on duty. But he professed not to know Richard Bollow by name, and when Susan described the lawyer carefully, the bartender shook his head.

"The one who drinks so many daiquiris..." Jack suggested.

Susan translated, but the bartender shrugged, as if to indicate that such a description applied to some large portion of his clientele. After the fat man with the white beard had taken to drinking daiquiris, *everybody* drank them now, whether they liked them or not.

They couldn't think of anywhere else to turn for the moment, so they hailed a taxi and were driven out to the racetrack in one of the western suburbs of Havana. This was one of the newer monuments to the decision of the Batista government to legalize gambling, and it was one of the less appealing. The racecourse was a large dusty oval, with some dusty flower beds in the center where dusty yellow roses bloomed. At one side of the track was a low grandstand, and directly behind this a low building where refreshments were sold and the bets were placed. The sky seemed very wide and high here, and the sun hung in it like a naked bulb in a cheap hotel room. An enormous crowd had gathered for the races that began at noon.

Jack and Susan decided to forgo both the refreshments and the betting, and went directly to the box to which Rodolfo's tickets admitted them, Woolf still in tow. To their discomfiture they discovered that their box was directly behind that of President Batista.

"Friends in high places," grumbled Jack. "Just what we need."

"He's not here yet," said Susan. "And heads of state have a habit of not showing up where they're expected. Especially dictators. It makes them better targets. Maybe we'll be lucky."

They were.

They sat alone in their VIP box for the next half hour, while the crowd of dusty unimportant persons roiled about them. A half dozen well-dressed persons, none of them Americans, showed up with tickets for the box, but Batista did not arrive. Nor did Rodolfo and Libby appear, which Jack and Susan found odd and rude.

Jack tied Woolf's leash to a metal railing, and the dog—who had spent his time in McGinty's licking up all the liquor that had so far been spilled that morning—fell promptly asleep in the hot sun.

Down on the track, the cars for the first race were being slowly paraded around to the scattered cheers of the crowd. Susan took a pair of mother-of-pearl opera glasses from her purse.

She shrugged. "I don't know why I packed these, but..."

• She and Jack took turns with the glasses, gazing down at the drivers and cars, and now and then scanning the crowds near the entrance, seeing if they could find Rodolfo or Libby or perhaps the dictator of Cuba.

"Here I am," said a small, low voice behind them, and someone was tapping Susan on the shoulder.

Libby Mather García-Cifuentes dropped into a chair in the row behind Jack and Susan. She was wearing a yellow silk suit, and a black hat with a thick veil. She slumped.

Libby Mather did not usually slump; she wasn't the sort.

"Where's Rodolfo?" Jack asked.

Libby pointed off vaguely to the left. "He'll be here."

"Look through these," Susan said, handing the glasses to Jack. Jack began scanning the crowd for sight of Rodolfo.

Susan got up and moved back to Libby and peered at her through the veil. A tear coursed down through the heavy makeup on Libby's cheek.

Susan reached out and lifted the veil.

"No, don't—" said Libby, pulling away.

"Shhh!" said Susan.

Jack didn't turn around.

Susan then saw that Libby's left eye was badly blackened. She let the veil drop. The crowd all around was growing more animated as the beginning of the race neared.

"Libby, listen—" Susan began quickly and earnestly.

A little sob twitched in Libby's shoulders.

Susan grabbed her. "Libby, did Rodolfo do that?"

Libby nodded, just once, and then said, "He said he'd do it again, if I..."

"If you what?"

"Susan!" cried Jack.

She turned to him. He was still staring through the opera glasses. Down on the track, the cars were lined up for the race, gunning their engines. Over the loudspeakers the announcer was calling out the names of the last driver and the number of his car.

"What is it!"

"I see him. I see Rodolfo. He's right over there by the entrance. And he's talking to Bollow!"

The starting gun was fired, and the cars took off in a fury of noise and smoke.

Roused at last, Woolf jumped up onto a row of empty seats, and began to bark uncontrollably.

CHAPTER TWENTY-FOUR

THE ENORMOUS CROWD at the track rose to its feet, inhaled vast quantities of dust and cigar smoke, and seemed to exhale it all again in one tremendous shout. Then, Jack could no longer see Rodolfo and the mysterious lawyer.

"I know that's who it was," he said, awkwardly climbing over the railing to stand beside Susan and Libby. He too peered at Libby's veil. A few feet away, Woolf strained at his leash.

"Rodolfo hit her," said Susan quietly. With all the shouting around them, however, Jack had no idea what his wife had said. "Rodolfo hit her!" she shouted.

Jack took a long breath, shook his head, and peered down at Libby. She had turned away in embarrassment.

Susan made a small subtle gesture, and Jack squeezed past Libby to get on the other side of her.

"All right," said Susan quickly and directly into Libby's ear, "you've got to tell us what's going on, Libby."

"I can't."

"Do it, Libby," said Jack sternly, "or I'll see that you suffer for having me fired from my job."

Libby's head shot up. "He made me."

"He made you have me fired?"

"He convinced me—he convinced me that you'd been stealing my money. I didn't really believe him, Jack, but..."

"But you had me fired anyway."

She nodded dismally.

The cars shot around the track and completed the first lap; the crowd rose again and cheered loudly. Woolf was barking at a little boy who was leaning over the edge of the box trying to sell little packages of candy.

"Jack forgives you," said Susan briskly. "I forgive you. But now you've got to tell us what's going on."

"I don't know," said Libby. "I don't *know* what's going on, but I think I made a mistake. I think I made a big mistake. And now I don't know what to do."

"It's a mistake that can be fixed," Susan assured her. "You can go back to New York with us."

"He won't let me."

"He can't stop you," said Jack. "When we go back—"

"I don't think you're going back," interrupted Libby.

"What?" said Jack.

"I said I don't think you're going back to New York either." She spoke quickly, almost breathlessly. "He's going to stop you. He's—"

"How?" demanded Susan.

"He's going to have you arrested—for murdering your uncle."

Jack and Susan leaned forward in order to exchange glances. Susan's glance asked: *Are you surprised?* Jack's glance replied: *Not a bit.*

Susan shook Libby's arm. "Are you sure? How do you know this for sure, Libby? How—"

"I *don't* know it for sure, but I heard him talking. And I heard another man talking. I didn't hear everything, but that's what it sounded like."

"When is he going to try this?" asked Jack.

Libby raised her veil and wiped away her tears. She winced as she inadvertently touched the bruised skin around her eye.

"Today," she said. "Here at the track. If he finds out I warned you, he'll hit me again." She looked from Susan to Jack and back to Susan again. "No one ever hit me before," she said simply. "I didn't know how much it hurt."

"They're coming this way!" cried Jack. He vaulted down the steps of the VIP box. He'd been at the top of the stands, to obtain a better view of the grandstand. "Rodolfo and about five policemen."

Woolf leaped at him, and the leash nearly broke his neck. Susan quickly began untying the dog.

"We have to get out of here," said Jack.

"Take me with you!" pleaded Libby, as she rose hastily. "I don't care if you did kill your uncle."

"We didn't kill him!" cried Susan. "In fact—"

Libby sat down again, hard. She stared at Susan. "You don't think..."

You don't think Rodolfo did it? was the sentence Libby didn't have the courage to complete.

"No, no," said Susan soothingly. "Of course not! Can you run in those shoes? If we have to run, I mean."

"Shoes or no shoes, we have to run," said Jack, grabbing Woolf's leash and starting down the steps toward the aisle at the bottom of the stands. This was not a very easy thing for Jack to do, since the stairs were a great deal shallower than was convenient for the length of Jack's legs and his left arm was still in its cast.

"Where are we running *to*?" demanded Libby, as Susan pulled her out of her seat and down the steps, after Jack and Woolf.

"Away from here," said Susan. "I can't believe—"

"I have a car," suggested Libby.

"Libby has a car!" Susan shouted down to Jack. Just then the pack of racing cars shot past the stands beginning another lap, so Jack couldn't hear over the cheering of the crowd.

Susan let go of Libby's hand and caught up with her husband. "Libby has a car. Maybe we can..."

Jack glanced back up at Libby, who nodded vigorously. "That way," she shouted, pointing to the right—away from the entrance to the grounds. And, fortunately, away from the direction in which Jack had last seen Rodolfo and the policemen approaching.

Now they were in a narrow aisle at the bottom of the stands, between the noisy crowd rising up in tiers to their right and the dirt track of the speedway at their left. The grandstand was raised above the track about fifteen feet or so to protect the spectators.

Jack stepped aside and Susan and Libby squeezed past him.

"Lead us to your car," he said to Libby as she went by. Libby nodded, and hurried along as well as she could in her impractical shoes.

With Susan in the lead the three of them made substantial progress toward the end of the stands, considering the number of small children, popcorn venders, and fat women wandering off to the comfort stations who blocked their path at every other step.

At last they reached the end of the grandstand. Behind a rickety little gate, a narrow flight of wooden stairs led down to a large field where a large number of automobiles and trucks were parked with no apparent system to their arrangement. Susan held Jack's arm to help him maintain his balance as he kicked open the lock from the gate.

Libby and Susan started down the stairs. Libby cried, "Oh, there it is. I see it now—I think..."

Susan stopped suddenly, grabbed Libby by the shoulder, turned her around and demanded, "Libby, you do have the keys to this car, don't you?"

Libby didn't have time to reply to Susan's question before they heard a voice behind them.

"Mr. Beaumont—"

Jack, just starting through the gate, whirled around, painfully hitting his injured arm against a railing. His good arm became entangled in Woolf's leash.

It was Richard Bollow, standing there, smiling.

Jack glanced over his shoulder, and exchanged another of those expressive glances with his wife: *Take Libby and get out of here.*

Susan's glance in return was: *I don't want to leave you alone.*

His turning back to Richard Bollow signified: *Do it anyway.*

Jack had barely time to reflect what a marvelous method of communication this new marriage of his allowed. It might not have been actual telepathy, but it was close, and it was much better than bickering and insults.

As Richard Bollow came forward a few feet closer, Jack said, "We went to your office this morning."

"I wasn't there," said the lawyer, if indeed that was what he was. "I have—" Three small boys knocked against him and for a second he was pressed against the railing. When he had recovered himself, he didn't bother finishing his sentence. "Mr. Beaumont," he said, "I'm sorry to say that the Havana police have uncovered some very distressing evidence concerning the death of your wife's uncle."

Jack glanced behind himself on pretense of pulling Woolf away from a cardboard carton of discarded popcorn boxes. He noted with satisfaction that Susan and Libby were already down on the parking field. Jack fervently hoped Libby *did* have the keys to that automobile.

"They found the boy who did it?" Jack asked.

Mr. Bollow shook his head sadly. He was now only a foot away from Jack, even leaning forward a little. Perhaps so that Jack could hear him better; perhaps for some other reason.

"No," said Mr. Bollow. "What they found was an eyewitness to the crime. He is a young man—son of a municipal judge—who ought to have been in convent school that morning, but wasn't. I'm sorry to have to tell you this, Mr. Beaumont, for despite our short acquaintance I've really grown quite fond of you and your lovely wife— in short, the truant boy saw you slash James Bright's throat and throw the knife in the water. Mr. Beaumont, I'm afraid that you and your wife are both in a great deal of trouble. And considering what I know of the Havana police and the Cuban court system, you're not likely to be *out* of trouble for some time to come."

Jack had a simple plan. That was to deliver a knockout punch to the jaw of Mr. Bollow. Then, before the police arrived, he would hurry down the stairs and through the maze of cars to where Susan and Libby were waiting for him—with the engine running, Jack fervently hoped.

Despite the plan's simplicity, it was weak on three counts. First, Jack couldn't remember the last time he'd delivered a knockout punch to anybody, and he was almost certain that with a cast on one arm, and a dog leash wrapped around the other, he was going to have some trouble. The second reason the plan might fail was that when he looked over the lawyer's shoulder, he could see the five policemen already standing in the VIP box, looking this way and that. It wouldn't be long before they caught sight of him, or before Bollow gave some signal. And the third reason that his plan was likely to fail was that concealed behind a bag of candy in his hand, Richard Bollow was holding a pistol pointed directly at Jack's stomach.

Now Woolf at last showed courage, acumen, and sheer physical prowess. Either sensing the danger to his master, or else lusting in his doggy heart after the bag of candy, Woolf lunged at the man and savagely bit his hand.

Woolf came away with the bag of candy, but not before Bollow had gotten off a shot.

Jack instinctively dived to the left, and was saved from a nasty tumble by plunging not down the stairs, but into the ample stomach of a man who was seated on the very lowest tier of seats, peacefully munching hot corn and paying attention neither to the race nor to the confrontation that was taking place only a couple of feet in front of him.

Bollow's pistol shot had gone wide, plunging with a little geyser of dust into the earth of the parking field. But a moment later, Bollow had recovered himself. Now with no attempt to disguise the pistol, he turned it on Jack with a smile.

"Sic him!" cried Jack desperately, still in the fat man's lap.

Woolf lifted his nose from the bag of candy he'd torn open, glanced at Jack, and returned to his business, thereby answering the question of why he leaped at Bollow.

Bollow smiled, and squeezed the trigger.

At that moment the fat man on whom Jack had fallen pushed Jack off his lap—and then looked very surprised indeed when the bullet from the lawyer's gun embedded itself deep into his stomach.

He screamed once, and then slumped heavily over on his side.

For a moment there was a look of bewilderment on Bollow's face when he saw that he'd shot the wrong man, and he looked at Jack as if to say, *See what you made me do?*

But Jack was already setting off down the stairs, his progress impeded substantially by the fact that Woolf did not want to go with him. "I'm leaving you," he called warningly to the dog.

Bollow positioned himself at the head of the stairs and pointed the barrel of the gun down at Jack—but he didn't get the chance to squeeze the trigger again. Events had caught up with Mr. Bollow. Events in the form of a gang of some seventy-five panicked and angry spectators who had watched one man get shot and now saw the man with the gun about to shoot someone else.

While half these excited spectators were fleeing in a direction that was generally *away* from the source of the danger, the other half were fleeing *toward* Bollow and Bollow's weapon.

Bollow, before he correctly realized what had happened, had been flipped over the protective railing, and dropped down onto the dirt track.

Most of the racing cars were on the far side of the track, and the two or three that were in the lead were able to avoid the crumpled, dazed obstruction that was Richard Bollow.

Jack, taking advantage of the small melee, hurried down the stairs, Woolf loping after him.

Jack paused halfway down and scanned the parking field. There, not far from the guard rail to the racetrack, was Susan waving to him frantically.

Thank God, he sighed.

And then Jack heard a squeal of brakes, a great crash, and a shout of anguish and horror from the crowd in the stands behind him. He looked over his shoulder at the raceway.

One of the racing cars, in an effort to avoid hitting the spectator who had wandered, apparently dazed, into the middle of the track, had veered, sideswiping another vehicle. Somehow they'd been locked together and the two drivers were now fighting to gain control of their vehicles as they swung into the turn at the end of the straightaway. Despite the drivers' efforts, the two cars moved as one drunken vehicle.

And, as Jack watched nervously, the two cars bumped a third as it was trying to maneuver its way around the two stricken racers.

204 JACK & SUSAN IN 1953

The third car managed not to become entangled with the others. Instead, the driver lost complete control of it, and it flipped sideways, up, and into the air. Knocking over posts, it flipped—with almost comical slowness—over and over in the air, but no more than six or eight feet from the ground.

In another second it crashed. Jack saw it smash down onto the roof of a green car, and then burst into flames and oily black smoke.

His head jerked back with the noise of the blast, and then he realized that he could no longer see Susan, who had been standing next to a car with a green roof.

"Susan!" he yelled, and rushed down the stairs.

"Susan!" he called frantically again, and tripped on Woolf's leash.

He would have fallen but that a Havana policeman caught him, and helped him to his feet with a smile.

CHAPTER TWENTY-FIVE

Reluctantly leaving jack alone to deal with Richard Bollow, Susan—more or less pulling Libby along—dashed across the parking field. Libby did, fortunately, have a set of keys to the car. But now that they were down on the field, she had lost sight of the automobile again.

Susan clambered up onto the bed of a truck that looked as if it had been abandoned in this field for months. She looked all around.

"What are you doing?" said Libby.

"I'm looking for your car."

"You don't know what it looks like."

"Then you climb up here and look."

Susan gave Libby a hand up, and after a few moments, Libby found it. "It's over there."

Susan glanced back toward the grandstand.

"Do you see Jack?" Libby asked. "Will he be all right?"

"Jack does seem to get into trouble easily," said Susan, climbing down from the back of the truck. "But I'm not certain that he always gets out of it so quickly."

They made their way in the direction of Libby's dark green Cadillac.

"Rodolfo bought it the first day we got here, and I got an extra set of keys, but I haven't driven it yet. Rodolfo and I—"

"Libby," Susan asked suddenly, "why on earth did you marry Rodolfo?"

Libby stopped stock-still to consider the question.

"No," said Susan, realizing that this was hardly the moment for this discussion, "we don't have time right now. Tell me later."

"This is it," said Libby, stopping before a dark green Cadillac. It was an enormous car, and looked quite new despite a dent in the right front fender, a smashed light in the left tailfin, a loose length of chrome on a rear door, and splashes of yellow paint on two of the tires.

"Try the key," said Susan.

Libby climbed into the driver's seat, murmuring, "I hope I remember how to drive." She turned the key in the ignition, and the engine fired instantly.

"Thank God," said Susan, and began waving, hoping Jack would see her. She stood on the frame of the automobile inside the open front door, and waved higher and harder.

It was at that moment she heard a tremendous crash and squeal of brakes. She looked toward the racecourse and saw two cars locked together, traveling at a tremendous speed. The two machines hit a third, and to Susan's astonishment the third car took off like a rocket.

Except rockets don't fly so low to the ground, they don't go sideways, and to the best of her knowledge, they don't perform slow flips.

She could see the driver inside, braced against the back of his seat.

He's putting on the brakes, she thought.

Except friction brakes don't work for airborne vehicles.

Susan ducked, and the race car did a slow flip right above her head, and with a deafening roar, smashed onto the roof of an old green Ford only about twenty feet away.

In another moment there was an explosion, and a rain of glass and pieces of hot metal poured down over Susan's back as she crouched beside Libby's car. In one place her dress caught fire, but Libby, thinking quicker than usual, got out of the car and beat out the flames with her purse.

"Oh, God," cried Libby, even in the midst of her efforts, "what else is going to happen this month?" They were both choking from the acrid black smoke that was roiling up out of the mass of twisted burning metal nearby.

"Let's get out of here," said Susan, standing up and making sure she was all in one piece and none of her clothing was still on fire. "We have to get Jack. Libby, you'd better let me drive."

She jumped into the car, and Libby ran around to get in the other side. But suddenly she stopped directly in front of the Cadillac, pointed, and screamed.

"What is it!" cried Susan.

"Rodolfo!" she cried. "He's coming—and the police are with him. Oh, God!"

Susan saw it was impossible to flee in the Cadillac. Even under the best of conditions, getting out of this field of vehicles parked helter-skelter would take careful maneuvering, and the best of conditions did not include a nearby conflagration of smoke and burning gasoline or a frantic heiress jumping up and down on the parched grass.

Susan's only thought was that she had to get out of there, and fast. On foot was impossible as well—the police could certainly run faster than she, not to mention that they doubtless had guns.

"Hide in the trunk!" cried Libby.

It was a stupid idea, but Susan knew she didn't have time to think of one that made more sense.

"Hide in the trunk," said Libby again, "and I'll get you out of here."

Susan pulled the keys from the ignition, pushed open the car door, and stayed low to the ground so as not to be seen by Rodolfo and the approaching Havana police. Libby took the keys and opened the trunk. Susan pushed aside two small, heavy boxes and climbed inside with misgiving and hesitation.

"Hurry, hurry, hurry," cried Libby. "They're coming."

"Remember I'm in here, will you," said Susan, as the lid was slammed shut and she was left in darkness.

An ambulance siren was blaring feebly from somewhere on the other side of the field, and from the racetrack came all the noise of the race. The race still continued, despite everything that had happened.

At the base of the wooden steps, Jack pleaded in English with the policeman to let him pass. The police either did not understand or pretended not to understand. But it hardly mattered, for the next thing Jack knew the policeman had snapped a cuff of steel around his right wrist.

This was accomplished with a smiling politeness, but then the officer faced the problem of how to attach the other cuff to Jack's left wrist, for it was completely covered by the cast.

Before the policeman had found a solution, however, the first wave of a vast crowd of people surged down the stairway on its way to gawk, wonder, and generally impede rescue efforts of the hapless race driver.

Woolf, frightened by the crowd, all of a sudden threw himself against Jack's back in an effort to escape. This propelled Jack forward onto the policeman, and the policeman in turn fell to the ground beneath Jack.

The policeman's head struck a little uneven outcropping of cement on one of the pillars that supported the stadium. He was stunned. Jack saw his opportunity and pulled himself out of the policeman's grasp, then quickly melted—as best he could despite his height—into the crowd that was headed for the site of the accident.

The crowd gathered around the wrecked racing car, which was perched neatly and upside down atop a decrepit Ford. Both cars burned sullenly, creating a column of black smoke. The driver of the racing car had miraculously dragged himself out through the window of his vehicle, and now was sitting on the ground, alternately coughing and spitting up shards of broken teeth.

Jack did not see any corpses lying about, which was a good sign. But he saw neither his wife nor Libby, and that was a bad sign.

The ambulance was snaking its way across the field toward the wreck as Jack backed away, keeping a lookout for the two women.

He began to circle the crowd, peering toward the wreck, but also peering under other vehicles, in case they were actually hiding.

Suddenly right before him was a slowly moving vehicle—a dark green Cadillac with a smashed red light in its left tailfin. He caught a glimpse of the person in the front passenger seat. It was Libby!

He ran alongside, and his shadow falling across her face alerted her. She turned, and her eyes went wide with fear. She shook her head vehemently, and mouthed the words *Go away!* through the closed window.

"Where's Susan?" he mouthed.

Even though the Cadillac was not going very fast, it was hard to run alongside it. Jack was also keeping an eye out for policemen, at the same time trying to keep Woolf away from the wheels of the car. He also had to avoid running into the fenders, bumpers, and other sharp corners of parked vehicles.

But he did manage to lean down and peer across Libby's ample bosom at the driver of the Cadillac. It was Rodolfo! And Rodolfo, having sensed some strange motion outside the car, turned his head.

Jack dropped to the ground out of sight, flinging out his bad arm so that he would not fall atop it. Nevertheless, it jarred nastily against the earth and cracked the plaster.

Jack looked up at the Cadillac as it sailed on toward the exit of the field. Just then a scrap of paper fluttered out of the window on the passenger side. After the car had disappeared, Jack sneaked between the crazily parked vehicles and retrieved it.

The paper was the foil from the inside of a pack of cigarettes. It had peculiar scratchings on it, and when Jack held it up, and turned it this way and that in the sunlight, he could make out the nearly illegible words:

SUSAN TRUNK FOLLOW.

Susan was in the trunk of the car, and Jack should follow them.

So much was clear.

What was also clear to Jack was that the Cadillac had not gone toward Havana, but turned toward the south— and Jack didn't have a car.

Keeping low, and doing a kind of duck-walk between the vehicles, Jack looked for a car or a truck with the keys left in the ignition. This search was hampered by Jack's height, his broken arm, and Woolf's conviction that his master had devised some new sort of man–dog game.

When Jack finally found a vehicle with keys inside, after examining a couple of dozen, he discovered why the owner had been so careless. The engine wouldn't start.

He might have spent the rest of the afternoon in this fruitless search, so he decided he'd have to take his chances. He stood up straight, walked out to the road, and got into the back of the first taxi waiting in line.

In a quarter of an hour he was back at the Internacional, having reflected on the way that if he survived this, and ever divorced Susan, and fell in love and married again, he would not spend his second honeymoon in the Pearl of the Antilles.

As he entered the lobby of the Internacional, he tried to appear inconspicuous and nonchalant. This was difficult, for not only were his clothes filthy, but he was holding his broken cast together with his good hand—the hand he also needed to hold on to Woolf's leash—and there was the dangling handcuff, still attached to his wrist, jangling loudly beneath the sleeve of his shirt.

He tipped the porter two pesos to hold the dog for fifteen minutes. He instructed the man at the desk to find him a car with an automatic shift, and to find it quickly and without regard to cost. He went upstairs, changed shirts, improvised a sling by ripping apart a pillowcase, gathered up all his and Susan's money and whatever jewelry they had that looked as if it might be possible to convert into money, and then walked out again. He went down the stairs, for he could easily imagine that if he waited for the elevator, the doors would open on half a dozen police with drawn weapons.

At the desk, Jack dropped off his room key, saying, "Just in case my wife comes back in the next few minutes..." He picked up the key for the Ford that was almost ready for him in the garage behind the hotel. Then he retrieved Woolf, returned to the desk for a map of Cuban roadways, and went whistling merrily out through the back garden of the Internacional.

In the garage he waited for a few minutes while the car, privately rented at an outrageous sum from one of the assistant managers of the hotel, was being filled with gas. Jack studied the map, tried to ask a few directions of an old man who, it soon became clear, knew nothing about English, Cuban geography, or the desperation of a hunted man.

When the car was ready, Jack opened the back door, shoved Woolf inside, and wound the end of the leash around the window handle. He got into the front and drove off with a grim smile.

Two dark cars pulled up in front of the hotel just as Jack was passing by, and he knew without even having to look that policemen were getting out of them.

The road south took him past the racetrack, where the wrecked racing car still smoldered in the field. The remaining automobiles in the Gran Premio still circled the dusty track.

Jack thought he knew why Rodolfo had turned the Cadillac south, instead of returning to Havana.

It looked as if Jack was going to get to visit The Pillars after all.

CHAPTER TWENTY-SIX

SUSAN HAD TIME for reflection in the trunk of the Cadillac. After an hour or so of travel, it became obvious to her that Rodolfo had not driven back to Havana, but was headed elsewhere.

Susan didn't like this conclusion.

She wasn't happy in the trunk of the Cadillac. Since the car was new, the space was tolerably clean, but it was small, and had hardly been designed for the accommodation of riders. There had been a time when Susan tended toward claustrophobia. That time had been until she climbed into the trunk; but now she knew that she could not allow that fear to overcome her. That fear of not having enough air to breathe; of having a small space suddenly lurch smaller; of walls bending inward and of sharp objects piercing through them; of locks failing to open; of gas seeping inside...

There were a great many things about the trunk of a Cadillac on a fairly long trip that were not pleasant, and in succession, Susan suffered every one of them.

She wondered if Libby had been playing a part, if her old rival somehow remained her rival still, despite the fact that they had neatly traded off Manhattan fiancés. Was Libby *ever* satisfied? Had she lured Susan into the trunk of the car, and was she now laughing in the front seat? Probably not, Susan concluded with relief. Libby was capable of the laughter, yes. Of making the plan and playing so consistent a part, no. Susan suspected that, uncomfortable as she was, with only the two small, heavy boxes as pillows, Libby might be almost as distressed though she had the freedom of the front seat of the Cadillac.

Through painstaking and dextrous investigation, Susan had discovered that inside the small heavy boxes were rifle cartridges. This discovery did not improve her peace of mind.

Her eyes had grown accustomed to the darkness, and she could see little slits of light here and there around the seams of the trunk. When she stretched and altered her position she even found a tiny hole where a screw had fallen out, through which she could see the rough road over which they were traveling.

It began to rain, and the rain beat deafeningly against the metal that was only a couple of inches over Susan's ears, making her feel even more trapped than before.

She tried to remember her geography. Cuba, unfortunately, was more than seven hundred miles long. And it would be just her luck that Rodolfo's destination was at the very tip of the island.

Then another danger occurred to Susan. Libby had obviously anticipated that Susan would spend a short time in the trunk. What if she began to fear for Susan's life back there? Would she reveal Susan's presence? Susan certainly didn't want that; she preferred claustrophobic metal walls.

Would Rodolfo realize, by Libby's nervousness, that something was wrong? And stop the car, and beat Libby till she told him what was bothering her?

An unpleasant journey became unpleasanter still.

The rain kept up, and despite everything, Susan fell asleep.

When she awoke again, the automobile was no longer moving.

Rain no longer drummed on the roof.

Her neck ached from her rifle-shell-case pillow.

She wished desperately that she had taken advantage of the ladies' comfort station at the racetrack.

Another hour passed. Visions of Libby's treachery ran through her mind alternately with fears that there might be some very good and very terrible excuse for Libby's not coming to let her out of the trunk.

Not only had the rain stopped, but now the sun came out, and it beat down hard on the metal trunk. Susan began to feel as if she'd been caught in the back room of a steam laundry. Then it felt as if she'd actually been moved in between the blades of one of the presses. She felt woozy, as though her brain were bubbling and boiling inside the casing of her skull. She no longer had any desire to visit the comfort station, but there was an easy and embarrassing reason for that relief.

Outside the automobile all seemed silent. She heard a few anonymous creaks and snaps, but they were muffled and brief and uninterpretable.

She slipped in and out of consciousness, but this wasn't sleep. This was something else. Something darker and more dangerous, but there was nothing she could do to prevent it.

Suddenly her ears were assaulted with a tremendously loud grating, which was actually nothing more—and nothing less—than the key being pressed into the lock of the trunk.

She breathed in deeply, as if fresh air were already hers for the taking.

The trunk lid rose upward with a sweep. Light and air and even the surprising smell of the warm sea poured in upon her. She was blinded with sunlight—and relief.

"Libby..." she whispered.

But when her eyes had adjusted, she saw that it wasn't Libby who'd opened the trunk.

It was a little boy—about nine years old.

Susan had seen him before.

He was the child who had slashed the throat of her uncle on the Havana pier.

He smiled.

Jack knew approximately where he was headed, even beyond the general direction of south and west. He had a map. He had a decent instinct about proper directions that worked most of the time. He also was driven by a compelling need to find Susan and make certain that she was all right.

He was convinced quite beyond his ability to explain it, that Rodolfo, with Libby in the front, and Susan much farther back in the back than people tended to sit, had driven down to The Pillars.

The problem was, he didn't know exactly where James Bright's plantation was. He had a province: Pinar del Río, which lay west of Havana. He even had a nearby town: San Cristóbal. He hoped that that would be enough.

Not very many miles west of Havana lay mountains. Very quickly, in his rented Ford, Jack was driving up steeper and steeper inclines. The roads got less-traveled and rougher, and when it began to rain, it looked as if the whole thing—roads, Ford, Jack, and Jack's vague plan of rescuing his wife—would all be washed down into the torrent that was tumbling along the side of the road filled with mud and debris.

But Jack didn't wash away. He drove and drove, stopping every few miles to check the map, and here and there to ask directions. Those men and women he bewildered with his Spanish eventually made out the name "San Cristóbal" but they never figured out that Jack was also looking for a new dark green Cadillac with a light broken in the left tailfin.

West and south of the mountains was a flat coastal plain, thirty miles wide, on which farmers raised tobacco to be rolled into cigars. Jack drove along the narrow road, beneath a wide drenching sky; low flat sodden fields seemed to stretch forever on either side.

San Cristóbal was about seventy miles from Havana, and Jack found it despite rain, despite his broken Spanish and his broken arm, despite the terrible mountain roads. His journey was helped considerably by the fact that the road he traveled lay directly alongside the tracks of the railroad that also went from Havana to San Cristóbal.

He didn't know what to expect of the town, but it turned out to be poor and small and flat and dirty. But if it was not as small as he'd anticipated—it was the center of a regional tobacco market—it exceeded his expectation when it came to dirt.

San Cristóbal was a fly-blown maze of streets and low buildings that had once been painted white. He had no more arrived in the town than the rain stopped, the sun immediately came out, and steam rose from the filthy streets in ghostly curtains of moisture. Remarkably ugly children and quite handsome women paraded the streets. Old men sat placidly in the front of the sad-looking buildings, and old women leaned out of the windows, resting their elbows on stained white cloths. Jack saw no young or middle-aged men of San Cristóbal in the village or the fields.

He stopped at a small store with a Shell Oil sign before it and bought gas. He got out of the car, released Woolf for a few minutes' walk, and asked the small boy who had come out to put gasoline into his tank whether this was indeed San Cristóbal. The boy pointed across the way to the railway station. A dilapidated sign, blistered with age and the heat, read clearly, SAN CRISTÓBAL. Jack then tried to ask the boy if he had seen a dark green Cadillac with a beautiful blond American woman in the front seat, but Jack didn't know the Spanish words for all those things, and the boy didn't understand anything but "Cadillac." He had seen that, and pointed vaguely off in what appeared to be several different directions.

Jack said, "The Pillars."

The boy shrugged.

Jack said, "Señor Bright."

The child suddenly erupted in a torrent of Spanish, gesticulating as he withdrew the nozzle of the pump from the tank. Jack's trousers were sprayed with the last drops of the gas.

As he was reaching for a handkerchief to dab at the gasoline stains, the handcuffs on his wrist slipped out of his shirt and dangled before the boy's astonished face. The sun shone glancingly off the metal.

Instead of getting out his handkerchief, Jack reached for his wallet, and paid the boy five times the cost of the gasoline. He hoped the boy would understand that the extra cash was a bribe for silence. The boy took the money and ran back inside the store. Looking around, and noting with relief that no one else appeared to have noticed the handcuffs, Jack climbed hurriedly back into the car, calling desperately for Woolf.

Woolf was interested in a small female dog of ignoble breed, who was wandering around the ramshackle railway station. Woolf would not come.

By the time Jack had made the hard decision that he'd abandon Woolf—at least until he'd rescued Susan—the boy had come out of the store with a man who looked to be his father.

The man, who was large-boned and muscular, stood directly in front of Jack's Ford; the boy had positioned himself directly behind it. Jack could not drive off without hitting the man, and he could not back up without knocking over the boy. Neither alternative seemed a good idea.

Woolf, humiliated by a stern canine rebuff over across the way, trotted up to the car and whined to get in.

Jack smiled a confident smile, leaned out the window at the same time that he was trying to open the door to let Woolf in, and said, very slowly, "I'm looking for the home of Señor James Bright, The Pillars..."

The man's expression shifted when he heard the name of Susan's uncle. He came around to Jack's door just as Woolf was scrambling across Jack's lap. The man reached in and grasped Jack's right hand, pulled the sleeve back, and thumped his finger against the handcuffs.

Jack didn't know the Spanish for, "This was a most amusing practical joke my wife played on me," and before he had time for another thought, the man had dragged him out of the car and into the store. Woolf trotted amiably behind.

CHAPTER TWENTY-SEVEN

SUSAN PUT HER hands on the edge of the trunk and raised herself up. She saw that she was in some sort of courtyard before—or perhaps behind—an immense white house. The surrounding vegetation was thick and green, and looked a great deal cooler than she herself felt. She was still woozy with the heat she'd endured while locked inside the trunk of the Cadillac.

The boy retreated a few feet, not, it appeared, out of fear, but merely as if waiting to see what Susan would do if given enough room.

He was much better dressed, she noted, than when she'd seen him last. He wore a little uniform, in fact, such as she'd seen in Havana on boys that attended private school. Short pants, white shirt, blue tie. But there was no doubt in her mind that this was the child who had murdered her uncle.

And unless she was very much mistaken this was her uncle's house, outside of San Cristóbal. There were doubtlessly other plantation houses a few hours from Havana that Rodolfo would have had some reason for visiting, but somehow Susan knew that this was The Pillars.

She said nothing to the boy as she climbed cautiously out of the trunk of the car and stood on the swept, even pavement of the courtyard.

Two possibilities presented themselves for escape from this killer-child. She could run into the house; the success of that plan rested on the hope that she could gain entrance by an unlocked door or window, and that once inside, she'd find help there. It was more likely, she knew, that Rodolfo was inside. Rodolfo, who'd tried to have her and her husband arrested for the murder committed by this boy.

She could dash into the forest that began just beyond the garden fringing the semicircular courtyard. That choice supposed that she was strong and rested enough to outrun the boy and then fight her way through a virtual jungle. Even then there would be no way to get in touch with Jack. Even if he had managed to avoid arrest, he wouldn't have been able to return to the hotel. Where could Jack possibly be?

They'd been foolish, Susan saw now, not to have had some plan, some place of meeting, some code for use in emergencies. But how could they have known?

Then Susan thought of something that made her heart give an extra beat. In absence of a plan, and with a return to the hotel impossible, there was one place where Jack might think to meet her—and that was here, at The Pillars.

She tried to walk to the house, but after only a few steps her legs gave way beneath her and she collapsed onto the pavement. She didn't know whether she was glad or sorry to think that Jack was possibly on his way here.

Strong arms raised her up, and Susan knew by the smell of his hair oil that the strong arms were Rodolfo's. "You are very foolish," he said, and she had neither the strength nor the inclination to disagree.

He lifted her up and carried her toward the house. Her head lolling over his shoulder, Susan watched the murderous boy padding silently after them. He smiled up at her again, as if pleased that she were going to be taken care of.

They entered through a set of glass doors into a room with whitewashed walls and bright carpets; it was filled with rattan furniture covered in chintz. A photograph on the wall—of her father as a very young man—confirmed her intuition. This was indeed her dead uncle's house.

It occurred to her a moment later that, as his heir, this house was now hers.

Rodolfo laid her on a sofa, and when she turned her head toward the windows at the other end of the room, she could see a pillared veranda and the Caribbean a few hundred yards beyond, down a slope of shorn grass and a strip of white beach. A pleasant place, she thought, under different circumstances.

"Very foolish," Rodolfo repeated.

"Where is Libby?" Susan asked—or tried to ask. Her voice didn't work as it ought to have. Her words were a whisper, hoarse and unintelligible. She cleared her throat and tried again. "Where is Libby?"

"Upstairs," said Rodolfo, sitting down in a basket chair across the rug from her, crossing one leg elegantly over the other. "I am very disappointed in Libby for not telling me that we had a guest in the trunk of the car. Armando," he commanded in Spanish, "bring Miss Bright—I mean, Mrs. Beaumont, some water."

In a few moments the boy appeared with a glass of water. He knelt delicately on the rug at her side, carefully lifted her head, and pressed the glass to her lips. She drank slowly, and when she fell back again, she felt much better.

Rodolfo smiled, and asked, "Would you like to see the rest of the house?"

Susan hesitated only a moment, then nodded. She raised herself up on the couch, and Rodolfo waited politely for her to recover herself. Then he rose, came over, and helped her to her feet.

"Lean on me," he advised.

He walked her through the rooms of the ground floor of The Pillars. These low-ceilinged rooms were long and comfortable, but relatively narrow, and windows opened both toward the Caribbean to the south and to a sheltered and shaded courtyard in the back. A house in the tropics needed as much cross-ventilation as possible. Everything was clean and bright and comfortable, and Susan had no difficulty imagining her uncle here.

"Where are the servants?" Susan asked.

"In mourning," said Rodolfo.

Which was to say, no one would come if Susan called for help.

In the kitchen, which was surprisingly modern and surpassingly pink, Susan drank a second glass of water and then felt still better. The disarray and general filthiness of her condition began to make her uncomfortable, even though she knew that conventional decorum should not apply in such a situation as this—when she was being held in the firm grasp of the man who doubtless had engineered the murder of her uncle.

Rodolfo took her out onto the lawn in front of the house so that she could see the six pillars that gave the place its name.

The house was quite beautiful; long, low, and rambling, with windows of different and odd sizes. The pillars served to hold up a wide porch roof that sheltered the front windows from the sun. They were thick and massive, disproportionate to the rest of the house, but in a place so pleasant, cheerful, and comfortable, matters of architectural purity seemed of little importance. Susan, for a few seconds, as she looked up at the house with the bright sun at her back, entertained a little fantasy of living here with Jack.

She could imagine long, lazy days in the course of which they hadn't a care in the world; no worries about being arrested, being trapped in small spaces, or being done in by nine-year-old boys called Armando.

"Why did you come here?" Susan asked Rodolfo.

"Here? The Pillars?"

Susan nodded. He had wound her arm tightly within his.

"To burn it down," he said.

Half an hour after he had been forced into the small dusty store in San Cristóbal, Jack came out again.

The handcuffs had been sawed from his arm, and given as a souvenir to the boy who had pumped his gas. With his good arm laid across the edge of the table—the better to be sawed upon—and his bad arm pressed across his breast in the broken cast and sling, he was fed beans and rice by a patient old woman who also put a bottle of beer to his lips every now and then. A daughter of the house had taken English in school, and Jack talked with her, hoping to explain his situation.

The daughter of the house didn't know *that* much English, but she made a real effort, for she did understand that Jack was married to James Bright's niece, and evidently Susan's uncle had been well liked in the area. There was something about his treatment of some infamous and hated band of sharecroppers, as nearly as Jack could make out. The old woman crossed herself, fork in hand, every time James Bright was mentioned.

Best of all, when Jack came out of the little store, he had a map of the area, with the location of The Pillars clearly marked.

He followed the map carefully, back out onto the lonely roads that wound past wide, dismal fields of tobacco. Sometimes he caught a glimpse of the Caribbean to his left as he drove west. It was now about four in the afternoon, and the sun was shining directly into his eyes, making it difficult to see. He'd been driving along with a low fence at his left for some time before he came to any break in it. He passed the break before he'd realized that this must be the entrance to The Pillars.

He backed up and looked for a sign. He didn't find one, but he did find a post that looked as if it had borne a sign, and that the sign had recently been ripped off.

He turned down the narrow dirt road and drove cautiously along it. On both sides, fields of sugarcane rose up to a height of eight feet and more. Jack could see nothing on either side of him but the forest of cane. If he had had a good arm to stretch out the window he could have touched the stalks. Above was the bleached sky, ahead of and behind him, the narrow road. Between the ruts of the road grew weeds so high and coarse Jack could feel them as they dragged along the chassis of the Ford.

Once or twice other tracks crossed out into the cane fields, and Jack thought it a good idea to stop while he was still out of sight of the house. He turned the car down one of these lanes—so narrow that the green stalks of cane brushed against the side of the car, and the foliage brushed against the side of Jack's face through the open window. Once Jack had hidden the car from the main road, he turned off the ignition, got out, and retraced his path.

The double-rutted road between the fields of cane wound on, and Jack was sorry now that he'd drunk that beer back in San Cristóbal. The sun was still hot, shining in his face; his left arm ached and itched under his cast; he was sweating and filthy. And he didn't know what he was going to face at the end of the road.

He had neither a weapon nor the use of both arms, and he had to admit to himself that Woolf, panting along behind him, was not the dog to attack on command.

Jack, despite his fears for Susan's safety, began to hope that this tiny rutted road would go on forever.

It didn't, of course. Soon Jack noticed the tops of trees over the cane field to his right. And by the time he had figured out this meant the cultivated fields were coming to an end, they stopped.

He found himself standing at the edge of a lawn. The road widened a bit here and led to a kind of whitewashed stone archway, and through this arch Jack could see a paved courtyard with beds of flowers.

He moved across the grass, trying to stay out of sight of the house, and peered through the archway into the center of the courtyard. There he saw the dark green Cadillac in which he had seen Rodolfo and Libby drive away from the racetrack. The trunk was open.

Jack saw no one, heard nothing. He stood still for a few minutes, leaning down to hold on to Woolf's collar to prevent the dog from running off.

Woolf lay on the ground, exhausted from the heat. Birds called in the trees that surrounded the house, and Jack could hear the soothing crash of waves on the beach.

Except for the evidence of the automobile, Jack would have surmised that the place was deserted.

Woolf suddenly jumped to his feet, and took off— with such alacrity that Jack lost his grip. The dog was headed for a leaking faucet he'd just seen on the far side of the patio. Jack instinctively started after him, but before he had taken more than half a step, the sound of a gunshot rang out from the direction of the house, and a chip of stone flew up just in front of Woolf as the bullet struck the pavement. The shard struck Woolf in the flank, and the dog skidded and yelped and plunged into a flower bed.

Jack jumped back to the protection of the archway.

The house was not deserted.

Now, having been lucky enough to escape this imme-diate detection, all he had to do was to find a way inside, disarm the person with the gun, and rescue Susan.

CHAPTER TWENTY-EIGHT

"BURN...IT...DOWN?" Susan repeated slowly. She tried to imagine the house in front of her in flames, and couldn't. It seemed such a waste, such a terrible waste. She tried to think if perhaps Rodolfo meant something else or if his very good English had suddenly given way, and he intended something quite different and innocent.

"Yes," he replied, understanding perfectly, "burn it down to the ground."

He led her gently back to the house, as if they were an affianced couple, strolling about the estate of some happy and well-situated relative.

"Would you like to see upstairs?" he asked.

"Before it's too late?"

There were times she wished she could bridle her tongue. She made a mental resolution to do better in the future.

Rodolfo didn't reply. They stepped inside, and after the heat of the sun, the marble-floored entranceway was cool and dim. He led her up a curving staircase that was carved of some dark wood; it appeared to have been polished recently. A stair carpet patterned in deep red and blue sank thick and soft beneath her feet.

Upstairs a long corridor ran along the front nearly the length of the house, with a row of evenly spaced windows overlooking the sloping greensward and the Caribbean. Gauzy white curtains blew in and tangled themselves across their path as Rodolfo led her toward a door at the end of the hall.

Along the way they passed other doors, to guest bedrooms and bathrooms, Susan surmised. One door was open, and yes, she'd been right. It was a bedroom, and on the bed lay Libby.

"Libby!" Susan called. Libby didn't stir.

Rodolfo guided Susan past. "Libby is sleeping," he said. He opened the door at the end of the corridor and Susan stepped into a massive bedroom. Her uncle's, she assumed, though its furnishings and ornamentation were rather more ornate than she would have predicted for a bachelor. The room was crowded with antique French furniture, a host of bibelots, engravings in gilded frames, many lamps and mirrors, and a vast mahogany bed with a graceful canopy of mosquito netting.

"Lie down," Rodolfo said, "you must be very tired."

The bed looked white and pristine, and Susan felt soiled. But there were other reasons for not lying down.

"Why?" she asked.

"I said, because you must be very tired."

"No," she said. "Why are you going to burn down this house?"

Rodolfo seated himself in a chair at a small desk that was arranged against a section of wall between two windows. He was turned so that he could face both the desk and Susan as well. He didn't answer, but pulled out a drawer of the desk and extracted its contents: two handfuls of folded papers and envelopes.

He began examining the papers, making no reply to Susan's question.

"Why did you have my uncle killed?" she asked. "I don't understand any of this."

"Ah!" he said, unfolding a document that had a legal stamp on it, "you recognized Armando."

"Yes," said Susan. "That was the boy who killed James."

"Armando is my brother," said Rodolfo. "Actually, my half-brother. We have the same father."

Susan had a sudden moment of panic. Should she run? Where would she run to? Rodolfo's casual insouciance suggested that he had no fear of her escaping. And if that was so...

"Tell me!" she pleaded.

"Tell you what?"

"Everything. I don't understand any of this."

As he went through the papers, Rodolfo merely dropped them on the floor, the way a man might do who knew they were soon to be destroyed.

"No," said Rodolfo, peering into another drawer, "there is no reason for you to be told anything, for in a little while..." He didn't finish his sentence for he'd become absorbed in the contents of a letter, which made him smile.

Actually, he didn't need to finish, because Susan understood him well enough as it was. *In a little while you will be dead...*

Some attempt at escape began to seem like a better option than simply letting this maniac kill her without her putting up a struggle.

Rodolfo seemed to sense this change in her attitude. He glanced up from the amusing letter. He was no longer smiling. "Lie down on the bed as I told you," he said in an icy tone she'd never heard him use before. "Or I will shoot you now."

Susan saw that he now held a small revolver, hardly larger than his hand; it had apparently lain out of sight in the recesses of her uncle's desk.

Susan sat down on the edge of the bed. Now there seemed to be nothing to do but put off the desperate moment; only the slender hope that Jack would arrive in time with more help than just that dog.

"What are you looking for?" she asked as calmly as she could.

"The deeds to your uncle's properties."

"What makes you think he'd keep them here?"

Rodolfo shrugged. "I don't think he did. I think they're probably in a safe deposit box in his Havana bank. But just in case he did keep them here, I don't want to burn them up."

"Rodolfo..."

"Yes, Susan?"

"Why did you come to New York?"

"To get you to marry me," he replied simply.

In a third drawer he found a sheaf of financial statements. He examined the one on top, glanced at the one on bottom, tore off a letterhead, and then pushed everything else off on to the floor. Old canceled checks fluttered over the carpet.

Susan remembered seeing more than one movie in which a hopeless victim persuaded her potential murderer to explain his motives, to detail a long and successful series of deviousnesses, to exult in his perfidious cleverness, and—because of the time lost in this egotistical display—to forfeit the whole game. The heroine was invariably rescued, and the villain, if not killed on the spot, ended up in jail. Of course those were movies from her childhood, the thirties. Maybe in 1953 things didn't work quite that way.

If Susan could only persuade Rodolfo to tell her the whole story—and it looked to be a complicated one—then maybe this would provide extra time for the cavalry, in the form of her one-armed husband and their feebleminded pet, to arrive.

"You knew I was going to inherit this house."

"Of course," he admitted.

"But if you wanted it so badly, then why are you going to burn it down? And what about Libby?" She wasn't so much concerned with his answers as she was anxious that he talk. If he was talking, and responding to her questions, then he could not also be setting about to murder her in that maddeningly unconcerned manner of his. But her plan didn't seem to be working.

"As I said before," said Rodolfo, calmly shutting the last of the drawers, "there's no need for you to know. Because in just a few minutes it's not going to make any difference to you at all."

He rose from the desk with the gun.

Susan tensed as he came nearer the bed.

"Lie down," he said once more.

Susan could see no help for it but to do as he'd ordered.

Still aiming the revolver at her, Rodolfo reached up with his left hand and tore down the filmy mosquito netting.

"Rip this apart," he commanded her, "and twist it."

Without getting up from the soft feather mattresses beneath her, Susan did so, making a small rope about half an inch thick out of the netting, but taking her time doing so. She tried to control the shaking she felt inside; she wouldn't give this Cuban cobra the satisfaction.

"Now wrap it around your ankles," said Rodolfo. When she was done he tugged at it to make sure the knot was tight.

"Now make another one."

A second makeshift rope was twisted out of the netting. "Turn over."

She thought she saw her chance. She knew that he'd have to put down the gun to tie her hands together, so when she rolled over, she counted *one, two* and then kicked out with all her might, hoping to catch him in that vulnerable place between his legs.

Her feet struck against air, and she succeeded in doing nothing but turning herself crossways on the bed and tangling the spread beneath her.

Then she heard a shot—and even though she feared that in the next moment she would die, she did not scream out. She felt nothing.

By the time she realized that the shot had come from elsewhere in the house, she felt a hard blow to her temple. Then there was blackness and there was nothing else.

It was the smell of kerosene that roused her.

She thought for a moment that she was back in summer camp at Lake Winnipesaukee. But that would make her no more than thirteen years old, and she knew that wasn't right. Which meant that she was in someplace other than New Hampshire. She opened her eyes and saw an expanse of white silk.

The odor of kerosene was stronger. The noisome smell did not help her headache. She could not move, and she realized that her legs and hands were tied.

Then she remembered where she was, and under what circumstances. She jerked her body about so that her head hung over the bed. She could see splotches of liquid on the carpet, and whole puddles of the flammable stuff on the bare floor inside the hallway door.

The light in the room wasn't much different, so she knew that she hadn't been unconscious long.

"*Libby!*" she screamed.

Rodolfo leaned in through the doorway, evidently to avoid stepping in the puddles. "It would have been better if you had remained unconscious," he said. He smiled a smile of slight embarrassment. "I don't really like doing this, you know."

"You're going to burn me alive!"

"You and Libby," he amended. "She *is* unconscious, I'm happy to say."

"Why don't you shoot me!"

"Because it must look like an accident," he explained. "The mosquito-netting ropes will burn completely, and no one will know that you were tied."

He reached into his pocket, and took out a small packet of matches he'd picked up from the Varadero Room at the Hotel Nacional. Susan even remembered seeing him place them in his pocket.

"I'm very sorry," he said with what appeared to Susan, even in her predicament, to be absolute sincerity.

He tore out one of the paper matches, struck it, held it beneath the book until the whole thing seared up in a *whoosh* of flame. Then he tossed the small torch into the center of the room.

His aim was good, and the amount of kerosene he'd used was substantial. The Oriental carpet on the floor of James Bright's bedroom suddenly exploded in a large circle of flame.

CHAPTER TWENTY-NINE

IT WAS JACK'S fervent hope that whoever had shot at the dog had not seen the dog's master. Jack could have run back across the side lawn to the shelter of the trees, but he decided against that. Someone inside the house would have been watching for another running target, canine or otherwise. So keeping himself low and using the ornamental plantings for cover, he crept up until he got to the house itself.

He now flattened himself against the side of the house, no pleasant sensation considering the sharpness of the stucco covering. He inched toward the front, ducked beneath a window, came up again, and ducked beneath another window. At the front corner of the house he paused for a moment using a large, blooming oleander as cover.

He crept around the front of the house, feeling absurdly exposed. It was well that poor Woolf was keeping away.

The first window he reached was open. He stood beside it and listened. He heard nothing inside. He took a chance and peered in. At this end of the house was some sort of long narrow storage room, dim and cool. Through the open window, even with the oleander at his side, he was certain he detected the odor of kerosene.

It was difficult, Jack realized, for a man with his arm in a cast to negotiate climbing through a window four feet off the ground, but he decided to try. For some reason he thought it was better to be shot at close range than to be picked off as he ran across an open lawn. He got as close to the window as he could, and then raised his left leg, and got it through the aperture. He gripped the lower half of the window sash with his good arm, and pulled himself up and into the storeroom, banging his head, getting splinters into his hand, and tearing a hole in the front of his trousers.

The storeroom was no more than eight feet wide, but it ran the width of the house. He could see a door at the farther end, and he moved carefully toward it, trying not to knock over any of the jars and bottles arranged on the sagging shelves, nor to cry out when a large spider dropped down from the ceiling, ran across his neck, and then squeezed into the small space between his broken arm and the cast that covered it.

Jack could feel the spider crawling down toward his elbow. It was cool and dark in there, and that spider— Jack was certain—intended to set up a colony around his elbow.

He debated a moment how he ought to deal with this door: cautiously open it, hoping the door would make no noise and that no one was in the next room. Go through boldly and quickly, and obtain another hiding space. Or press his ear against it, to listen for movement on the other side.

He decided on the first option, but as he placed his hand upon the knob of the door, he felt it already turning.

He immediately stepped back and flattened himself against the wall beside the door. The door swung wide, into the storeroom, concealing him behind it. He heard two voices speaking in Spanish, a man and a boy's, and they were just on the other side of the thin door that was his only protection. Jack held his breath. He could now feel the spider creeping down his arm toward his wrist.

Jack recognized the man's voice as Rodolfo's. Jack heard them pick up what sounded like metal canisters filled with sloshing liquid.

The kerosene.

They went away, leaving the door to the storeroom open. Jack was about to move from his hiding place when he heard footsteps approaching again, and he quickly dropped back tight against the wall. It was either Rodolfo or the boy getting more cans of kerosene.

Whoever it was again did not shut the door. Jack remained motionless for several minutes. He listened intently, but could hear nothing. Once he detected a foot-fall in the room directly above, but it wasn't repeated.

He eased the door back enough so that he could get out from behind it. He could see no more canisters of kerosene, and figured therefore that Rodolfo and the boy would not be coming back. It was still possible that one of them—or even a third person—was sitting very quietly with a gun in the very next room.

Jack's eyes had already searched out the corners of the storeroom. The only thing that resembled a weapon was a garden trowel, which wasn't much of a weapon.

He picked it up anyway, thinking that he possibly could throw it hard.

He peered warily around the doorway into the next room. This turned out to be the kitchen, pink and empty. Jack stepped silently in and exchanged the garden trowel for a butcher's knife.

There were two doors here to choose from, and he picked the one toward the front of the house.

It opened into a formal dining room, and though the window onto the sea was open, the chamber reeked of kerosene. The yellow damask cloth covering a massive Sheraton table was soaked with it, and the liquid dripped from the corners of the cloth. The draperies had been splashed as well, though not far up, so Jack surmised that this was the child's work.

Jack crept to the next door and peered around. He was at the entrance hall now. He could cross it to what looked like a parlor on the other side, or he could ascend the stairs to the second floor.

He listened for some clue that would tell him what to do next, but he heard nothing.

He decided on the parlor, so he started carefully and quietly across the foyer.

Halfway across he heard the voices in the next room, Rodolfo's and the boy's. They were coming his way.

As fast and as quietly as he could, Jack mounted the stairs, giving thanks to James Bright's unhappy ghost that he had installed such thick carpeting on the stairway.

At the top of the stairs, Jack had another choice. Right or left? To the right, at the end of the hall, he saw an open door, and that made his decision. All the other doors, after all, might be locked.

Below him, he heard Rodolfo giving what sounded like a command to the boy in Spanish. Then Rodolfo's voice grew closer; he must be coming up the stairs.

Jack moved down the hallway as quickly as he could.

One of the doors he passed was ajar, and he swung it open and jumped inside, thinking that even if Rodolfo came inside he could once again hide behind the door as it opened. He closed the door till it was again just barely cracked.

He wasn't alone in the room.

Libby lay on the bed, staring at him stuporously.

"Jack?" she said.

"Shhh!" he said as he flattened himself against the wall beside the door.

"Jack!" Libby was vastly relieved to see him. In another moment, Jack knew she would begin a wholesale retelling of her latest round of woes.

"Shut up!" Jack hissed as loudly as he dared.

He heard Rodolfo moving along the hall outside.

Jack held up his hand for Libby to lie still and quiet, but Libby had begun to writhe on the bed.

Jack saw for the first time that her hands and her wrists were bound beneath her. He also noticed that this room had been given the kerosene treatment as well.

He listened for Rodolfo but heard nothing. The Cuban had evidently passed on down the corridor.

Jack crept over to the bed, turned Libby over, and with the butcher knife sliced through the ropes that held her. This was not easy, for the ropes were strong, Libby was writhing, and Jack had still the use of only one hand. Once her wrists were free, he went to work on the ropes that bound her ankles.

"Where's Susan?" he whispered.

"Did she get out of the trunk?" Libby whispered back.

"Yes."

"I don't know where she is."

From out in the corridor, came a kind of *whoooosh!* They both looked up in surprise. Jack, knife in hand, dropped to the floor and pulled himself across the slickly waxed floor till he was hidden beneath the bed.

"Pretend you're still tied up!" he cried in a whisper he hoped would carry up through the mattress but not outside the confines of the room.

Looking toward the door, Jack saw it swing open, saw what he assumed were Rodolfo's shoes and trouser cuffs. And then he saw a lighted match drop to the floor, where it promptly extinguished itself.

But a second match did the trick. A puddle of kerosene near the door went up in another *whoooosh* that told Jack exactly what the first noise had been.

CHAPTER THIRTY

LIBBY SCREAMED, and Jack heard Rodolfo's well-modulated laughter disappearing down the hallway.

Jack rolled out from under the bed, scrambled to his feet, and clamped his hand over Libby's mouth

Libby bit him. On his good hand.

The bedclothes were already on fire. Jack dragged Libby off the bed, and she landed with a thump on the floor. He dragged her up past the flames and toward the door of the room.

"Shut up!" Jack cautioned her. "He thinks you're still tied up!"

"I should have married you," Libby said. "I really should have."

Holding Libby back, Jack peered out into the hall. He caught a glimpse of Rodolfo as he turned down the stairs.

Jack stepped out and down the hallway toward the room at the end; Libby followed at his heels, as close as Woolf would have done under similar circumstances.

"Jack!" cried Susan from the bed.

They were separated by a low wall of flame, fanned here by the sea breeze blowing in through the open window. The wallpaper had caught as well, and little yellow tongues of flame were licking upward. The torn mosquito netting above Susan caught suddenly and burned as quickly as a spider's web with a match put to it.

Jack ran to the opposite corner of the room, picked up a small rug, and threw it across the burning floor. Almost immediately, small flames began leaping up through the webbing, but it was enough to allow Jack to cross to the bed. Libby began coughing with the smoke.

"I want to get out of here!" she cried. "I don't want to burn!"

Susan flipped herself over so that Jack could get at the netting ropes with the knife. In a few seconds she was free.

The carpet over which Jack crossed was burning fiercely now, and the room was filling with smoke.

"Cuba was your idea for a honeymoon, wasn't it?" Jack remarked.

Without another word, they grabbed hold of the bed, Jack at the head with his good hand on a post, and Susan at the foot, pushing with both hands. They moved the bed over the worst of the flames, jumped up onto the high mattresses, and then crossed over to relative safety.

Now the hallway was beginning to fill with smoke. The bedrooms where Susan and Libby had been tied were burning brightly now, and smoke was pouring up the stairwell from the first floor. They saw that the entire staircase was on fire.

Quickly, the three of them moved down the hallway on both sides of the staircase and tried all the doors; all the rooms were unlocked, but there was apparently no other staircase to the ground floor.

"We'll have to climb out of a window," said Susan.

"Fine," said Jack, holding up his broken arm, "you two go ahead. You'll also be able to draw Rodolfo's fire.

I'm sure he and his little friend are out there somewhere watching, just to make sure that nobody makes a last-minute escape."

"Sorry," said Susan, "I wasn't thinking."

Fortunately, because of the strong cross ventilation, it was still possible to breathe in the upstairs hallway. But that also meant that once the various fires had really established themselves, they would spread with dangerous rapidity.

Jack stood at the banister beside the burning staircase and peered over onto the marble flooring of the entryway twelve feet below.

"That's how we'll have to go," he said, and began kicking at the banister.

After a moment, Susan joined him, and then Libby. Together they managed to loosen a section of banister. "Don't let it fall," Jack warned, "because we'd have to fall on top of it." They lifted it up and flipped it over onto the burning stairs. A little more fuel at this point wasn't going to make things much worse.

"Libby," Jack said, "go find as many blankets and bedspreads as you can carry."

Libby and Susan dashed down the hall into some of the rooms that weren't burning; in a few moments they returned, arms laden with comforters, pillows, and other bedding. They dropped them onto the marble floor beneath.

"Who's first?" Jack asked.

"Libby," said Susan.

"Absolutely not."

"It has to be you," said Susan. "So do it."

Libby got down on her hands and knees, and inched backward over the edge. Jack held one of her wrists, Susan the other. She was so achingly slow about it that Susan gave her a little shove, and the margarine heiress shot out into the empty space and Jack and Susan were nearly pulled over with her. She dangled for a moment, then Jack and Susan's grips began to slip.

Libby fell to complete safety atop the pile of quilts and blankets.

Jack and Susan looked at one another.

"You next," said Susan.

"Hardly gallant," protested Jack.

"I don't have a bad arm," Susan pointed out.

She was right. Jack sat on the edge, legs dangling down. He tossed down the butcher knife, their only weapon, and Libby retrieved it.

"There's no way to do this properly," said Susan, for Jack's balance was all off because of his broken arm.

"I know," said Jack. "So just push."

Susan did, and Jack fell, flailing and crying out, and landed square onto the pile that Libby had rearranged beneath him. He was jolted a bit, but he did no further damage to his arm.

As soon as Jack had rolled out of the way, Susan sat on the edge and pushed herself off.

At the bottom she twisted her ankle, and Libby helped her up. It was impossible to stand, much less to walk, without considerable pain.

The dining room on one side of them was on fire, as was the living room on the other side. Here on the first floor the smoke was much thicker, and all three of them were coughing.

The smoldering curtains on either side of the front door suddenly burst into orange flame.

"What about Rodolfo?" said Libby, choking as she inadvertently breathed in the thick smoke. "You said he was waiting out there with a gun."

"I'm sure he's gone," said Susan. With that she pulled open the front door.

A wonderfully refreshing breeze immediately fanned away the worst of the smoke around them, and allowed them to see that Rodolfo stood there, revolver in hand, right outside the door.

Because the setting sun was in her eyes, Susan couldn't see the smile on his face, but she knew it was there.

"One. Two. Three," he said. "I do not like shooting people."

"Then don't," cried Libby. "I'm your *wife!*"

She took a step forward, and he raised the small weapon at arm's length—aiming it directly at the center of Libby's head.

Libby stopped, then burst into tears. As if being shot between the eyes by her husband just before she was about to escape from a burning building were just one terrible thing too many to happen to a young woman who was *supposed* to be enjoying herself on a romantic tropical honeymoon.

At this critical instant Rodolfo flinched—flinched because directly behind him, a sopping wet Woolf barked loudly. Woolf barked not because Jack and Susan were about to die and he was upset; he barked because he had just discovered the pleasures of saltwater surf, and wanted to share his happiness.

Rodolfo, nonetheless, flinched.

And Jack and Susan took advantage of that momentary falter. Together they rushed forward, both of them hitting Libby in the back. Libby lurched forward out of the burning house and fell against her husband, and knocked him to the paving of the front porch of The Pillars.

The pistol discharged and the bullet shattered one of the panes of glass in the dining room window.

Jack had fallen atop Libby who was still atop Rodolfo. Susan jumped to her feet, and as hard as she could, stomped Rodolfo's hand that still held the revolver. It clattered to the paving, and Susan gave it a strong kick, sending it several yards away into the yard. Armando, seeing his opportunity, appeared suddenly around the corner of the house, and charged after the gun.

Woolf, however, got there first, and snatched it right out from under Armando's grasping hand. He ran back to Susan with it, hoping she would continue the game of throw-and-fetch.

"Over here, Armando," Susan said with a thin smile as she pointed the revolver at him.

The boy obeyed, not realizing that Susan could never have brought herself to shoot a child. Not even one that she had seen murder her own uncle.

CHAPTER THIRTY-ONE

THEY DROVE BACK to Havana in the Cadillac, a tied-up Armando in the back seat between Libby and Woolf. Jack sat in the front seat and slept as Susan drove.

Rodolfo was in the trunk, and Libby grinned with irrepressible satisfaction every time she felt him kicking against the partition at her back.

Back in Havana, the difficulties with the police were eventually settled, though Jack ended up spending two nights in jail, Woolf was very nearly put to sleep in the Havana pound, and an assistant manager of the Internacional threatened to throw Jack and Susan out of their room because Jack had abandoned his Ford in a cane field in a remote corner of Pinar del Río province.

Richard Bollow had not died on the racetrack, but he was in the hospital. He had been, in fact, James Bright's lawyer, but he was also a member—more or less—of the

García-Cifuentes clan by marriage: he was the stepfather of a brother-in-law of Rodolfo.

It was Bollow, renouncing his allegiance to the family in exchange for clemency and a promise of protection and a large amount of cash from Libby, who provided the details of the story: the García-Cifuentes clan had started out years before as sharecroppers on an estate not far from James Bright's, and had gained a substantial amount of money through the surreptitious cultivation of illegal substances—marijuana and coca, to be specific. With this money, they'd also rented land from James Bright, who for this sort of thing was the ideal landlord, since he didn't personally oversee the use of his property. The patches of marijuana and coca they grew interspersed in fields of sugarcane were profitable. With the profits, the son Rodolfo had been sent away to Catholic school. Proving himself there, he had gone on to college, though not—as Jack had discovered—to Harvard.

Though they were by all accounts a handsome lot, the members of the García-Cifuentes clan were not known for their polished manners. Thus, Rodolfo was often useful in the negotiation of certain exchanges, the implementation of certain devious plans, and the establishment of connections between the family and members of the Batista government, who not only demanded bribes but appreciated a handsome and well-mannered courier to deliver them.

Through a confederate in the provincial registry the García-Cifuentes clan had discovered the contents of James Bright's will and that Susan Bright was his legatee. The original plan had been for Rodolfo, already in the United States, to meet Susan, woo her, and wed her. The uncle would then be killed, and the García-Cifuenteses would come into the possession of the land they so much coveted, and from which they had already made so much money.

It was at this time—shortly after Rodolfo appeared in New York—that James Bright had discovered the fields of marijuana and coca on his land. He also found out that his beach was being used as a dropping-off point for arms shipments to the antigovernment rebels operating in the mountains of Pinar del Río. The García-Cifuenteses were evenhanded when it came to dealing with the dictatorship and the rebel cause.

James Bright had burned down the fields and set watches on his beach. It was not because he supported the Batista regime any more than he did the rebels—he simply thought that no sane man got involved in politics.

Out of simple vengeance, and out of an even simpler desire just to have the meddlesome old man out of the way, the García-Cifuenteses delegated certain members of the family to assassinate James Bright. Three attempts failed; the fourth succeeded. It had been nine-year-old Armando's first blood; the child, the García-Cifuenteses considered, was promising.

Back in New York, Rodolfo would have gone through with his plan to marry Susan, but he suspected her distrust of him, and he'd learned from home that James Bright had accused the García-Cifuenteses of the attempts on his life. With Susan no longer a possibility for him, he turned his attention to Libby—and persuaded her in joining him at the altar. In Cuba, he learned of the death of James Bright with satisfaction. It would now be possible, with Libby's money, simply to buy the land from Susan when she inherited it. But when Jack and Susan showed up—married—and began making troublesome inquiries, he altered his plan. It had been Rodolfo's revised intention to have Jack and Susan convicted of the murder and then to have the will suppressed. Because Susan was James Bright's only living relative, the property would have reverted to the Cuban government. Rodolfo's family had already made preliminary bribes to ensure that the property would be sold to them at a price far less than the actual market value.

In short, Rodolfo had had a surfeit of plans and contingency plans. He would have won if he'd married Susan, and he certainly won in marrying Libby. If he'd succeeded in burning Susan and Libby up in The Pillars, he would have ended up not only with that property but with Libby's fortune as well.

"As plots go, it was a bit *ex tempore*, wasn't it?" Jack said with a gesture of his cast—a brand-new one, all in one piece and lacking a resident arachnid.

"A bit," said Susan. "I'm quite embarrassed that I didn't see through him immediately."

"I did," put in Libby. This was in the first-class section of the Douglas DC-6 that was taking them back to New York; Libby had paid for the tickets, as well as for all of Jack and Susan's other Cuban expenses. "I saw through him the second I laid eyes on him. Don't you remember, Jack? In that terrible restaurant in the Village."

"Libby," Jack pointed out, "you married him."

"Yes," agreed Susan, "at least I didn't marry Rodolfo."

"I was confused," said Libby. "Jack, after all, had just tried to commit suicide and Rodolfo *was* very good-looking in a Rudolf Valentino sort of way, and I liked his voice. Besides, I had never gotten married before and I thought it would be a sort of interesting thing to do. And it was certainly a very nice way of getting away for the summer. I loathe summers in New York. I do wish one thing, though."

"What?" said Susan.

"I wish one of us had killed him. Oh, I guess I don't mean that. I mean I wish that little gun had gone off accidentally and shot him through the head. I'd make a much better widow than a divorcée, I think."

Jack and Susan exchanged glances.

"Widows have to wear black," said Susan. "Divorcées can wear any color they like."

"Oh!" said Libby, reconciled, and no longer particularly regretting Rodolfo's remaining alive. "And Jack," she added, "I'm going to make sure you get your job back."

Jack smiled, and said, "Thank you, Libby," though he was by no means sure that he wanted it.

He did take his job back, however, and even managed to wrest Maddy away from Mr. Hamilton. Susan inherited her uncle's wealth, which was substantial: two million dollars. This was exclusive of what was left of The Pillars and the land surrounding it.

A few weeks after the probating of the will, Susan received an offer of nearly a million dollars for that property from a large American corporation that had been looking for land on Cuba's Caribbean coast on which to build a gambling resort. Jack and Susan speculated that Rodolfo had known about this company as well, and that had been one more reason he was so anxious to get his hands on The Pillars. It also explained why he was so willing to burn down the plantation house; he knew that it would be razed anyway.

A few months later Jack made inquiries on behalf of Libby regarding her soon-to-be ex-husband. Rodolfo had been indicted, tried, and convicted on numerous charges, including attempted murder and arson. He was sentenced to a term of eighteen years in jail, but he soon escaped with the aid and connivance of his brother Armando, and joined a growing band of guerrilla rebels in the hills of western Cuba.

Jack and Susan moved to an apartment on Park Avenue that was a bit too near Libby, whose story of a frightening marriage to an unscrupulous Latin American appeared, with many photographs of Libby past and present, in the tabloids and several weekly magazines. When they'd recovered a little from their Cuban exploit, Jack and Susan decided they deserved a real honeymoon, and with the money to do anything they wanted, the choice among so many possibilities was daunting. Eventually they decided on Paris. Paris was lovely, but it was dull compared to their adventure in the tropics and they came back sooner than they'd planned.

Even after an absence of only three weeks, Woolf pretended not to remember who they were.

THE END OF
JACK AND SUSAN'S ADVENTURE
IN 1953